Alan Gould is a poet, novelist and essayist who lives in Canberra. His recent publications include the poems in *Mermaid* (1996), *Dalliance and Scorn* (1999) and *A Fold in the 'Light* (2001), the collection of essays, *The Totem Ship* (1996), and his fifth novel, *The Tazyrik Year* (1998). Among his awards are the 1999 Philip Hodgins Memorial Medal for Literature, the 1992 National Book Council Banjo Award for fiction, and the 1981 New South Wales Premier's Prize for poetry.

The
Schoonermaster's

The
Schoonermaster's

ALAN GOULD

flamingo
An imprint of HarperCollins*Publishers*

An extract from this novel appeared in *Quadrant*, December 1998.

Flamingo
An imprint of HarperCollins*Publishers*, Australia

First published in Australia in 2000
This edition published in 2001
by HarperCollins*Publishers* Pty Limited
ABN 36 009 913 517
A member of the HarperCollins*Publishers* (Australia) Pty Limited Group
www.harpercollins.com.au

HarperCollinsPublishers
25 Ryde Road, Pymble, Sydney NSW 2073, Australia
31 View Road, Glenfield, Auckland 10, New Zealand
77–85 Fulham Palace Road, London W6 8JB, United Kingdom
Hazelton Lanes, 55 Avenue Road, Suite 2900, Toronto, Ontario M5R 3L2
and 1995 Markham Road, Scarborough, Ontario M1B 5M8 Canada
10 East 53rd Street, New York NY 10022, USA

National Library of Australia Cataloguing-in-Publication data:

Gould, Alan, 1949- .
   The schoonermaster's dance.
   ISBN 0 7322 6823 0.
   1. Historical fiction. I. Title.
A823.3

Cover and internal design by Darian Causby, HarperCollins Design Studio
Typeset by HarperCollins in 12/16 Fairfield
Printed in Australia by Griffin Press on 70gsm Bulky Book Ivory

5 4 3 2 1   01 02 03 04

Acknowledgments

In creating this narrative I would like to thank various people and institutions for the helpful advice they have supplied on maritime and other technical or geographical matters; these are Russell Vasey, Barry Feldberg and Margaret Lillywhite, Maree Boland and others connected with the Maritime Museum of South Australia, Frances Prentice of the National Maritime Museum, Julia MacFarlane, Peter Langridge, Peter Cornhill, and Dr Ilya Englin.

I am indebted to that most readable shipping authority, Basil Lubbock, whose account of the ship, *Foyledale*, in his book *The Nitrate Clippers*, I used as a guide for certain events in this novel. It was as a result of reading Ron Thiele's equally engaging account of the sailing ketches of South Australia, *Ketch Hand*, that I began to contemplate a novel based, in part, on that trade.

Finally, my thanks go to Les Murray, Margaret Connolly, and my wife, Anne Langridge, for their encouragements after reading the manuscript of this work.

I saw that if I went to sea when I should be grown in years I should be little better than a slave, going with many a hungry belly and wet back, and being always called 'old dog' and 'old rogue' and 'son of a whore'. But all people are not born to live at ease. My desire was from my youth to see strange countries and fashions and I must with hunger and cold pay for it.

Edward Barlow, 1668

… a past that's personal as yesterday,
vast as the tent of stars
where the sanguine navigators
vanish to be our present,
being elsewhere deeply here.

Alan Gould, 'A Catamaran on Lake Coila',
The Twofold Place (1986) and
Selected Poems (1992)

I'll cross it though it blast me. Stay illusion.

Hamlet

Establishing Sarah

I

I will tell you the story of a woman who was brave and high-spirited and oddly detached from the social and personal ties that occupy the lives of most working and family folk. She was my friend, Sarah Tilber, and only now, with her life complete, am I aware of how acutely I miss her vivid presence and the lively illumination of far-off places that her letters used to bring me.

Sarah's story will concern one of her forebears, but I shall begin with a recollection that involves Sarah and my own grandmother. This was when we were both about seven years old, a wet Saturday when my father drove us to Lowestoft to visit this old lady.

'She is blind, Sal,' I informed her solemnly as the rain flecked the windows of the car. 'Her eyes have been . . .' I paused before supplying the word I had been taught on previous visits to the harbour town, '. . . enucleated.'

'Which can make Jennifer's grandma seem rather formidable,' my father quickly added from the front seat.

'What's enucleated?' asked Sarah.

'When they take the eyeballs out,' explained my father more fearsomely than was his usual manner with children.

I remember Sarah contemplated this information for some moments as the frowning, redbrick villas beside the road flashed past us. Whenever she was in the company of grown-ups, she had a certain 'mature' tone that she adopted. 'How impossible not to be able to see,' she stated, and in the rear-vision mirror I saw both my parents smile at this.

In due course we arrived before my gran's grey house and went through the hall to where she sat in what was still (in 1954) called the parlour. This was a dark, high room, dusty, cobwebby, with thick, floor-length curtains that were, despite the daytime, pulled shut. A standard lamp with a tasselled shade highlighted different brass and porcelain objects on the mantelpiece which were arranged around a clock in a marble cabinet decorated by carved figures playing pipes or carrying pitchers. Gran sat, huge, slab-faced and unseeing, in her high-backed chair. She wore a black dress with beige lace around the neck which resembled the froth on a glass of stout. Her stockings were thick and the colour of milk tea, and her feet bulged from her round black shoes like two buns from their baking trays. Never could I quite bring myself to look at the place where her eyes were.

'Gran, this is Sarah.'

The great head tilted towards where Sarah and I stood before her and nodded once or twice. 'Then Sarah must come and stoop just here,' Gran instructed. My friend did so, and held herself rigidly as the massive old lady felt all over the tensely serious face and around the contours of Sarah's shoulders and arms. 'I have to establish your *presence,* young lady,' said my grandmother in the odd strained voice which Sarah was later to say 'did not belong to our century'. My parents and I watched the progress of Gran's hands as they gathered information, methodical, careful, like those of a vet handling an animal.

'It's all right, Sal,' I remember assuring her.

'I know that!' She smiled quickly to disguise her impatience.

We were given tea and required to render a clear account of ourselves to the old lady, schoolwork, hobbies, holidays. Later, while the grown-ups talked and the teacups clinked, the two of us went into Gran's bedroom and devised a game of clambering around the room from dresser to chair, from wardrobe to the bed with its high mattresses and eiderdown. Under our rules, touching the floor was prohibited. We shut the door on ourselves so that the room was in darkness, and, in our absorption, lost track of time. All at once the door opened and Gran stood there, silhouetted with her stick in one hand and the other on the lintel.

'You girls! You girls! I can't see you.' Her voice was querulous. For perhaps a minute Sarah and I remained silent, balanced on the furniture in our respective corners. Then Gran shuffled into the room and stood near the bed. 'I say that I can't see you,' she scolded.

'Yes you can,' replied Sarah's voice from the darkness above the tallboy, 'because you established me.'

There was a further interval of silence before Gran informed Sarah that she was a forward young lady. The admonition was enough to distract her from the chastisement she had intended for what she must have guessed was our disarrangement of her bedroom. We each descended from our perches and slunk past her and out of the room.

The rain eased, we were encouraged outside, and walked together along the seawall with our hoods up. Sarah was subdued. 'I don't like being touched all over,' she decided at last. After an interval she said, 'I looked at them, Jenn.'

'Her eyes?'

'Yes. It was awful. Like when you open up a prune with your spoon. Like ... like her centre had been scooped out. But I looked at them.'

We watched the brown water slap at the sides of the fishing boats until it was time to go home. And she did not accompany me on our visits to Lowestoft again.

You have established me.

Thirty-five years later, in the last phase of her life, Sarah embarked upon a personal quest that involved her attempt to establish the presence of a vanished forebear, the seafaring great-uncle, Charles Tilber, whose elusive presence we will follow on these pages. Her quest gained in momentum and intensity as the months unfolded. Nonetheless she left it unfinished — *undetermined* might be the more exact word — at the time of her disappearance in July 1990, near the border of Peru with Chile.

During this final period of her life I was, I believe, her only confidante. It had been Sarah's custom to write to me two or three times a year, but during 1989–90 her correspondence — chatty, bulky missives, postcards crammed with black handwriting, her final, haunting audio cassette from Valparaíso — used to arrive at my kitchen table at the rate of one or more items per week.

Sarah's quest, you must understand, was founded upon an intellectual passion to do with the past. I have one handwritten letter, posted from Australia in October 1989 when she was some four months into what she was then calling her 'Retrieval Project'. In this she tried to describe for me the complex nature of her preoccupation.

Semaphore, October 4th 1989

Dearest Jenn,

No! I think in your last to me you are missing my point. It is this.

If, without loss to the vividness of my present life, I can take my *shrewdest* sympathies back into oblivion (as we must suppose Orpheus did) and restore Charlie Tilber's quickened presence from my family's past, together with the people of his life — Milliken, the *Kilbride's* Captain Yuell and his family — what an adventure of the mind! I would be rescuing for the light of day all that *may* be rescued of that lovable old seafarer's actuality, and *that* would bring me, surely, the potency for *all* former, inconspicuous lives to be recovered for the human mind, each in its delicate individuality.

It is for this reason I will then be able to say: *The past completes me.* How shall I bring home for you the emotion this possession of the past arouses? Be patient.

I start with this present moment. I am on Semaphore Beach again. It is untidier than the last time I wrote. Strewn in the tiderows of sea-grass are broken thongs, glittery rags of cellophane, waxy sweetpapers, crushed drink cans. Not far away I can see a half-eaten hotdog which seagulls, in a blizzard of wings, are fighting over (as no doubt seagulls did a century ago when the people in frock coats and muslins dropped the sandwich crusts of their picnics, the butts of cheroots, scraps of lint, broken shoelaces).

Beyond this the sea has an austere beauty this afternoon. There is some sheet lightning on the horizon in the direction of Yorke Peninsula. The ocean is flat in the pre-storm, with lovely, pewtery patches intermingling with dark velvety striations, while the sky has a dramatic, furled, charcoal front coming my way with a great milky curtain of rain behind it. I can see the dipping triangle of a lone boardrider's sail, striped fluorescent red and green. And just now a man in shorts, singlet and the kind of straw trilby you can buy at chemist shops here, came past and advised, 'You'll get a wetting any moment, I'd say, lady,' in exactly that tone which Australians of this era like to try on authority while pretending to be one's equal. 'Yes. Thank you very much,' I told him, and he shrugged, and called his dog, and squeaked away across the white sand towards the car parks and the Norfolk Island pine trees. (You see! Despite your worries, my welfare seems to get well looked after.) Apart from me, and Mr Trilby, the beach is empty of people north and south, and the wind is not yet high.

There! Presto! You are here. I can establish this for you. I can hold the present in my hands like a quantity. Yet this is not sufficient, not for me, not for anyone, because I am unwilling to overlook that what is present glitters with what *has been* present.

So I go back to my Charlie Tilber. Can I confine my purpose with Great-Uncle T to a biography at all? Yes, I say, if it begins and ends with simply wanting to capture a person's life story. But my impulse towards bygone matters is altogether more peculiar when I examine it closely. I think it is to do with wanting to *inhabit* more of time than has been given me, to inhabit Charlie T's time as intimately as the moments of my own I have just described. Perhaps everyone hankers after this *identification* with what has gone before.

You see, it is this reflex to put me, Sarah Tilber, in the picture that makes me want to attempt more than an objective life story. I want to be on the *inside* of what he would have called his own time. Can I thus transfer my sympathetic self? I think so.

Better than anyone, you know how I love the atmosphere of those old ships and docklands because you used to share the feeling. Yesterday I was looking at a collection of historical maritime photos, and came upon a double-page photograph taken in 1881 of shipping in London's South-West India Dock. It is before my mind's eye as I sit here writing to you. It shows such a bristling, chaotic palisade of masts and yards. There are barges and lighters jumbled together beneath the great steel hulls of the merchantmen, whose lower yards are 'cockbilled' as they sway their cargoes out of the holds and into the hands of the waiting Londoners. There are bales and tarpaulins, and gantries disappearing into the London fog. I find it so *moving,* Jenn, to contemplate the scale of what is so precariously present in the old photo, and how all the far-flung places of earth are incipient in the cavernous holds of those ships. Timber or tins of salmon from Puget Sound are being discharged here, jaggery from Madras, jute from Calcutta or Manila, wool from Geelong or Lyttelton, guano or nitrate from Iquique or Antofagasta. I see this. My beach and my photo, 1881 and 1989, the one combines with the other as naturally as atoms in a molecule or light and shade on the surface of the sea.

So, how *automatic* it is for me to sit here on this beach, yet imagine myself present, viewing this spectacle of 1880s' shipping in the photo, coal smoke brought to my nostrils on the damp river breeze, Great-Uncle's short figure beside me in a shore-going bowler hat, and a watch chain looped from buttonhole to waistcoat pocket. He has family traits I would recognise: habits of mind, a genetic make-up identifiable with my own in the colour of his eyes, perhaps, or the texture of his hair. I am enmeshed in the same genetic and cultural pattern he was! Not that he will talk to me or do his thinking in my head. Hah! Not yet, at least.

You see, what I want to find out is how one might manage such an identification across the borders of a lifetime; how, with lots of tact, knowledge of detail, and as much shrewdness as I can muster, I might tune my imagination to conducting it. Is this vicarious? Is this just play-acting? Do write and tell me.

The first rain is coming down in big splotches. I must run, or these biro'd pages will be ruined. Love, S.

❧

Passion-of-the-intellect. Despite what might appear in this story, Sarah was averse to the mystical. Once, at a college party in our late teens, we both sat in a circle on a wooden floor in a big, empty house and smoked opiated hashish from a gurgly brass pipe.

'How did you find it?' she asked me next morning, leaning her back on the tree that supported the hammock where I reclined.

I was quite definite that I had found the experience nauseous and vile. 'No-one seemed to be able to do anything but grin. And at one point I was aware of some creature snuffling at me. He had some impediment in his nostrils and was like a big, long-nosed dog. I hated the grinners, and hated myself for hating them. How about you?'

'Swimmy,' she pronounced, 'and a most extraordinary derangement of my time sense.'

'Like how?' She was rocking the hammock for me, gently.

'As I walked home by myself along Wherstead Road I lived, no, *was being lived*, through aeons. I couldn't say if it was late, or nearly dawn, or a Saturday in summer, because such considerations would have been so trivial. I seemed to be trailing immense centuries, flaking them off me. Like a comet.'

'You sound very spiritual about it.'

Absently she pushed the hammock and said, 'I could start a religion based on the distances I seemed to see last night. But Jenn! It was hateful. I want to choose where I am. I insist on it.' We became careful about the parties we went to.

Sarah's insistence that she should choose where she was informs her part in this story. But I sense there to be more to the story itself. When I came to re-read the letters in the light of her disappearance, I was perplexed. This was because the nature of Sarah's quest, begun in a spirit of such buoyant curiosity, appeared to me to have gradually enclosed her in an atmosphere of fatality and to have foreshadowed the end that overtook her. In a way that I find unwelcome, it made that fate, if no less atrocious, somehow determined and acceptable.

Sarah and I grew up as neighbours near Ipswich in East Anglia and it is my impression that our friendship dates from at least the time we were toddlers, able to babble our first articulate thoughts to each other. We attended the same schools, the same university, sharing in some cases identical courses and tutorials. Sometimes, on the macadam surface of the playground, the girls would dance to a particular jingle, and they would do this more pointedly whenever they saw Sarah and I nearby.

> *My mother said I never should*
> *Play with the gypsies in the wood.*
> *If I did she would say*

'Naughty girl to disobey,
Disobey, disobey,
Naughty girl to disobey.'
The woods are dark, the grass is green,
Here comes Sally with a tambourine . . .

'The Twins', 'The Conchies', 'The Left and Right Pocket' were various epithets used to describe or deride our inseparableness. Other companions came and went from our circle; the casual spite from peers could not assail the simple liking we had, one for the other, and our friendship endured, with its sustaining in-jokes and shared phantasmagoria and, in truth, a certain defensive spite we ourselves showed towards those outside our confidence.

We lived not far from the navigable Orwell. Towards this river we used to wander, abandoning our bicycles to descend, wading through two cornfields and a wood tangled with blackberry, to the bank with its low gnarled hawthorns and dilapidated fences. There, at low tide, we might heave one gumboot after another from the suction of the blue-grey foreshore mud, on the lookout for interesting flotsam, or, with squeals of glee, fish out on the end of a stick the ghostly white condoms that floated down from Ipswich docks.

'Sal! It's a whopper!'

'It's a sock, surely! Or a rubber nightcap!'

'It's from a person who must need special trousers!'

In holiday time, with our legs dangling over the wooden Cathouse Road Hard, we chewed a stick of liquorice or, later in our teens, experimented with cigarettes. There was, I remember, a slender fellow with blue overalls and a shock of white-blond hair who, invariably, could be seen at work in the well of the clinker-built cutters, pinnaces and launches that were tethered to the jetty. We had nicknamed him Floss, and used to enjoy sitting above him, offering bits of impudent advice, watching with delight his neck grow redder as he wrapped his leather strop around a propeller shaft and then pulled manfully in his efforts to make a diesel engine work.

'Hey bo-uy!' we called, imitating his broad accent. 'We'z embarrazzin' ye-ou?'

'Not that ev remarked on et,' he would reply stolidly, not unbending from his task.

Out on the river's broad reaches were the bobbing dinghies with red or sky-blue sails which belonged to the nearby boarding school. These would scatter before the great cream and black steamers that loomed upstream, spiky with masts, derricks and ventilators, their slab-sided hugeness somehow out of scale with the riverbank trees and the black and white cows on the far bank. I recall how the glimpse of a peaked hat high on the superstructure of these thrumming monsters, or the different national flags fluttering at their stern rails, used to prompt in the two of us an odd, charged emotion, in part yearning, in part an exhilaration that such clues of an exotic, further world could pass back and forth before our eyes, betokened by no more than an arrangement of colourful stripes, crescents or stars on a rectangle of flapping cotton, or a remote foreigner in a blue uniform with a splodge of white on his head.

On calm Saturday mornings we used to watch as one of two London barges, moored downriver in Pin Mill Bay, hoisted its quadrangular cinnamon-coloured sails beneath the varnished sprits, forever preparing to depart without ever seeming to do so. We used to amble home from the Pin Mill sweet shop beside the small cabin boats moored to the bank by their long painters which were hung with beards of luminous green seaweed. If it rained, we sheltered under the chocked-up hulls of yachts, kicking wood shavings, smelling the new marine paint, idly trying out various dreamy futures.

'We'll buy a boat and sail to the Andaman Islands.'

'Won't we need someone who knows about boats?'

'We'll bribe Floss to come.'

'What with?'

'Cigarettes. Sherbet lemons.'

'He's a man. He'll want more than that.'

'I don't see why.'

'Sal!'

'Then we will make sure he behaves.'

'He'll be useless for conversation.'

'He can be trained.' And then Sarah would call out to Floss, who might be painting red lead on a nearby hull, 'We'z for takin' ye-ou to the Andaman Islands, Flozi! Goo'n awee'n pack.'

'No thang-hyou,' he would reply.

For always, of course, we were at this banter, provoking, conjecturing, daydreaming aloud. In all our acquaintance I cannot remember having had a serious quarrel with Sarah and, as I say, we remained in correspondence after she moved to Australia in 1978.

This was our 1950s' and '60s' pastoral. I depict it in some detail because the milieu of a working river was so much a background to our childhood and teenage years, and it qualified Sarah well for the story which, two decades or so later, and on the other side of the world, she decided she wanted to tell. Like many children who grow up in a vivid environment, for all that we suffered our odd bouts of despondency, we were never seriously unhappy. And we took for granted the river commerce until we both, in turn, moved away from it and, as a result, found in our vacant moments that we longed for its proximity and colour.

Teacher and schools librarian that she became, I want to say that in the *force* of her being, Sarah was ever the historian.

'...Because I can remember things finely and am shocked when I hear other people recall them coarsely,' she once explained.

Fiercely, of course, she insisted she was an amateur in historical matters, but I could observe how spontaneous was her curiosity about bygone things, how sure was her instinct for the atmosphere of a given epoch. 'There is properly no history, Jenn, only biography.' She used to come from lectures quoting this Emerson to me.

'You're holding forth again, Sal,' she liked to be reminded on such occasions.

'Surely not!'

And if there was one aspect of the past which most fascinated her it was that period just slipping from view, the era not quite our own, rich in archival photographs and documents, 'still warm from use', as she used to say, yet from which the minutiae

16

of mind, of gesture, and expression, had already been all but effaced.

Let me illustrate for you this cast of her mind. During her last visit to me from Australia in 1989 we had gone walking one misty November morning along the Suffolk lanes near my husband's school. The trees were all but bare and the brown leaves were gathered in sodden, oily-coloured drifts in the ditches beside the roads. For some time we spoke little, taking a rest from conversation after having talked late the previous night. Passing over a stile into a field, Sarah paused on the wooden step and, taking up the topic of our late-night discussion, she looked down at me and observed, 'For instance, Jenn, you might ask what has happened to the word "wallah"?'

She dismounted from the stile and we continued down a muddy track. 'I *might* ask that question,' I remarked. 'But *you* do so to clinch some point you were making last night.'

She laughed, and then proceeded in her characteristic headlong way. 'As in "punkah-wallah", "box-wallah" or "desk-wallah",' she said, 'or as in the jolly, spectacled fellow on that Christian camp we attended near Cromer. We used to call him "Ping-pong Paterson, The Games Wallah". Do you remember him?'

'Of course.'

'You can probably think of other words like that.'

'"Scullery",' I tried on her, 'where people used to black their boots and put the wash through the mangle. Or "skiffle",' I thought of another, 'as in the rattly music which those fellows with slicked hair used to play on a washboard.' The essence of our friendship, I was all too well aware, lay in the enjoyment I took in amplifying or, more rarely, gently puncturing a train of thought Sarah had initiated.

'Exactly!' she rejoined. 'Do you see the fleeting thing I am trying to catch?' and glanced at me searchingly.

'We-ell.'

'Almost all words illuminate authority. Think how the history of our time must be a complete blank for anyone ignorant of the term "wallah",' she declared.

'Not a *complete* blank, Sal, surely.'

'*Complete!*' she insisted.

'Complete, then.' I smiled.

'And that is not to mention the slippery difference in tone with which "wallah" might have been used by Major Bloggs in Delhi in 1943 and by his daughter, Dorothy Bloggs, at a Norfolk camp in 1963.' We walked for several yards before she repeated emphatically, 'A *complete* blank'. The lifted eyebrow and a hint of humour at the corners of her mouth allowed me to know Sarah was enjoying the effect her vehemence had on me.

'I won't argue.'

But she would be serious again in a moment, and her countenance could become energised, uplifted almost, like that of a person in the presence of their beloved.

'The *real* point is, not only have the expressions slipped away from us, but look how a whole configuration of attitudes and authority has gone with them. Especially authority. It's so negligent, the way the past sheds all its fine detail, all its . . . its pointillism. Don't you agree?'

'How can I not!'

She paused in her train of thought for a moment.

'Jenny Happle, you can be mostly but not entirely in accord with me!' This was said good-naturedly.

'I reserve the right to listen with my own smile, Sal,' I replied carefully.

She watched me for a moment or two before continuing. 'Of course you do. Anyway, it's this moment-by-moment that I'm resolved to recover around the life of Great-Uncle. If I can discover what he thought, I might be able to discern dimly the things it never occurred to him, as a person locked into his time, to think. For you see ...' Companionably she tucked her arm under mine and I was pleased by this because such casual physical gestures were rare in the headlong verbal style of her friendship. We had entered a small wood. The mist had created a film of droplets on our collars and woollen hats, but it was thinning, and there was a lovely, delicate bronziness perceptible now in the bare trees as the sun tried to shine through. '... That configuration is so *almost* reclaimable.' We slushed among the wet leaves for several moments before she spoke again. 'It is like ... like looking at an expanse of water and trying to remember *exactly* how it appeared a moment ago. Sad, and thrilling too, don't you think?'

'Yes,' I replied, for in the end I did not need my own lightly subversive smile. Sarah's conviction, the entire force of her being, was too moving for me to wish to impede her enthusiasm. 'Though people ridicule words like "wallah" now,' I thought to add.

'They're history too!' was her cheerful reply.

19

A time still warm from use. Sarah pored over old photographs, and I knew her to buy up tatty family collections when they were offered in junk shops or at jumble sales. This was one of her enthusiasms in the period before she emigrated to Australia as a not-so-young wife. It little mattered who was being depicted in such carefully posed sepia pictures· Sarah could construct *that* part of things herself, for this, after all, was the very point of purchasing them. What was attractive to her was the material evidence of bygone clothing, the characteristic postures of once-living people that gave clues to the temperament of an era, the differing traits of physique, hairstyle, complexion, that had now become submerged by a generation or two of small genetic modifications and several layers of fashion.

'How can I tell what this child's life was like until I see the kind of shoes she wore,' was a remark Sarah once made to me during university, as we peered at a late-Victorian girl's picture in one such album.

For this reason, then, I will now describe a particular photograph I once took of Sarah herself. I possess several pictures of my friend, both as a child and as a woman, but as I contemplated the task of turning her various papers into this memoir, the photo which I chose to set before me on my desk as a reminder of her presence was by no means the best I had. It shows Sarah at the age of seventeen. Her hair is longer and bushier than the bobbed style she adopted later. Her figure is a little plumper, her cheek more youthfully rounded than that of the more angular woman she became, and she has on some cheap, oddly fetching spectacles which she used whenever she was out walking. It is a black and white snapshot, taken in our last year at school, and the sun shines fully upon her pleasant face, causing her to frown in the same moment as she is smiling for the camera.

This 'crossover' in her expression has always disconcerted me slightly. Once, in a newspaper article about a young Australian journalist killed during the Tet Offensive in the Vietnam War, in the caption under his photo I learned a term the Vietnamese people use when they deem there is tragedy foreshadowed in the set of a particular face. They described the young Australian's aspect as being 'Sô', and I know of no equivalent expression in other languages. Sô. Do I see just such a vulnerability when I look at my snapshot of Sarah? I prefer not to think it.

Yet it is an impact made more poignant because Sarah has moved at the shutter instant so that her features have blurred just slightly. The result is indeed to make her presence look somehow unstable, like those laboratory photographs depicting the transience of an electron. Furthermore, on the day when, during the school lunch hour, we broke bounds to collect the prints of this film from the chemist, I recall Sarah looked over my shoulder as I went through them, and coming to this representation of herself, with a laugh she exclaimed, 'No, don't keep that one, Jenn. I couldn't bear anyone to think I am a blurred sort of a person!'

Nor, in the force of her personality, was she, even though I disobeyed her in this and the rather inferior snapshot passed into my album.

As I am able to reconstruct the Retrieval Project in Sarah's mind, it seems to have formed unobtrusively during her years of marriage, and to have become more compelling at the time of her first flight from her husband, Kieran Fawne.

I want to be on the inside of what he would have called his own time. This, in practical terms, meant she wanted to write about her seafaring great-uncle. Her research commenced in Adelaide, took her in her hard-used Datsun around the harbour townships of the South Australian gulfs — Ardrossan, Edithburgh, Port Victoria — and I was sent snapshots, taken with her own camera by some willing local, of herself standing perhaps on a dilapidated pier, or beside the rusted skeleton of an old ketch. In the fierce Australian sunlight Sarah looks back at me from under her fringe of hair, hatless, self-conscious and, to my mind now, vulnerable.

These field trips were directed towards uncovering the last twenty years of her great-uncle's seafaring life. To trace Charles Tilber's years in deepwater sail between 1875 and 1900, Sarah returned to this country in 1989 on the visit I mention above. She wanted to see documents.

'...Or rather, smell them, Jenn, let the edge of my hand feel the texture of the pages that the writer's own hand moved across with the pen.'

'So you won't actually read their contents?'

'Secondary,' she laughed. For was she not, on this occasion, fresh from the archives of the Greenwich Maritime Museum, and the Kew Public Records Office.

And how could I doubt her absorption in her task. I had known, from childhood onwards, how Sarah could focus her willpower with such intensity. *'I looked at them, Jenn.'* 'Her eyes?' *'Yes. It was awful. Like when you open up a prune with your spoon. Like … like her centre had been scooped out. But I looked at them.'* And thirty-five years later …

'What an *intent* time of it I've had, Jenn.'

We drove away from the railway station in my car. 'Kew was all shipping registers, official logs, certificates of discharge and other maritime whatnot. I spent my time making guesses about character on the basis of whether a signature was flourished or plain, scribbled or painstaking.' Thus she chatted.

'And Greenwich?' I asked.

Ah, Greenwich! Here she had come upon Captain Yuell's own logbooks from several of his voyages, page after page of wind directions, distance covered, noon positions, the taking in of this sail, the clapping on of that. 'Ordinary vanished routines. Marvellous stuff! Why, just from the captain's deliberate handwriting the whole Victorian ethic of self-improvement revealed itself to me. Marvellous.'

I commented that it was also marvellous the way she could turn a museum detail into an x-ray of an entire era.

But the animation of her spirits caused by Kew and Greenwich could not be checked. 'In the same box I found …' She allowed a moment of dramatic pause, and I glanced at her from my driving.

'What?'

'A letter by Mrs Yuell to her sister, together with a long postscript from Little Miss. Actually written from Valparaíso Bay and dated May 31st 1900.'

'That was luck.'

'Think! That killer storm was probably already building strength as they wrote! Unposted, of course, and eventually returned to the company by the British Legation. I spent the afternoon copying that poor woman's handwriting, word for word, into my notebook, and I swear I never felt more committed ... no, I have to say *transposed*! Just hours before she drowns, she is chatting to her sister in the perfect confidence that her future is a long, placid certainty. She mentions the ship's first mate, Fordyce, her dearest, overstrained John, various crew members, though not much of Great-Uncle ...'

'And Little Miss?'

'Little Miss, I discover, collects vocabulary in the same way she might gather seashells. For her aunt in this letter, she offers "boisterous", "akimbo" and "tumult". I surmise these words were used by Mama to describe what was then becoming visible outside the porthole of their cabin. You see how one can take these historical snapshots?'

'Yes.'

'The vital thing, though, is that I have discovered their actual voices, don't you see? They're ...' Sarah broke off. 'Oh, I can practically feel my people stepping out before me. I mean it!'

'I believe you,' I assured her. Somehow her enthusiasm gave a sense that my car was full of people.

'Not their *entire* lives, of course, but moments of them, and with all the delicacy of their last-century attitudes intact.' I glanced at her quickly. For a moment her face was pensive in the dashboard lights. 'It is so moving, you know, seeing their underpinning, their *necessity*.'

Thus she had exulted as the headlights swung this way and that along the lanes to the school. Later, we sat at my kitchen table with a glass of wine and she grew more self-conscious about her enthusiasm. 'I should not flaunt these discoveries, should I, Jenn? For am I not preying on their misfortune?'

'It was long, long ago, Sal.' My assurance was ineffectual.

'It was yesterday,' she replied, 'or as good as.'

But her moment's self-doubt was, I thought, being unfair to her own talents and integrity. I used to wonder how her talents, her force of character, had eluded the workforce after she left Canberra, and in one of the letters I wrote to her in 1989 I asked, 'Why, now that you are free, do you not pursue a career as a producer of TV documentaries, or become a high-profile academic historian with a round of conferences to attend?'

She replied in a prompt postcard. 'And be surrounded by people who can violate how I wish to construe things? No fear.'

As she herself foresaw, Sarah's project eventually refused to become a satisfactory retrieval. There were not enough recorded facts. Her solution to these cul de sacs was typically Sarah, as one late postcard I received from Valparaíso reveals.

'Jenn,' it reads, 'with the archive on the Yuells now exhausted, I know all I will ever know about them. Time now to find that trance where I can invent reliably. Love, S.'

And invent she did, with a historical imagination of great resource and tact. Sarah believed her imaginings. That is to say, she took it for granted that whatever entered her imagination was possible. If that imagining embodied all the available evidence, then it was probable. Simple.

This has meant that I inherited a story that had not quite resolved itself between what did happen and what might well have happened.

❦

I couldn't bear anyone to think I am a blurred sort of a person, she had said in that moment of self-regard. But the circumstances of her disappearance *are* blurred and will probably remain so.

In the company of a chance-met old acquaintance, she was making her way to Lake Titicaca in the Andes. In one of her last letters she had posted me snapshots of the terrain in northern Chile. 'Hills and ravines, Jenn, the colour of blotchy human skin. They fold into each other, and not a sprig of vegetation. Meagre concrete houses by the roadside, bunkers more than homes, all defaced by apparently meaningless graffiti. This, under a flawless blue sky, does nothing to lighten my gloomy mood . . .'

Written on the minibus that took her to Arica, this is the last glimpse Sarah provides me of herself.

It is known that the two of them hired bicycles from a shop in Arica, then vanished somewhere in the mountains between there and Pizacoma in August 1990. Despite investigation by the Peruvian authorities and the Australian and British embassies in Chile, no trace of either person has been found and the inquiry has concluded they met their deaths by misadventure. It is hard for me not to imagine some sordid atrocity was committed against her. Sarah was forty-three.

So I return to the snapshot on the desk before me. And I should say this. Through conviction, I live and teach with my husband at an Anglican school, but I am not, I think, a credulous person, nor am I a fatalist. Yet there is, I find myself compelled to acknowledge, a more troubling, almost pagan aspect to the mystery of Sarah's disappearance. From her vivacious correspondence, and from our conversations during her 1989 visit, I perceived the degree to which her biographical project absorbed, exhilarated, and, at a less calculable level, troubled her. As her letters will show, quite early in her researches her ancestor's story took an oddly fatalistic turn. A superstitious reader might believe the material she uncovered about her relative actually presaged the fate that caught up with her in those barren mountains. As I say, I recoil from this idea. Why should my friend not be imaginable as a lively old woman?

I have chosen to keep this memoir in the form of the original letters, month by month, in the order I received them. In addition I have solicited reminiscences of Sarah from several people who knew her and their responses preface Sarah's own letters. Quite deliberately I interplay my own portrait of my friend with that she created of her seafaring forebear, Charlie Tilber. They belong together.

And I grieve and puzzle over what has happened to her. For I have been unable to rid myself of the very superstition I mention above: namely, that the nature of the material which so absorbed the last year of Sarah's life inevitably appears to implicate itself in the fate which has befallen her. Her nonchalant spirit would pooh-pooh this idea, yet one of her letters declares:

'Think! An animal will forget its parents in a twinkling. Yet we live with the past like we live with the sea. It moves and breathes all around us. Why will it not be at rest? So deep am I in the life of Great-Uncle T, that at times the past's message seems implacable. *You can neither stop nor still me, so there!* I tell you, it is not the particular ghost of Charles Tilber that haunted dear old Albert during our recording session, but the heave and sway of the past itself, with all its unfinished business. My particular business was to seek friendship with a once-living ancestor and somehow it seems to have emptied me, hollowed me out. Why does that business glitter so at the same time as, obscurely, it wearies me?'

And in that postcard from Valparaíso where she speaks of inventing Maie Alice Yuell, having discovered an old photo of the girl in the Museo del Mar, she asked me the question: 'Do you think a person's face can have its fate written on it, like poor Maie Alice?' Like *Sô*?

To the postcard I wrote back impatiently, saying that I would never accept any view of misfortune being so destined that you could see it printed in a person's features. It would have been one of our few real disagreements, but I know now she had left Valparaíso for northern Chile by the time it arrived, so it is likely she did not receive it. In the card I further told her I repudiated this primitive determining of human lives. And I do so now.

Yet I cannot make it go away.

2

'You should have been Mum's daughter, not me,' Sarah once remarked during our teens. Certainly I perceived my own relationship with Hazel Tilber was an easier one than Sarah's appeared to be, and two or three times in a year I will keep up my contact with Hazel who has continued to live — now on her own — in the Tilbers' stuccoed, semi-detached house in Hardacre Street, Felstone.

Sarah's papers were returned to this address by her estranged husband, Kieran, and these included my own letters to her. On one of my visits, after Hazel and I had talked at length about Sarah, I borrowed them. A day or two later I received this letter from her, supplementing our conversation, but also touching upon the awkwardness in the relationship between mother and daughter which Hazel had been reluctant to talk about with me face to face.

Hardacre Street 28/7/96

My dear Jenny,

It *was* nice, and a comfort, to see you and your

youngest again when you popped over on Tuesday last. She is so bonny, and I am able to assure you she looks just like her mother did at the same age. One advantage about growing old is that one is able to say things like that!

It made me sad to talk about poor Sarah, but probably did me good. Since then I've thought of one or two more things I ought to have told you for your proposed book.

I once heard Father say to Sarah, 'You must have some guardian angel looking out for you, Sally-girl, because you sure don't look out for yourself.'

This was after she went with her two brothers to the swimming pool in Fore Street and got into difficulties. She was about eight and maybe she told you all about it. Brian and the attendant had to jump in and rescue her, then turn her upside down to shake out the water she had swallowed. The boys were going to keep it a secret, but Sarah could not be stopped from chatting merrily about the mishap. You may imagine how it gave Ben and I a scare.

More so because, you see, it was the second time something like this had happened. Our earlier fright is one Sarah would not remember, her having been not quite three at the time. We had gone in the old car to Felixstowe for the bank holiday, and hired deckchairs. Ben read the paper, the boys played in the sand, and the sea glittered so picturesquely. All at once we noticed that Sarah, in her frilly swimsuit, had run down the beach and was already in the sea. This happened so quickly. I dare say the breakers were not very big, but still they were almost Sarah's height. We saw her fight the first one, and then get knocked over by the next. By then, of course, Father and Brian had reached her and pulled her out. You can imagine how our little girl was crying piteously. But were her tears because the waves had frightened her? No! It was because Father and Brian had interfered with some fancy she had set her mind on. At supper, the boys made jokes about how 'Bub', as they have continued to call her (even though she has quite grown up), had been trying to swim to Holland. But Father told them they should button it because it could have been serious.

That's one thing I remember.

Talking of crying, it was always when she was cross that Sarah cried, never when she was sad. Once, when she was about nine, and away with you at the church camps, Father, the boys and I decided we would re-paint her room for a surprise when she got back. It was such a pretty job when it was finished. But what was young madam's reaction when she came home? She took one look at it, then cried and cried with vexation because she had liked it the way it was. 'Boo hoo, I can't see my country now,' she wailed, which apparently referred to some marks which the damp had made on one wall.

Nor would she get upset at a telling off. Once, when she was about six, she went into Derek's room and trod square on one of his model aeroplanes. Derek, seven years her elder, gave her such a rocket you could hear it all over the house. I went upstairs to see what was amiss, and there our little girl stood, Derek shouting at her, Sarah looking him straight back in the eye, stony as a chapel, not even blinking, and certainly not going to go away until the storm was over. She was such a fearless wee thing. Later I found her in the coal shed with a book.

I said how Sarah was our late child and how Father, being a few years older than me, was more like the grandpa Sarah never had than he was a dad. Ben was a fair man, and treated the two boys and Sarah equally, but it was clear to me that Sarah was his favourite, and if her brothers had been teasing her, he used to slip her a sixpence when they were not looking. I still have all those books that she and Father used to read.

She always ate with appetite and her school reports used to please Father no end. You asked me when you were here if I thought Sarah grew away from me and I know I didn't give you a very good answer. Yes, I think it is true, and from quite early on. She used to say crossly, 'I *know*', if I tried to remind her of anything. She wasn't very interested in the things I did and didn't want me to take an interest in the things that took her fancy. It's as simple as that, and can't be helped, I suppose. But she was still my child. You, with your own, will understand what I mean.

I will make myself an old misery if I keep this up, so I'll stop. I have the two boys, and the garden may be small but it is always wanting something. It's a pity you saw it in such rain last Tuesday. When the sun comes out the foxgloves are a picture. Come over again soon.

My love to you all, Hazel.

PS: I think you should have all Sarah's papers and letters. I mean, to keep. They will go into the attic and be forgotten if they stay with me. Did you know Sarah used to write out long stories about someone called Rolf in exercise books when she was a teenager? She kept them in the drawer where she had her jumpers and didn't let on. I found them there, but never read them. And now I don't want to. But you will have known about them. The two of you were so thick together. H.

❧

I should say that I was unaware of these stories. However, even more than her mother, Sarah preferred to deal with sensitive personal matters in writing rather than conversation.

Her younger brother, Derek, wrote to me as follows.

Briton Ferry 9/8/96

Dear Jenny,

You ask me about the time when Bub stayed with us during her 1989 visit.

It was a hectic time for us so somehow we missed out on catching up. The boys were younger, and very lively. Bub used to sit in an armchair and try and read. She would look up every now and then if the squabbling got very loud, and, while I wouldn't say she was off the planet, she looked as if she wanted to be.

There's not much else I can say. Bub was always Bub. You don't have to have a lot in common with someone to wish they were still around, do you? We called her Bub, which got to be short for Bubble as much as for the fact she was youngest. Yours, Derek Tilber.

❧

'I discovered just the other day why I married Kier,' Sarah wrote to me not long after arriving in Australia in 1978.

'He's thoroughgoing. Like me, he wants the fullest picture! A detail lost and we fear the whole fabric will unstitch itself. This means we take time to listen to each other, and it is fun!'

The long letter from Kieran Fawne that follows is thoroughgoing. But then I had encouraged him to be so, and the result is I received from him this generous response to my several enquiries regarding his life with Sarah once I had begun to determine how I would tackle this memoir of her. For many years Kieran has been a Professional Officer in the National Library of Australia.

Canberra, June 16th 1996

Dear Jennifer,

I am not sure how long a sufficient answer to your three questions will take me. This is because I sit down and think about them, and my memory swells with startlingly fresh recollections of Sarah. Is it very forward of me to want to commit these recollections to paper and pass them on to you? We have met but once, after all. Yet spouses inherit their partner's schoolfriends, and Sarah always allowed me to read your letters to her as they arrived over the years.

Anyway, I have set aside the next few evenings in order to reply to your letter. My thanks for both the outline of your proposal to turn Sarah's correspondence with you into a memoir, and for the forewarning about some of her comments touching our married relationship.

You need have no concern about the latter, for I am perfectly aware that she was not, by nature, a malicious person. Indeed, her cheerful detachment, punctuated by short bouts of uneasy conscience, was quite the opposite to malice, as you well know. That is not to say that the effect of her insouciance could not sometimes hurt those of us who found ourselves in her vicinity.

For all that the event is now six years ago, Sarah's disappearance continues to make me feel numb and unwilling to believe it, especially so given the outlandish role played by that Barney person. Never, in our twelve years together, did I meet anyone who wished Sarah ill. In fact the reaction to her was often strangely protective. Take my mother. With innumerable purchases of useful household items, she intervened to 'save Sarah the trouble of the marketplace'. But the spell affected other, chance-met people too. Twice Sarah had wanted to buy a secondhand car, and on both occasions (the second resulting in the battered Datsun you mention in your letter), I recall there was some chance-met, ginger-haired tough with mechanical nous at hand to volunteer himself as an adviser.

Then again, observing her self-possessed air, some of the women staff at the library once decided she needed female companionship and tried to enlist her for their 'ladies' nights'. Out of cheerful curiosity Sarah even went to one or two of these evenings before, apologetically, she excused herself from interest in their society.

As her friend, you are easily able to imagine how Sarah ambled through these attentions: well-disposed, essentially untouched, perhaps a little puzzled that she should attract such solicitude from people.

'Doesn't Sarah sometimes want another person to confide in?' my mother asked me once, rather hopefully. I replied that Sarah was a very self-possessed person. 'A little off the planet is what you really mean,' was my mother's rejoinder.

Of course I remain hopeful that, even after this time, some happy outcome for the two of them might still emerge from Peru. For who knows what could have happened in those mountains? My thanks for sending me one of Sarah's photos of the terrain. I didn't like the look of the Cordillera Occidental one bit — it's a pinkish version of the moon, no? — and why she would want to bicycle through it is a crazy whim only she could account for. Even so, it is simply too hard for me to imagine some malevolence trailing her bicycle along those mountain roads and intending her harm.

How easy this is to say. And yet we both know her temperament, how she was quite capable of turning her life around in a moment. Was not her decision to marry me in 1977 one such instance of this? And is it impossible, I find myself wondering, that back in 1990, her spirit made weary by all that questing among past things, Sarah decided, spur of the moment, that she would drop all her former contacts and disappear like a hermit into some austere Andean village, no doubt thinking that, at a future date when it suited, she would send us each one of her long letters detailing her adventures and telling us how her life had been renewed?

How easy it is, when you want someone back, to dream up these scenarios. And can we not, both of us, foresee Sarah's genuine surprise when we each in turn wrote back to her Andean shack, infuriated, declaring how concerned we had been for her safety?

Of course I know, like you, that such optimism is forlorn, for she exposed herself to danger quite recklessly on this occasion, I think. And there is the Barney person to account for. Yet something in the sheer casualness of her fate (do you feel it *was* casual?) puts me in mind of a well-meaning but not especially responsible spirit slipping from view on a fancy. One day, no doubt, a peon will find some ghastly human remains shoved into a gulch in the Cordillera Occidental, and we will be informed. I dread the finality of it when it comes, but I suppose it will resolve our doubts.

One effect her disappearance had on me was to make me join Amnesty International. I am not quite sure why this should be cause-and-effect because I still consider myself a selfish person. But when I used to think of Sarah's fate in those mountains, something in its loneliness gave me visions of innocent men and women being imprisoned and outraged. I help with a mailing list, sell badges outside supermarkets on Saturday mornings, and give some money. Strangely, this makes me feel not quite so helpless in the face of Sarah's arbitrary end.

And so, to your three questions.

I can answer the middle one shortly. Yes, I knew one of the Tilbers was supposed to have come out to Australia, and yes, I was aware that she had further information about him in one of the letters her father sent her not long before he died. That letter is among the items I returned to Hazel. But I paid this detail of Tilber family history no special mind, and never during our marriage did I hear Sarah talk at any length about this seafaring ancestor, Charles Tilber. She liked having photographs of old ships on the walls of our house and I knew, of course, of Ben Tilber's genealogical hobby, for I had seen the famous family trees on my first visit to Hardacre Street in 1977.

Equally, I was aware that Sarah had an imaginative life going on most of the time. As you will hear, it was the most striking feature about my first meeting with her because it seemed to detach her from the rest of us. This detachment was a most forcible impression. It is not even as though her imaginings were especially guarded matters. Rather, they were a mental set she slipped into, more abstractly, more unreachably, I'm bound to say, as our marriage progressed. I've known her go into the bathroom intending to have a shower. Forty minutes later, if I put my head around the door, I would find her naked to the waist, hugging herself abstractedly, not yet having turned on the taps. So raptly could her attention focus on some inner object. When this happened she used to remind me of Coleridge a little, whose distracted 'absences' I never quite believed in until I came to know Sarah in the intimate circumstances of a marriage. These 'absences' became particularly frequent after the death of her father in 1987.

However, while being aware of an Australian connection, I was not privy to much of the imagined substance in Sarah's mind. (I was keener that she should finish with the shower so I could use it myself!) Nor could I guess the intensity of the historical interest which I encountered in the documents I found in her Semaphore flat when I cleared out her few things. It is quite probable that her Great-Uncle Charles was featuring in her imaginings towards the end of our relationship, given the energy with which you say Sarah researched his life after she deserted me in 1989. In my phone calls to Adelaide after her flight, she answered my enquiries about how she was living by mentioning the adult writing classes she taught. I tried to say how this new role sounded both right for her and a refreshing change from the library. She said, well, she supposed it *was* refreshing. But we were like strangers talking by then. No hostility. Just clumsiness. Transmitting weak signals to each other, you might say.

So I knew very little of the old mariner, and I did not really pay much heed to the details in the Tilber family genealogy beyond the polite interest I showed towards her father's documents in '77.

Monday evening

Requiring greater detail was your first request that I recall for you the circumstances by which Sarah and I came together. Forgive me if, for the sake of orderly progression, I repeat here some of the things you may have learned from Sarah herself when you attended our wedding.

My jokey version of events (with which I used to tease her sometimes) is that I was her 'pick-up', her 'toy boy'. Though 'pick-up' and 'toy boy' hardly convey the innocence with which our relationship commenced.

On a luminous July evening in 1977, literally while we were sitting at each end of a park bench beside the Brayford Pool on the River Witham in the middle of your English town of Lincoln, she talked me into going with her. You could not imagine anything more chaste.

This was the year when Sarah was attending her postgraduate course in school librarianship at the Bishop

Grosseteste Teachers' College there. You will know she was twenty-nine in that year. For my part, I was a twenty-two-year-old Australian who, having completed a degree in history and philosophy, was now making the conventional grand tour. I had bussed from Scotland by a roundabout route through various cathedral towns — Durham, Beverley and York. After Lincoln, I intended to look at Ely before heading south for Canterbury, Winchester, Salisbury, Wells, etcetera. With my methodical habits I suppose you could say I was 'collecting' the English cathedrals. I was certainly buying, then sticking down in my travel diary of the time, all the postcards I could find of these magnificent places of worship.

I remember when she first saw me writing the journal at her breakfast table on the morning after her 'pick-up', Sarah asked me, 'What makes you want to keep that?'

I quickly learned that you could not give this person pat answers because when I complacently offered, 'So I can tell where I've been,' she probed further. 'Yes, but *what* makes you want to do that?'

To this I replied, 'I don't know. To make me feel my visits to these places are authentic, I suppose.' Sarah considered for a few moments, then asked, 'Do you think that events lose authenticity once they have happened?' I was not ready for the question, and replied that I did not know, whereupon she stated that she rather thought they did not, and pursued the topic no further. I had a vague sense I had just failed a test.

But to take you back, I had arrived in Lincoln to find the youth hostel was booked out. This unsettled me, for I did not enjoy the prospect of camping beneath some

English hedge. You'll think this very timid behaviour for the tearaway Australian spirit, no doubt. Well, I am not a tearaway, alas. Perhaps my life hitherto had been sheltered. I had done no backpacking in Australia, and to my imagination there was something incalculable about hitchhiking in overcrowded Britain that allowed me to conjure up scenes of being pinned inside my sleeping bag while crew-cut toughs went through my belongings, or, worse perhaps, having some tramp settle with his meths bottle uncomfortably close to my camp site while he treated me to his interminable and incoherent life story. Because it was more populous, more instinct with dark deeds and associations (more thoroughly televised perhaps), your country seemed to me so much more menacing than mine when it came to the prospect of sleeping on my own in the open. I mention this because, presently, I will describe the effect on me that Sarah's company would have.

Being summer, the twilight was drawn out and this gave me the illusion that my day had been unusually long and encompassing. (I had been up since dawn and had visited two of the above-mentioned cathedrals that day.) Every south-facing surface was touched by the lemony light, which also suffused through the big leaves of the English chestnut trees and glittered in the dense copper beeches. Both voluptuous and delicate, it was also, to my Australian eyes, just a little unreal, like a scene already composed and translated into art, and it evoked in me an odd sensation, as though I were distant from myself. (Dare I say, like a prince in the land of the not-so-good faerie queen.)

So I wandered about the Lincoln streets and eventually found myself beside Brayford Pool, unwilling to meet the expense of a hotel room, and not knowing quite what else to do.

As I contemplated the water in this mood, partly estranged, partly aware I needed to resolve where I was going to stay, I first noticed Sarah. She sat on a park bench, breaking off bits of crust and throwing them to a group of swans which converged towards the bank. There was a satchel beside her from which protruded several folders. I'm a shy person. My instinct in a public place is to find an unoccupied bench where I can sit alone with my thoughts. But for some reason I went over, dumped my pack with its little Australian flag sewn onto the flap, and sat down on the other end of her bench. She seemed not to object.

How is an amorous attraction first kindled? Can it occur, not when you meet the image of your ideal partner, but when you encounter a person whose appearance and manner sets you agreeably free from that ideal? I had grown accustomed to think my preference was for (don't laugh) a dreamy film star type of girl, neat in figure, serene in manner, who brushes back a long sheaf of fair hair with a negligent hand before saying, soulfully (and probably with an American twang!), 'There's something troubling you, Kieran. Won't you tell me?'

Well! This person beside me now had a bob of dark hair, unbrushed. She was, I suppose, more burly than petite, and it was clear she wore her plain skirt and blouse without the slightest interest in creating an impression. Yet I was immediately conscious of finding her pleasing.

Amiable rather. Her eyes, especially, had a lovely animation, hopeful, alert for what might present itself.

We sat for some minutes. I believe the words 'I beg your pardon' were the first I exchanged with my future wife, for I was aware she had said something to me.

She repeated that I was welcome to throw the swans something too, and a brown paper bag was being proffered.

We tossed the bread at those big, gliding birds. To make conversation, I told her that I found their long curved necks and silent glidings on the water more threatening than graceful.

'Reptilian,' I said, then qualified, 'just a little at any rate.'

'You're being fanciful, surely,' she replied to this, which, in the light of what I was about to hear, was a little rich, you'll agree.

The evening luminescence had grown more saturated, more yolk-like in colour, for it was after eight now. Again we did not talk for some time. Then this person beside me indicated the view towards the town and Lindum Hill that faced us across the water, and asked me what I thought I saw when I looked at it.

'Are you an art student?' I asked, thinking that I was being challenged on some matter to do with visual perception.

'Just say what you see,' she insisted without answering my question.

So I responded warily that I saw swans, pleasure boats, an ice-cream kiosk on the far side, parked cars, houses climbing the hill towards where there stood, what I recall emphasising, the *awesome* cathedral and its three towers.

She looked at me with a level gaze, waiting to see if I

had completely finished, before she began telling me her own version. When this came, it was my first taste of Sarah's 'hurtlesome' style, and I saw how, in the manner perhaps of a land developer issuing directions to surveyors, she used her arms to section off the scene before us.

'This is what we are looking at,' she opened. (I can recall it practically verbatim.) 'From there to there against the far bank you can see blunt-bowed, wooden rivercraft of various kinds, wherries, keels, cobles. That deep-laden one over there,' she pointed to an empty space of water, 'is a vessel called a Humber keel. You will note how these several vessels are in different stages of derigging, having arrived from Boston. For instance, look how the one to the left has its creamy rectangle of sail still set, though hanging slackly now that the wind has dropped. Now look at the one in front, how blackly its sail profiles itself in the shadow of the other. And there,' she pointed towards the ice-cream kiosk, 'is another Humber keel with its canvas slack and so heavy on the spar you can almost feel the texture of the cloth. Over here to the right you can see how the sail of the smaller wherry is collapsing into ponderous folds as it comes down the mast. Look, there's the silhouette of a fellow against it, the watchman, do you think? I have always loved the crowdedness of this wharfside, and the way at this time of evening all the sails of the shipping are tinged with the ... what would you say? ... the *smeary fire* of the sunset mingled with all the chimney smoke from the houses of the town. And how these colours reflect in the water and flicker towards where we are sitting! It is like lacquer on some warm timber ...'

You can imagine how I looked at those eyes to see if I was in the company of a loony. I asked her, 'You say you have *always* loved the way ...?' But those eyes were animated and intelligent.

'Shush,' she instructed. 'Look, you can see more bare masts in the penumbra, and behind them the two redbrick buildings.' She pointed to two which appeared in a very whitewashed condition to my eyes. 'How orange they are in the smoky light, as though illuminated from below by the glow of braziers along the wharf. Now,' she put a hand on my sleeve, 'we will direct our attention upwards across —'

'You sound like a schoolteacher on an excursion,' I interjected.

'*Shush!*' she instructed again, then relenting, she added, 'I am, sort of,' and paused, as a teacher will pause in order to restore order. Then she resumed her description. 'We will direct our attention upwards across the higgledy-piggledy of roofs and the smoky atmosphere created by their chimneys, to where the cathedral is catching the light along its southern facades. It is peppery in colour and yes, you are right, it is awesome.'

Again I wanted to chime in, but she was not yet ready to be interrupted. 'And so to the sky. To our east you will note the patch of blue, then a *gorgeous* swathe of fawn cloud (or would you say it was tan?), which is the crest of the dark mass of indigo storm you can see coming in from the west. That's it.' She finished with evident satisfaction.

'But it isn't,' I laughed.

'It is. Plain as peanuts.' And she had a smile at the corners of her mouth. I was being played with.

'I don't understand.'

'Anno Domini 1867,' she said, then added with the same cheerful informativeness, 'And by the way, I'm Sarah.'

I was prompted to ask, 'Are you 1867 too?' and my flippant question brought a playful expression to her eyes that suggested I could believe what I wished. So I told her my own name, we shook hands briefly, and I said, 'For a pure fantasy, you sound so very sure of your details,' whereupon she took a lecture folder out of her bag and from it produced a postcard on which there was a rather fine, albeit romantic, painting by one Henry Dawson of the scene that confronted us.

'You transposed that?'

'Shall we say it was my prompt. I was rehearsing it when you came along.'

'Rehearsing? Why?'

'Don't you sometimes like the sensation of living in parallel? Then you can take what is and what was, and twist a single plait out of them?'

'I've never thought about it. Besides, you can't live in parallel, not really.'

'Of course you can. What's *really*?'

I told her that a large part of my honours thesis had been about trying to determine exactly that.

But Sarah's interest in time was eccentric, egotistical, rather than academic. She said, 'When I want to feel a bit more complete in myself, I find somewhere like this bench where I can sit and practise.'

I suppose I could have taken this person as being just a little cracked, if it were not for a look in her eyes and a set to her mouth that suggested she was also amused by the effect she might be having on others. Yet she stated these odd views with such crispness that one complied with her lead automatically, and in my case you might say I did so for the rest of our lives together. For it is still Sarah's version of the view across Brayford Pool that is most vividly in my memory rather than the one which was actually before us. Also, I confess, I had promptly slipped her into that stereotype of the forthright English lady which allowed me, in my turn, to be amused as I was being led.

Now she looked at me sidelong, and drew attention to my Australian accent. This required me to give an account of myself, and led to Sarah quizzing me about my travels in Britain. She had been to many of the historic sites I enumerated, and all at once I found myself talking uninhibitedly with her, basking in the attention and the exchange. I heard about her several 'grisly' years of teaching, her school librarianship course, and disclosed how I, myself, was toying with the idea of a librarianship course on my return to Australia.

The twilight persisted, we talked, and then, in that abrupt British fashion, the sky darkened and there came down a shower of rain. So we ran for shelter to a pizzeria, ordered an evening meal and bought a cheap Portuguese wine to go with it. When Sarah heard about my accommodation anxieties, she promptly invited me to stay in the house where she rented a room.

'You're taking me very much on trust, you know,' is what I recall responding to this invitation.

But she was confident and playful. 'Am I? I have beside me a gentleman, somewhat nervous. He has the good, but deprecating, manners of a colonial of the better sort.' (I winced at this blithe patronising.) 'He seeks temporary refuge and ...' (I swear I saw her eyes twinkle) '...companionship with an eligible English spinster.' She looked at me with that steady gaze for a moment, and I realised she was probably older than I was. 'Don't worry. I keep a flick knife in my bag. I think I'll cope,' she finished.

We laughed, and I made a mental note of the simple practicality of that flick knife. (Only now does it occur to me to wonder whether this weapon later led her into trouble up there near Pizacoma.)

We continued to talk amicably as we ate. For the meal we paid a scrupulous half each, then we wound our way up Lindum Hill along various narrow cobbled ways that gleamed from the rain. By the time we had reached her attic room in the Pottergate house and she had made us coffee, I felt I had been a friend (should I say rather, a follower?) of hers for years.

That, then, Jennifer, is how we met, and my thanks for your question because I find I have enjoyed recollecting it. So much so that I very much want to say a little about the days that followed in order to account for the effect Sarah had on me. But my fingers are stiff from typing, so I will resume this tomorrow evening.

Cont'd Tuesday

Those first days of ours were very chaste. In an elusive way, they set a theme for the whole of our relationship.

I was given what, you may remember from your own visits to Sarah in Lincoln, was termed 'the prayer room' at the back of the house. Indeed it remained in use throughout my visit. It was alarming, for instance, on that first night to wake and find a fellow in a yoga position at the foot of my bed. Despite the night's chill, he was bare chested, disconcertingly thin, with a lupine face that ended in a strand or two of beard. He stared at me intently.

When I called out, 'What do you want?', he appeared to sway slightly, but was otherwise unaffected by my presence for a minute or two. I wondered whether I might have been safer under that hedge. Then he went and sat on the chair where I had earlier piled my clothes.

'Are you with Sarah?' he asked.

I replied that I supposed so. 'She has allowed me to stay for a night or two,' I added, feeling absurdly that I had to establish some credentials with this yogi-looking fellow.

'She brings people back here sometimes,' he informed me. 'She finds them.' I was allowed to consider this, and then was asked, 'Do you like her?' The question seemed all the more intrusive because I could barely see my interrogator in the dark.

'I think so. Why?' I said.

He was silent for a few moments, and following this last question, to my relief, he had ceased to scrutinise me quite so intently. At length he said, 'Sarah is a very nice person, would you believe.'

'That is my conclusion,' I offered.

'But whenever she has to be sociable,' he continued, 'she comes across like someone in a play who hasn't got used to their lines. Are you with me?'

'I don't believe I am,' I replied.

I sensed rather than saw him furrowing his brow in the

obscurity. 'It's as though she has to think out what to do in order to be social. Do you see?'

I had to admit that I didn't.

Again I felt the scrutiny on me for some moments. Then he stated, 'I think I will go now,' and in an instant had slipped out.

It was the social ease of the bare-chested fellow rather than Sarah's that I reflected upon in the dark. In the morning I learned that this was Barney (no surname, it seems, neither then, nor post-Peru). He was described to me as a mild loony who slept all day and went about dressed like a holy man at night. There was some medication that he took. Though as a matter of fact, I now think his observation of Sarah was quite astute. And I am, like you, disconcerted by subsequent events.

More immediately, however, I was struck by the contrast between Sarah, with her homespun skirts and forthrightness, and the stagy meditations, joy-in-life singsongs, and the light-as-air clothing of psychedelic orange or purple chemises and pantaloons of her Aquarian Age Christian fellow lodgers. You saw them on your visits. Would you not agree? Yet how obvious it was that Sarah was the *true* free spirit there. You see, I had detected something sovereign in her and had already begun to love it. If she had a backwoodsy manner in her dealings with the Aquarians, she was also in splendid self-possession.

On that first morning she gave me a tour of the great cathedral. We wandered under the lofty fan vaulting and among the great arches with their inlay of Purbeck marble. She knew, of course, all about the catastrophic fire of 1141, and the rebuilding under Saint Hugh. She could tell me, for instance, how each of the village churches beside the Witham between Boston and Lincoln had an unwarrantable wealth of Purbeck marble as a result of what had been purloined from the barges bringing the material all the way from Dorset. When we stood beside the Angel choir, admiring the carving in stone and wood, I remember her explication.

'Gangs of stonemasons used to troop across Europe from job to job,' she told me. 'You can imagine them, standing in line here, one fellow perhaps from Norway next to another from Holland, and beside him perhaps a Fleming or a Londoner. They would have spoken some common, crude lingua franca to each other, much like I've heard the Russian, German, Scottish, Icelandic cod fishermen do today when they meet mid-Atlantic for a Christmas drink. And whenever a mason wanted a model for the imp or devil he was carving, what did he do but take the features of his immediate neighbour. See here! How's that for a seven-hundred-year-old historical snapshot?' And she tapped a pair of heads.

She moved me on. 'I think I like your headlong commentaries,' I declared to her rather weakly, though already, with the atmosphere of the great church all around us, and with that hint of detached amusement at the corners of her mouth as she held forth, I wanted to say I found her entire person rather lovable.

'Are you a churchgoer?' I asked, connecting her knowledge of the cathedral with her New Age housemates. 'By that, I mean a believer?'

She shook her head. 'I'm a pagan. I believe in what I imagine,' she said, 'but I believe it *is* imagining.'

'You mean 1867 and all that?'

'And *all* that.' Then she thought to add, 'Though sometimes my curiosity has moved me to sit at the back of a congregation in order to observe what priests actually do.'

'Why?'

'People who have arrived at a set of religious beliefs intrigue me. Priests particularly.' Then she gave me a quick glance. 'And are you a churchgoer?'

'No,' I replied quickly, then decided to trust her with the declaration that I sometimes thought I might be moving in that direction.

'Why?' she pounced.

To which I then managed this reply. 'I'm not sure. To be made secure from disappointment? I think it is something to do with wanting calmness. The kind of calmness that goes together with deep orderliness.'

Her response was mischievous. 'I think you look like one.'

'One what?' I enquired, naturally.

'Priest. Father. Vicar. Yes, vicar.'

I asked her what a vicar was supposed to look like.

'These days?' She considered my features for a moment, taking my chin in her hands and, with an impish tilt to her head, moving mine so that she could regard my profile, before deciding: 'Scholarly, and with a tentative good nature that is asking to be put to work in a good cause.'

Having thus assessed my person she grinned and I did not take her flippancy amiss. This subversive lightness in her mood was another theme that lasted into at least the early years of our marriage, for she was ever quick to prick my earnestness and I enjoyed this. We moved on to look at the chapterhouse, and it was in this round chamber that Sarah first mentioned your good self, Jennifer, and the Anglican camps at Cromer where the two of you went each summer.

'But you said you're a pagan.'

'I go in order to give Jenn some irreverent company, which she appreciates, and I enjoy the singsongs. When the girls all pray, I watch their faces.'

I have to say that the sheer detachment of this delighted me.

I also felt her efforts to give me a history lesson obliged me to respond in kind. So, when we were out in the open again, I parrotted happily from my Australian undergraduate curriculum about the flickering shadows on the walls of Plato's cave, about what Descartes said could be doubted and what could not, and other bits and pieces of catchy philosophy. Did she guess this was a tit for tat? As I say, I was conscious of her being older than me. Nonetheless, I found myself being listened to, and this was gladdening. I had never had much success with girls and now, miraculously I was enjoying myself, wandering among those mullioned windows and escutcheoned doors in the precincts of Minsteryard. We bought bread rolls, cheese, a jar of black olives and cans of lemonade for lunch and consumed them on a low wall that had pink valerian growing from the cracks. With a sharp thoom! Sarah spat the olive pips onto the grassy slope below and, catching sight of my amusement at this, asked, 'Does the colonial gentleman think the English spinster is being indelicate?'

'Not in the least,' I assured her, and sent a pip down the slope in the same manner.

'When I was small, my dad and I used to have competitions with plum stones to see how far we could spit them.'

'Should the English spinster not call her dad "papa", or "pater" or some such?' I asked, airily. 'Anno Domini 1867 and all that.' I was brought up short.

'No. He's my dad and he's real.' She looked at me and her smile no longer had quite the same nonchalance.

Recognising I had bumped against more serious matters, I gave her a quick apology, and for a few minutes we gazed at the outlook. From our vantage there on the wall we could see across a shimmery view of slate roofs and then the broad chequerboard green of England steaming to the south.

In the afternoon Sarah had her last tutorial for the year, and in the evening she worked on her final essay. She also put a proposition to me.

'Tolerate my swami friends interrupting your sleep for another three days. Then I'll be finished at the college, and we can bicycle down the B roads to Ely. From there we could travel on to my parents, where you could stay for a few days. They're always relieved if I bring home a male friend.'

My objection that I had no bicycle was promptly met by Sarah saying we would get one from the police sales. It needn't cost me much more than a train fare. This established another theme which persisted into our years of marriage: that *my* role became one of foreseeing difficulties, Sarah's to override them. But I was glad to accept the invitation to remain in that rambling Pottergate house. I felt the human contacts I had made on my travels hitherto had been bland and timid, but that with this new live-wire acquaintance I was 'onto a winner' as the Australian expression was. In part I could not believe how effortlessly my good fortune swept me along, how naturally the knack of forming a friendship with a woman came to me. And in part I wondered if it was shabby of me to regard Sarah as 'a winner'.

A rattleshake bicycle was procured for me at small cost. Sarah sent off the trunk of her belongings by rail to Ipswich, taking nothing but a sleeping bag, wash bag and change of clothes, while I attached my pack to a rack behind my saddle. Then we set out down the deep lanes of Lincolnshire and Norfolk.

Shall I tell you my mood as I pedalled after Sarah, or coasted down some long slope behind her? I felt like a canary, suddenly uncaged and flying in pursuit of my liberator. That night, and for the next two, despite my earlier qualms, we camped under hedges or piled high the mown hay in a paddock and lay on top of it, side by side in murmurous conversation, until we slept. Such was Sarah's breezy effect on my preference for a roof during the hours of darkness. It was not the flick knife in her bag that made me feel safe, but the fact of her companionship that never gave me time to consider how vulnerable we might have been. I recall the names of villages — Brothertoft, Hoffleat Stow, Friday Bridge — and how the moon popped up from behind a hedge, orange as a mandarin through the dust of the day's harvesting. At one point in the fen country she boasted how her dad's family had come from Holland and drained these squared-off fields. On the second day we stood together under Ely's lantern tower and I found it more marvellous, more ingenious, than anything I had yet seen. Late in the afternoon of the fourth day we leaned our bicycles against the coal-house wall of her parents' house, and I was introduced to the Tilber seniors, Ben and Hazel.

Thursday evening

Yes, they did seem to take some pleasure in the fact that Sarah had brought home a male friend. You will guess how they were as hospitable as that confined house allowed. I noted Sarah's sometimes peremptory manner with her mother, who was a homely soul, and the oddly distant banter of jokes with which she engaged her father. I had been prepared for a special relationship, and my impression was that she adored him but lacked an easygoing adult manner of expressing this. As you will confirm, he evidently thought the world of his 'Sal', and set his own considerable self-education at nought beside the various diplomas of this, his youngest child.

He had suffered, some weeks before, the first of the strokes which would eventually take him off in 1987. While I was a guest, his armchair had been placed for him to convalesce where a patch of sun streamed through the drawing room windows, and I used to sit beside him, looking at the chart of his family tree spread on his lap, but also watching how his eyes followed Sarah's movements with an attentive sadness. Ben was well disposed towards me, but I didn't quite know what to make of his arrayed ancestors, and our odd attempts

57

at conversation never quite meshed. I felt myself to be a clodhopper. So I was uneasy during the time I stayed at Felstone. The elder brothers, whose qualifications I gathered were technical, had both left home. As for yourself, you had already left for the Cromer camp where you were a coordinator, and where Sarah was due to add her irreverent company in a week.

'I'm coming on your cathedral binge in the southern counties,' was how she told me she was going to spend the intervening week.

So she borrowed her mother's little red car, and in this we travelled down the English motorways, circumventing London in order to take in Canterbury, Winchester, Salisbury, Wells, Gloucester and lastly Exeter in a westerly figure of eight. One thing I remember, somehow more significant now than it seemed then, is when we came before the tomb of Edward II at Gloucester Cathedral. His murder, as your own historical knowledge will tell you, was ghastly. We looked at the alabaster effigy of the sleeping king behind its web-like canopy. I was quite moved by the touching repose of the murdered man, and said so.

Sarah replied, 'I don't feel a thing. Piety repels me. You can't talk back to it.'

My response was to express surprise. 'I thought you were the one who was able to conjure up the past.'

'Some doors are closed.' She was already moving on.

In contrast to this was her animation whenever we reached some of the small harbour towns of Devon and Cornwall, through which we drove beyond Exeter. At Bideford, after poking around the seafront, we found an antique shop, and Sarah quickly discovered a group of photographs of the old town showing various craft berthed at a wharf, their decks cluttered with nautical paraphernalia, and fellows in waistcoats standing about. 'And some doors are open.' She took me by the elbow and turned the pages of black and white pictures. It was expected I would connect the open and closed doors, for all that a day and a half separated the two conversations.

Whenever I drove the car, Sarah would jerk the passenger seat back as far as possible (she had a brutal way with anything mechanical, I was to learn — cars, cassette players, washing machines) and place her bare feet up on the dashboard so that her white and blue patterned wraparound skirt fell back over her strong thighs. She had such battered feet! I loved the nonchalance of her gestures and postures, and wanted to touch her. Yet another inner voice was saying to me, 'No, this is different from those infrequent sexual opportunities of university. Here there is time. This is special. Let matters unfold as they will.' I could hardly believe how unlibidinously I behaved. Again we often slept out, once or twice scrambling into the car when a downpour filled the woods with its crescendo. Sometimes, as we sat watching the flickering needles of rain coming through the great trees, I would lean across and kiss her. She was happy to allow this. Indeed, she would hold her head back an inch or so and look at me a little wonderingly, as though kissing were an activity she had heard about but not yet encountered. She said she preferred it not to be on the mouth for the practical reason that she felt she could not breathe properly while the kiss was happening. Nor, my intuition told me, was she one for holding hands or casually resting a head on a shoulder. Her person was a most sovereign matter.

Then one evening on the homeward leg of our trip, as we lay side by side in our respective sleeping bags, passing a bottle of cider between ourselves, looking up through the branches of an oak tree, we had an exchange which still feels dreamlike in my memory of it.

Sarah said, 'By the way, I'll marry you, if you like.'

And in a calm, dazed voice I heard myself respond, 'What for?'

She laughed at the bluntness of my answer. 'Because I enjoy the way you can talk about things and you have an arranging sort of a mind.' I heard her voice from the dark. 'I believe I could live with that.'

I said, 'But what about Australia?' and her reply was that Australia would be perfectly fine, she would come with me there if I liked. One of her dad's uncles was supposed to have gone to Australia. She might try and look him up for her dad's family tree. Who knows, there might be a distant Tilber cousin with a gold mine at Kalgoorlie or a block of flats at Coolangatta.

'You see. It can all fit if you want it to,' she remarked.

Do I convey the dreamy atmosphere of this conversation? After a silence I confided how I would always be apprehensive that, when all I had to say about Plato's cave and Descartes' systematic doubts had been trotted out, there would come a day when she would find me a rather dull sort of a person. But she laughed, and said that, all right, when that day came, naturally she would leave me. Here was that alarming detachment again. And so I said, yes, why not get married, because my cavilling at the idea had not disguised the fact that I was thrilled by it.

Well, Jennifer, you know most of the rest. We told her parents on our return. Her dad was happy enough with me, but not with the prospect of his youngest being out in Australia. We took six weeks to think about it. I hitchhiked around Holland, northern Germany and Denmark, while Sarah joined you at your camp. Then we were married at the Woolverstone church in late September. My own parents, taken aback by the suddenness of events and the fact that my bride was seven years older than I was, came over for the celebration. Sarah and I took jobs, she as a school librarian, while I had a succession of night-cleaning employments. Then we decided to return here to Canberra, which we did in mid-1978. Within three years we found ourselves working in the same building: Australia's National Library.

Sunday morning

Your last question asks me what my thoughts are on why Sarah left me, and you mention your qualms in probing me on such a personal matter. Actually, I feel a certain freedom in describing these things for you because, as I say, I have followed your correspondence with Sarah over the years and know the quality of your friendship. Obscurely, I feel you have a right in the matter, since you, like me, thought the world of her. Besides, I think I can answer the question concisely.

As I had predicted in that dreamy wood, her interest in me lapsed. I have kept on file the note she left for me to find when I returned from the Library that day in 1989 and it says it with almost comic plainness.

'Kier,' it reads, 'I'm taking a break from your company, I'm not sure for how long, probably for good. I don't feel properly alive here any more. *Of course* this makes me feel mean, which is why I have chosen to leave this note. *Of course* the gutsier option would have been to look you in the eye. Though surely you've seen this coming? Well, maybe not ... I'll let you know my forwarding address. *Of course* you are an admirable person. It's just that our lives are on divergent paths and argument about that fact is useless. Sorry. What a furnace of a day to land this on you too. S.'

This manner of leaving *was* sneaky of her, and quite uncharacteristic. I think it was the result of a panic. She wanted a particular, *romantic* kind of freedom (one more usually sought by males, by my observation), and could not resolve how to take it without doing hurt.

Is it fair for me to say I was surprised and baffled by this note? Not quite. For a year or so before the envelope was left on the telephone table I knew our involvement with each other was persisting through a kind of helpless inertia. We moved around our weatherboard house, exchanged the conventional remarks, occasionally stole glances at each other across the formica table. But during that time I could see from day to day her dissatisfaction. Indeed, visually Sarah seemed to be shrinking, no, *hunching* into herself almost. You know she had in her movements such a free, upright, natural poise — 'carriage' is the old-fashioned word. And I did not know what I could do about it, so I used to bring home lots of work, and sometimes a day might go past where we hardly said a word to each other, even though we worked in the same building and went there each morning in the same car, usually Sarah's. In the evening the television would cover our silences.

Once I tried to remark jocularly, 'Do you realise we haven't talked to each other since anno Domini 1867?' But she shrugged, and allowed the flickerings of the screen to absorb her.

I cannot say I could detect a particular alternative focus for her energies. But it is now clear she was looking for an interest in which the essential life, as she perceived it, still inhered. And where did this alight? Upon a dead relative! Never did it enter her head, I think, to seek this interest in another lover. I'm now convinced that when Sarah, in her whimsical . . . her abstracted way, took me up in Lincoln, it was her one life experiment in living as man-and-woman. As abstractly as she dropped me, she dropped the idea of a partnership with anyone else. 'Do you see anyone?' I could not stop myself from asking her on one of the occasions I phoned Adelaide. 'I didn't leave you for any reasons that could make you jealous, Kier,' she assured me. Perhaps I should be grateful. For as you know, I have remained under the spell of her cheerful, outlandish innocence.

Having no children spared both of us from the moral consequences of her restive intelligence.

I think our marriage of twelve years was a case where an inconsolably lonesome person teamed up with an inveterate solitary. It is unpleasant (and self-indulgent, I suppose) for me to have to put this construction on things, but that is how I now see them. We did have our moments of joy. As much as Sarah's strange detachment, it is probable that my own lack of imagination when responding to Sarah meant that these moments never became quite expansive enough for our marriage to have survived as a source of sufficient stimulation for her.

Well, I must close now and get this off to you. Your original letter to me mentions the slender, dark-haired Australian with sallow complexion who you met outside the Woolverstone church in 1977. Still slender, I can assure you, though I have lost some of that page-boy hair. Within the last year I have been fortunate to meet someone else, also called Sally — Sallyanne — and to be accepted by her teenage children. I still work at the Library. As you can see, the house was not sold in the end. I have no idea how to answer your kindly meant question, 'Am I happy?'

Let me close by making one observation on those letters of yours that used to arrive for Sarah and which she let me read. I think I understand something of the spontaneous joy you took in each other's company. That quality was present, certainly at the outset of *our* life together, and, I like to believe, never entirely absent during our more difficult years. I remember her with gratitude and, for that reason, permit me to say I remain your friend.

My best wishes to your husband and family, Kieran Fawne.

Of the people Sarah met in South Australia during her researches, I wrote to several, including Mr Albert Prideauz, whose taped interview with Sarah will appear on these pages shortly. Despite an uncertainty about his address, I received a short note back from him which was largely unhelpful.

Vale Park, SA [no date]
    Dear Mrs Happle,

When I told Miss Fawne the things I knew about her relative, she said they were going to be for one of the museums here. She has never placed them in one that I can discover. Maybe you will set that right with your book.

You ask about her flat. She lived in a bedsitter with a kitchenette off. You expect a woman to make a place look nice, but except for some pretty teapots on a shelf, she just had a bed, a desk and a couple of chairs. Funny sort of a home, I thought, when I went there.

You also ask, did I like your friend? I don't think I thought about it one way or the other. She was the right person to tell what I knew, so I did. She was pleasant, and as keen as mustard about our tapes. I didn't like to hear what happened to her. Who would?

Yours sincerely, Albert Prideauz.

Warmer, and more forthcoming, was the letter I received from Nina Musson who had been a nurse attending Sarah's great-uncle in his last years, and who Sarah interviewed at some length.

Victor Harbor, July 1st 1996

Dear Jennifer Happle,

I must thank you for your letter. Yes, I remember Sarah's visit well, and I was saddened to hear from you what had become of her.

On the occasion she came here we spoke for some time about 'the Captain', her great-uncle. She will have told you about the nights I sat with him in her letters to you which you mention, so I do not need to repeat any of it. I was glad I was able to tell her about the 'smoke drawings' and enable her to recognise what she already had in her possession.

I found Sarah a very pleasant person, and very bound up with the business of researching her great-uncle. Some of her questions surprised me. It was as though she would have liked to have done a drawing of the old man herself. I'll give you examples.

Did I remember what his hands looked like, his fingernails? I told her they were very arthritic when he was with us, and therefore stiff and clawlike. We used to keep the fingernails of all the old gentlemen trimmed.

Did he eat his food in a distinctive way? 'He ate very little. At the end we needed to feed him a little soup each day,' I said, and reminded her that the Captain had probably suffered at least one minor stroke sometime before his admission to Rostrevor Rest Home, the effect of which was the disarrangement of some of his memories.

These answers, I could see, disappointed Sarah, who was looking for clues to what she called the Captain's 'essentialness'. Some of her questions were harder to answer. *Did I ever hear the Captain tell anything like a joke?*

Was there anything characteristic in the things that made him laugh or smile? I could see how earnest her enquiries were, but could give her nothing useful here. She was interested in the odd bits and pieces I was able to learn from the Captain during those night shifts when I sat with him.

One little thing she would not have mentioned, and it only occurs to me to remember it now that I have heard about the evil fortune which has overtaken her.

The morning she left we had stood at the porch of our house here at Victor Harbor. Then Sarah went to her car and put her recorder into the back. She was, I suppose, about twenty yards away and, as I watched her, I felt a sensation of great sadness on her behalf. I am not certain why this feeling should have come upon me so suddenly, except that it was accompanied by the perception that I was watching a person who was unusually alone. I think this was the outcome of her very thorough and searching interview with me.

She returned to say goodbye and I made the comment: 'You are very attached to these matters of the past, my dear, aren't you?' She agreed with me and looked at me in a way I cannot quite express, as though she were saying that this could not be helped and was not altogether to her liking. And I found that I wanted to say to her that she would feel happier if she could concentrate her obvious energies and goodwill on things of the moment.

But instead I simply said, 'Well, you must take care, you know,' and with that she left.

You see, during the war I was taken from my home in Czechoslovakia and put into different labour camps. Several times I came across women who were like this, friendly enough, but detached from the rest of us who used to rely on each other to keep cheerful through the work in the propeller factories, and the cold and the dangers. They did not survive so well as we others did. Sometimes a sickness took them, typhoid or pneumonia. One I knew, who was repatriated after the liberation, simply seemed to give up living despite nothing obvious being wrong with her health or faculties. I used to watch this and feel so helpless to intervene. Sarah reminded me of these experiences. She seemed to me to be so unattached. I had discovered that I liked her, for she was kind and unafraid, I thought, and, in her own fashion, deeply attentive. But she wasn't properly present, somehow. I wish I could explain it. I'm so sorry for those of you who tried to be her friends.

Yours sincerely, Nina (Kovacs) Musson.

Establishing Charlie Tilber

June 1989

The spate of Sarah's correspondence began in this month, and overwhelmed me just a little. Sometimes the letters were typed in dense paragraphs; more often they were handwritten on pages which were torn as a piece from their pad with the bright red sticky tape keeping the sheaf together. I used to unfold and read them at the dining room table, and, as I did so, the individual pages would curl, almost as though transmitting the nervous energy with which they had been written. The first told me of her sudden flight from marriage.

Semaphore, June 2nd

Dearest Jenn,

Yes, I know. It has been *several* months between letters. I have decamped to this Adelaide beach suburb. I wanted, no, *craved,* sea air and an unimpeded horizon. You may have heard from my mother that, after testing married life for twelve years, I have separated from Kier. Nothing filed or legal yet, merely indefinite leave of absence.

'Might you come back, do you think?' he asks on the phone each Sunday night.

'Look. Probably not,' I reply.

'I only said "Might you . . . ?"' he insists.

'Please,' I say.

'Sarah, I don't understand why you left here so abruptly,' he asks me reasonably, and the phone seems to pulse gently with the nine hundred miles between us.

'Neither do I yet,' I respond. But I do. That's the pity.

Oh dear.

I am composing this to you at the end of the Semaphore jetty with my legs dangling above the green water. It is a mild winter morning and I feel as if I am aeons away from both Canberra and Hardacre Street. I do wish Dad had not passed on when he did, for I miss his letters. I hate the phone: it is too claimant. Letters — his, yours, mine — give me the distance at which I feel most comfortable when dealing with people. You know you couldn't doubt my attachment to Dad. Yet it used to worry me that I found him harder to talk to from my late teens. It wasn't Dad's fault. Some part of me just became harder to offer. He was canny enough to cross that distance in his letters to me.

Here are my new surroundings. Below me the little waves sidle to the beach, each ruffed like a poodle. Among Norfolk and Aleppo pines is the amusement park, behind that the Esplanade and its sandy bungalows. North is Largs Bay, and further, a trio of huge gantries marking Port Adelaide's Outer Harbour. If I look to the seaward I can see an anchored vessel with the livestock pens in ungainly tiers high on her decks. Beyond that ship, the Investigator Strait, and then hundreds of sea miles of unbridled ocean until, perhaps, you might bump into the remote Kerguelen Islands with their white bracelets of surf and sea birds. The wonderful openness of this prospect!

I look at this and for reasons I do not understand, but which I think are to do with my feeling the loss of Dad, I experience a sad yet somehow *exultant* feeling that tells me: 'Sarah, you are better off having no place, for any one place is quite the equivalent of another.'

This freedom became impossible in Canberra with Kier.

God knows, the break with him could have been messier. We didn't fight much, or even bicker. It was more the *pallor* of our lives that oppressed me. From the postcards I sent you after I migrated to Canberra in 1978 you will have seen the grandiose building where Kier and I were employed. I used to sit at my allotted desk and watch the earnest joggers in their colourful singlets plodding around the pretty lake. I yearned for the scruffiness, smokiness, *industry*, of a real waterfront, say Ipswich's Albion Wharf, or our Cathouse Hard.

For an age, it seemed, Kier and I dwelt in this strobe-lit archive like silverfish, nibbling and scurrying among the folds of interminable dossiers and bound volumes. Then we went home with a stack of files to prepare for the morrow's conferences. I almost expected some providential finger would come out of the air conditioning and squash us each into a small, powdery smear. Worse, I observed Kier to be content with this.

'Unfair, Sal!' you'll say. Yes, of course it is, but I can trust my intolerance with you.

The result of my discontent is that in February I resigned from the library, put my electric typewriter, my teapots, Dad's letters, a couple of suitcases of clothes and books all into my Datsun and, on a stinking hot day, bolted.

All day the dear little car took me across the endless Australian plains. Mirages glittered on the road in front of me and created broad, phoney lakes on either side. I would see a shimmery blip on my horizon and ten minutes later a monstrous truck would roar past me, causing the Datsun to shudder in the air rush. Very alarming.

That night I camped by the side of the Murray River at Mildura. I slid from my sleeping bag into the water like a crocodile whenever I wished to cool off, watched the stars above me and felt grateful for those huge interstellar distances. A restored paddle steamer thrashed by me once, lit up and crowded with revellers who called out greetings to me. Close by was a concrete bridge on high pylons across which the pantechnicons roared all night, making for their far-flung destinations. I woke early, saw an eagle patrolling the river bank on still wings, found some coffee in an early-opening café, then drove to Adelaide, where I bought a map at a petrol station and decided on this beach suburb because I liked the name Semaphore. A visit to a real estate agent secured me this flat, which I took because, past the walls of further apartments, stands a slender column of ocean, blue-green like azurite. I felt so decisive, and so free.

Now I have been here four months. Every three or four weeks I hear Kier's voice on the telephone, polite, withheld. He is being brave, of course, which makes my conscience prickle somewhat.

I'll not try you with any more of this grey marital matter. I have begun some research and will have things to tell you. Do you mind being my sounding board for a few months? Like old times, you'll say, with that tolerant sidelong look you used to give me from the hammock in your parents' garden. Love, S.

⤜⤝

A second letter arrived a week later. She was using her unattached state, she explained, to delve into a byway of Tilber family history. But so that I might be fully briefed, she would trace for me the origin of her interest in that childhood of hers which I thought I already knew quite well.

Semaphore, June 8th

You see, Jenn, my intention is to try and repossess a palpable human being, namely my great-uncle, Charles Harling Tilber. It is not that there are unresolved crimes or lost fortunes in the case. Who needs such commonplace riddles anyway when there is the more absorbing mystery of locating a personality among the multitude in Hades?

What *is* all this, you might ask. Do you remember from Hardacre Street days how keen Dad was about our family genealogy? Typically you could find him at the dining room table, busy with his charts of the Tilbers and the families they had married into: the Kippises, the Lackfords, the Femisters and Beards, Tollivers and Haughs. Scattered about him used to be his set square, a sharp pencil and the ultra-fine rapidographs with which he used to enter the minute names, dates and places on these extensive documents, one charting the Tilbers, one the Lackfords, and so on.

'If we could only go far enough back, we might find ourselves related to everyone,' he used to tell me with a smile. 'What do you think of that for a grand idea, my Sal?'

I thought it grand indeed.

And so, to take ourselves back (though not as far as the trees), there were weekend excursions to parish churches and town halls all around East Anglia. You came on some and will recall how, at Dad's direction, we copied into the exercise books he had provided the inscriptions on wall plaques, and the dates and names in church registers or shire rolls. On the return home, he would lead us in a relay singing of:

> *London's burning, London's burning,*
> *Pour on water, pour on water.*
> *Fire! Fire!*

Meanwhile Derek and Brian sat in the back, holding their plastic aeroplanes out of the windows such that the propellers might spin in the car's slipstream. Invariably my mother was absent from these occasions, having not one scrap of curiosity about her own (Tolliver) ancestry or anyone else's. She gardened, sat at the sewing machine, dealt with the present, you might say. How was such a one-dimensional life tolerable, I sometimes wondered.

The information we gathered Dad then transcribed onto his charts, or typed on a black Olivetti so that it might be ready for the printer in Ipswich to run off two dozen or so pamphlets bearing such titles as *The Tilbers of*

Saxstead Green or *Martha Kippis and her Descendants,* documents which Dad handed around to his elder nephews and nieces as gifts at Christmas.

'You Tilbers are a hobby-oriented outfit,' your own father once remarked to me when I presented him with one of these.

In my teens I recall I grew impatient with Dad. 'I don't see why you are taking all this trouble,' I complained once, feeling grouchy at the sight of him amid all those documents, so patient, so passive, so *docile* as I then thought.

'Don't you want to feel it's all there if you need it, Sal?'

Whenever Dad detected that I was trying to provoke him, he always replied with a mild question. And when I said brutally, 'Not especially,' he looked away and I could see I had hurt his feelings. This made me feel both remorseful and unrepentant. I never meant to disappoint him, but I always knew I could do so far more easily than Derek or Brian, which burdened me with a responsibility I felt was unfair.

Besides, a part of me also wanted 'it' to be all there if need be.

Continued later

Once (in the year we visited your blind grandmother), Dad and I sat together at the table. I was in dressing gown, he was in shirt sleeves. A reading lamp illumined the genealogical chart, and I remember a smell of beeswax, and a clatter from the kitchen where Mum and the two boys were shining up the forks and spoons with Silvo.

Leaning over the chart-in-progress, with my head on my hands, I said to Dad, 'All done, Dadda?'

His reply was, 'Never *all* done, my Sal.' For of course it was never *all* done. How do you complete an enthusiasm?

I watched and loved the pictorial aspect of the chart. Broad, ancient tree it certainly depicted, a vertical trunk connecting one generation of us Tilbers to another, the lateral lines of each generation drooping their foliage of names, dates and the lineages of the families they had married into. And there at the bottom my own generation of brothers and cousins supplied a foundation of tiny rootlets.

That, at least, is how my childish fancy construed it, though what I actually recall complaining to Dad was, 'I can't read the writing. It's too small.'

Promptly he provided me with his magnifying glass and then guided my hand along all those branches and tributaries. He made me recite the names as a test of my reading ability, and I can recall some of them still: 'Willem Tilbers, a dyke reeve (born circa 1683, in Holland), married in 1704 to Martha Kippis (christen'd 1685 in Ashby St Mary) ...' I recall stumbling over all those syllables, and Dad, with his delight in such terminology, explained to me that a dyke reeve was an officer responsible for drains, sewers, sluices and sea-banks.

What I *do* remember noting beneath the heavy magnifying glass were the long laterals of the eighteenth- and nineteenth-century families with their multitudes of Christian names, the Williams and Stephens, Marthas and Harriets, and the grim proximity of the christening and burial dates of so many. It was just a little creepy, all that fatefulness.

You'll wonder, Jenn, why these matters did not spill more fully into our talks along the Cathouse Road. Well, this was my other life and my excuse is that I keep dark *some* of the things which excite me so I don't lose the tension they create in the mind. That's pure instinct, don't ask me to explain it.

Equally inexplicable, *some* emotion did thrill me as Dad and I focused each name within the lens's circle, noting the professions, a generation or two of those dyke reeves, before the nineteenth century brought along the Tilber thatchers, pig farmers, domestic servants, a baker or two. All were village and market-town folk, provincial, sociable and inconspicuous, with a tendency towards self-education and, in some branches of the family, chapel worship and baptism by full and fervent immersion of the body!

Was my exhilaration to do with the intimacy of possessing my own little place at the bottom of all that micro-history? Yes! But the reverse too, the *expansiveness*, the thought that those multitudinous lives were included in me!

'They're in your bones and you can't get them out,' Dad informed me. They had got into my imagination too.

Does the past affect you in a similar way? Like my mother, you'll say no, won't you? Yet for me it's the sensation of being somehow ... hived with former lives. It's a power.

In the lamplight Dad and I proceeded across and down the broad chart. And when I touched the name at the outermost edge of the line that also contained Dad's own father I was able to read out 'Charles Harling Tilber, seaman, born in Lakenheath, 1859, died question mark, in Adelaide, South Australia, question mark.' There was no mention of wife or children against this entry.

Furthermore the entry was still in pencil, giving me the fancy that this Uncle Charles of Dad's was more provisional than all the names on the chart which were done in black rapidograph. As for those two question marks, they were — so thought young Sarah — unsatisfactory.

'Why have you put those?' I asked Dad, pointing to them.

'Because until we know for certain as to when and where Uncle Charles passed on...' He left the sentence unfinished.

'But if he's your uncle,' I reasoned, 'you *must* know all about him. I know all about my uncles.'

Dad was patient. 'Sometimes, old girl, a historian has to admit a person has lived the kind of life that slips below the notice of everyone else.'

'That's unfair,' I decided.

'I suppose it is,' was Dad's unhelpful concession.

'Perhaps Charles Harling hasn't died,' I ventured.

'I think it's safe to say the old boy's well and truly underground, my Sal,' Dad declared, indicating the ninety-five-year-old birth date. 'Whatever his fortunes in life might have been.'

Being fixed in my ideas at that age, I wasn't so sure. In my scheme of family relations, uncles were as everyday as forks and spoons. They dropped by at Hardacre Street with a carload of cousins. On birthdays the name of an uncle might appear with some best wishes and a date on a book token. Why, one uncle, Dad's elder brother, Luke, had passed away within even the short span on earth which, at that time, I could remember.

'How can you not know what happened to your very own uncle?' I objected.

Dad shrugged and brushed his hands across the mass of other names on his chart. 'Because this lot had homes, I suppose.'

Still unsatisfied, I said to him, 'Didn't *anyone* know him?' Dad looked helpless. So with the pedantry of a seven year old, I persisted. 'He was the uncle of...' and I ran my finger along the line of Dad's siblings and cousins, reeling their names off one by one. 'He was the brother of...' and this time I moved my finger up a branch to the extended rank of Charles Harling's brothers and sisters. Each had their professions, their marriages, their dividing lines of descendants, and included in its tiny black-ink capitals the name of Dad's own father, my grandfather, James Peverel Tilber, who was an ordering clerk, born 1867, died 1937, which was ten years before I was born.

Some 'chinks of light' squeezed through upon Charles H, Dad acknowledged. Lowestoft may have been where Great-Uncle Charles had signed on, or Boston, or...

'One day we could enquire up there,' Dad offered, rather lamely, I thought. 'My own father claimed to have no memory of this older brother, though he could recall the old Tilber cottage at Lakenheath before the family moved to the larger home at Thetford in 1873.' Dad paused, shook out a cigarette from its box and lit up. 'Curious how some things get passed down, though. Report has it that your Great-Uncle Charles was short in stature and had immensely strong arms, even as a young boy. Golly only knows what authority has passed down to us the fact that Uncle Charles was so constructed.'

Dad impressed upon me how important it was to rely on an authority when it came to the genealogy business. Then, drawing on his cigarette, he proceeded to explain to me one feature of our lineage.

'Look. Your grandfather, James Peverel Tilber, marries late in life your gran, Alice Phemister (b. 1883). Gran, you can see, is much younger than him. Now, mark this...' He guided my hand and our lens to the previous generation. 'His father, John Tilber, does the same thing: marries late to this younger woman, Maud Lackford (b. 1829). In the nineteenth century you did that if you were a sober fellow wanting to prove to a girl's family that you possessed the means and the steadiness of character to deserve her hand in marriage.'

He paused so that I might take in the long tradition of this sobriety. Then Dad moved in upon his point. 'Now just look at how *that* practice stretches a family across a century.' And with this explanation he adjusted the position of the magnifying glass so that it made the birth date of my great-grandfather, John Tilber, as bold as possible. 'What does that read?' he asked me.

'Eighteen hundred and twelve.' I recited the impressive date.

'There, you see!' Dad clinched his homily. '*My* grandpa was born in the year the famous Charles Dickens was also born, the year in which Emperor Napoleon's soldiers trudged with their cannons all the way to Moscow, then trudged back without them all the way to France through the terrible Russian winter. Trudge trudge trudge. They were ordinary fellows, just like my grandpa.'

These were Dad's exact words, and I must have had

such a serious expression on my face because I remember he glanced at me before he added, 'Of course all three of these gentlemen were long in their graves by the time you and I came on the scene.'

I was *so* impressed, by the actual history, yes, but also by Dad's tenderness towards the subject. How he loved it, my dear old dad. Actually, what he loved was the idea of pageant, where Napoleon and Dickens each had their places not so very far away from the humbler dyke reeves, thatchers, launderwomen, ordering clerks, who were his own ancestors. The Tilber tendency for self-education was strong in Dad, and history was his subject. This meant that his tone of voice when speaking on historical matters to his seven-year-old Sarah invariably had the respectfulness of the amateur, and that, put simply, Jenn, communicated to me the same lifelong urge to dig around in the minutiae of past lives.

Back to that evening. Obstinately, I recall, I drew our lens back to the name at the extremity of my grandfather's family.

'Didn't your Uncle Charlie visit you?' I imagined a short man with huge biceps standing in a door with his sea bag on his shoulder. For *surely* I could rely on Dad having known his uncles with the same familiarity I knew mine.

Dad would not admit my imagining of his uncle to the case, and it *was* unsatisfactory to me, the fact that I could visualise sailor and sea bag framed in a doorway and yet lack this thing called 'authority' for my image. How could Dad be so vague about this name and so precise about almost all the others?

'He had gone into the world, my Sal. Who knows what

it did with him? In those days a fellow might leave home to seek his fortune with no more feeling than when a young cat leaves a litter.'

'But you have written here, Adelaide question mark.'

'Well, yes.'

'Did you have authority?'

Dad eyed me in a way that indicated he thought my question pert. 'Again, one hears . . .' He stopped.

'Hears what?'

'Sometimes . . .' Dad contemplated me for a moment. '. . . A thing floats in the mind and you don't know how it got there . . .'

'That's what I do,' I triumphed.

'Just so. Well, it is *handed down* that Uncle Charlie might have owned his own ship out in South Australia. If it's true, then it stands to reason that someone in our family heard about it from somewhere. But what if it's not true? Without documentation, how do I know I did not imagine it?'

'You've written it in: *Adelaide question mark.*'

'In pencil,' he qualified.

What had impressed me, however, was that phrase, *out in South Australia*. Somehow that 'out' conformed with this man's name being on the outermost edge of our lineage, and his remoteness suggested itself to me as being at once mysterious and sad.

'People don't vanish, Dadda,' was the simple but firm proposition I put to Dad at the end of that evening. 'Someone will know all about it.' What cute *sagesse*. I looked at Dad for a few moments, his braces and rolled sleeves, his crinkly hair and round, shiny face which, whenever he grinned, you'll remember, seemed to crease suddenly like water where a stone has been thrown. And he glanced at me quickly, before folding away the chart and gathering together his implements.

Well, that is what I can recall, Jenn. *People don't just vanish* I had decided. What I meant was that I didn't accept the injustice that people should.

As a matter of fact, Dad's interest in his Uncle Charles was reawakened not long before his death, and I had a letter from him on the subject in 1986. But I'm going cross-eyed from staring at the keys, so I'll go and post this off to you now, and continue what I have to say in a follow-up letter in a couple of days. If I am too thoroughgoing in all of the above, forgive me. I feel companionable when I write to you. You could be swinging gently in that teenage hammock and me chattering on the tree branch above. Love, Sarah.

This was midway through the summer term and, for my husband and me, a busy time of year. So I had still managed no reply to my friend when a third letter, longer than the first two, arrived a week later.

Semaphore, June 15th

Dear Jenn,

Did I mention in my last the contact I have made here? We have met in a teashop. He is an ex-merchant seaman, an 'ornery' gent as the Americans might say, and has some information to disclose about Charles Harling Tilber. More on Albert presently.

If, in my last, I made researching Great-Uncle C sound like a lifelong mission, that would be inaccurate. Instead, what I have is an agreeable sensation each time I contemplate the *archaeological* care with which I will need to recover his person from oblivion. The fragile evidence of his existence has to be somewhere and, more particularly, *somehow* in the world. All I have to do is find it. Why? So that it may be a lively presence in the mind. My mind, at least, yours too, I hope, and available to the world. Why should one *not* be able to penetrate oblivion and retrieve a person's presence, in compelling likeness at least?

But my move to Adelaide was not with a very *deliberate* idea of doing this project in family history. It was more the attraction of putting a vast, shimmering Australian plain between myself and my former 'silverfish' life in Canberra.

Now to Dad's letter of 1986. I'll make you a fair copy, and you'll recognise how Dad, ever the hobbyist, comes straight to the point.

Dear Sal,

Do you remember, years ago we talked about one of my uncles called Charles who went off to sea? Something has turned up here in the post. It is from Beth (née Crowther), your Norwich aunt who, before she remarried, was the wife of my brother Luke (1904–53).

She gave me some of Uncle Luke's books, which she has kept all these years. I took them home and had them in a pile by my chair. Bound volumes of *Illustrated Weekly*, for the most part. I had gone through several of them when a folded piece of paper fell out of one and, guess what? It turned out to be an actual letter from my Uncle Charles to his sister Mary, written in 1875 from China. One hundred and eleven years ago, and from China! What a turn-up! You can see the paper is good quality notepaper with lines, though a bit grubby because he has made a blot or two. I bet his fingers were inky as he penned it. What do you say?

Dad then goes on to tell me about my Great-Aunt Mary (1861–1950) and the family she married into (Haughs), and ends by saying:

> Just as I am getting fired up about old Uncle Charles, the doctors tell me I am not allowed to drive! So I'll get Mother to motor us up to Lowestoft and Boston and see what they might have on the old fellow there. Send his letter back when you've had a good look. Your loving Dad.

Guiltily I hung onto the old document, and then Dad passed on in 1987. The result is that I have the original before me now as I write.

Whampoa Reach, China, 16th of July 1875
> Dear little sister,
> You may imagin my supprise when skipper came back on board and handed me a letter from you all the way from dear old England. Im glad about fathers chickens, and that Matt now is old enough to help him at the thatching.

Yesterday we rowed skipper fifteen mile upriver to a big city called Canton, and had two hours on shore there. So many Chinee along the waterfront it takes your breath away, and them scolding us if we took the paint off their sampans with our boathooks as we tried to get through with the jollyboat. They all of them have pigtails no shorter than yours, men and women alike. Down the alleys here you can buy a little macack monkey to carry on your shoulder, and you can choose a serpent from a box of others to have for your dinner. For five corses, our dinner cost about thruppence in English money, but I wouldnt touch them snakes.

Where our ship is anchored is called Yellow Anchorage on the Pearl River and youve never seen such a jamboree of grand ships together. There must be a hundred tea ships at least. And the grandest, let me tell you, fly the red ensign from the gaff. Today weve been down in the hold with the Mate and weve got our shingle all levelled and the ground-chop shipped, ready for the 'Flowery Pekoe' and other 'top-chop' teas to come on board tomorrow.

The washer-girls come around the ship in their sampans, and we call out from the rail, 'Hey Missy, you washee washee our gear,' and theyre quick to take the shirts we hand down, wash them, press them until they might be new.

Your brother Charlie hopes youll do your sums and writing well, Missy, and that youll be a smart little help around the place.

I cant say when Ill see you next for we are bound for New York. The first mate works us pretty hard, but

hes all right. As for skipper, hes a remote kind of a
cove, but the apprentices say he could sail old *Theseus*
to the moon if he had a mind. As for me,
Ive learned myself to be on the other side of the world
to the thing I love and it neednt be so bad as all that.

Signed, your brother Charlie.

It is that last sentence that quickened my feelings most.

Cont'd evening 14th

Last week I went to this city's Mortlock Library, and
learned that a certain CH Tilber had been the skipper and
part owner of a two-masted schooner called *Bicheno*
during the first three decades of the century. This was a
splendid start, and I wondered whether there might be
Australian Tilbers going back a generation in Australia. At
the very least I thought there might be people still alive
who had known a CH Tilber.

So, firstly I searched for Tilbers in the phone book —
no good. Then I looked up the names of people associated
with his ship, *Bicheno*. What followed was some very dry
research in the archives until I came across the name of
my 'ornery' gent.

He is Albert Prideauz, listed as cook and deckhand on
CH Tilber's vessel from December 1927 to March '28.
His age at the time is given as sixteen, and it was one of
several names connected with this schooner over a
twenty-year period. I chose it from various others because
I thought its slight unusualness would help me track it
down in electoral roll or phone book.

What an odd chimerical confidence there is about good luck. Don't you agree? One expects it to run, like a fish swarm or a seam of valuable ore, and I have been high on this for several days.

Not that the electoral roll was a help. And the phone book was all false leads until I came upon my one *providential* exception. This was a lady telling me that her husband had once been rung in mistake for an Albert Prideauz. Her caller had wanted the Mr Prideauz who lived 'in the caravan'.

'Caravan?'

'Yes, definitely caravan, though some months ago,' added my informant.

Tenuous information, you'll think, but nothing daunted, your Sarah began working through the Yellow Pages under 'caravan parks', asking, confidently, that she be put through to Mr Albert Prideauz. I tried seven before a receptionist at Vale Park stated that the best she could do for me was to chalk a message on her blackboard for 'Old Albert' to ring me back. Bingo! Three days later I got my call.

'I wish to speak with the person who was enquiring about the old *Bicheno*.'

The voice I heard had an old man's deliberateness. I explained to this voice who I was, the nature of my interest. Could I ask, did he, by any chance, remember my ancestor, a Mister Charles Tilber?

He perked up. 'How would I not?' These were the actual words he used in reply, Jenn. Imagine it. *How would I not?*

Was he willing to talk to me, I then asked. The voice at

the end of the line did not respond immediately. It was a public phone box and I could hear the sound of cars passing. Then he said that he had thought the Mister Tilber he knew didn't have any family, and there was another silence on the line. I explained my place in the family tree.

'He had the air of a man without family,' the voice insisted. 'Very definitely.' This was followed by further silence for a short time.

'We could at least meet,' I suggested. I was agonised lest he should lose interest in me and ring off.

'Perhaps we could,' he said. And then informed me that, as a matter of fact, he had tried, on and off, to put down on paper his own thoughts about 'the skipper'.

'So maybe your phone call has been a bit of luck for me as well as you,' he suggested, and I accepted the fact of his jottings about Great-Uncle as blithely as I did the rest of my good fortune in finding Albert Prideauz.

A day later, on this city's Rundle Mall, we sat opposite each other at a teashop — he had been pernickety that it be a 'teashop' and not a 'café'. We chatted and I explained to him my circumstances, how I was Sarah Fawne by marriage, but Sarah Tilber by birth. For himself, he was mid-seventies, spry, rather slender, and accompanied by a bundle of dog-eared papers which, he informed me, 'belonged to the case'. Yes, it seems he has his own reasons for being interested in Charlie Tilber.

'We'll bumble about in oblivion together,' I joked.

'Not oblivion, young lady,' he reminded. 'I was there.'

From his merchant navy days he knew our River Orwell

and the port of Ipswich, and this allowed me to enthuse about all that maritime traffic of our dreamy holidays, and how it had impinged upon my view of things.

He came back with, 'Your memory has got you in a spell, Miss Fawne.' He has a sharp intelligence.

Next I showed him my copy of Great-Uncle's letter from China. He read it through, then gave it back, as though the contents were already a part of what he knew. I asked him what he made of the last sentence, and he replied to the effect that it tallied with the person he had known.

We agreed on a further meeting. The date for this is so far unfixed. We even mentioned the possibility of making an oral history project out of our subject. He'll keep his eye on the chalkboard for my messages.

And the point of all this, Jenn? 'People don't just vanish, Dadda.' Oh how I wish Dad were still alive that I might tell him so. I'll breathe life into the forlorn name down there on the edge of that chart.

Now I'll stop to catch breath, and give you time to write and assure me you do not mind perusing whatever, in my egotistical way, I will dig up about this ancestor of mine. Do say you're agreeable to hear out my enthusiasms. It all might fizzle, of course. Best wishes to your hardworking Mike, and to each of your brood. Sarah.

⌘

I wrote back to Sarah by return post, and received this reply.

Semaphore, June 28th

Dear Dependable,

Could I doubt you'd write back so positively? Thank you for saying that Dad was a kindly presence. Yes, he was. If death *is* merely the event that translates us from a material to an immaterial existence, dare I suggest, he still is … just that. Yet it's odd, isn't it, how slight the imprint that people who are both good and ordinary seem to leave in the mind. I forget whole bits of Dad's life, as others must have let slip their knowledge of Great-Uncle Charles.

You report that your eldest is going up to the university in September! It seems only yesterday when … etcetera.

And you ask how, post-Kieran, I live. The answer is more vitally, and more frugally. Kier asks if we should not 'settle over property'. He will be honest and legalistic and paltry. Somehow I can't get interested. I have some savings of my own — money accumulates without children — and since March I've had my group of writing pensioners on two mornings a week.

This last, unexpectedly, leads me straight to my second encounter with Albert. At our first teashop meeting, it seems I so interested him in my writing course that he turned up at my class with his bundle of yellowy papers. Could I help him turn them into a memoir that 'rang true, like'? I could try, I assured him.

Albert's appearance among my old folk, with several sharp pencils in his top pocket, and a certain defensive mien, was, I'm bound to admit, short-lived. He listened attentively to what I had to say to the group about the importance of vivid and precise imagery. But when the class began a writing exercise, he looked unhappy behind the modular desk.

'What can I do to start you off?' I leaned over his shoulder.

'I'll be jake.' And he stared ahead stolidly, like a non-believer at a prayer meeting. As we broke up he waited at my shoulder until after the rest had left, and apologised, rather formally, for being an uncooperative old sod. He told me he thought he ought not to come again, and left. I feared I might have lost him for good. Ten minutes or so later I spied him walking along the pavement, and offered him a lift to his caravan, which he accepted. We were mostly silent as we drove. But when we had come to a stop outside his home-on-wheels, he confided that he didn't feel inclined to pursue the thing on his mind as part of a *group* of old folks. The objection was delicate. He didn't want his material to become (his word) 'unsprung' by treating it as 'something for people to mince over'. Would I care to come into the caravan?

'I would,' I accepted, and mounted the step behind him.

As caravans go it was capacious, and every cupboard was chock-a-block with non-perishable foodstuffs, boxes of cornflakes, tins of beans, spaghetti and meatballs, tuna, jars of marmalade and peanut butter. I was invited to sit down at a formica table and we chatted. He owned the van itself outright, he explained, but paid a rent out of his pension for this site next to the river. The position entailed a bit of a tramp to the shower block, chilly in winter, but the early morning music of ducks, coots, water sidling over itself — well, that beat anything offered by a retirement village.

'Oh crikey yes!'

No, he could not be bothered with owning a car. Had never owned one in his life. If he ever felt like a move, he would hire a truck and be towed to a new location, any agreeable spot so long as it had a terminal where he could plug in his small TV and electric jug, and a tap from which he could draw water. At seventy-five, too old to move? I asked. Not a bit.

'You must have saved a nest egg after those years at sea. So why not some plush apartment in Largs Bay or Port Adelaide with a view of the shipping?' I asked.

Shipping? He'd had his fill of shipping. After a certain point, going around the world was a bit like a bus route, he declared as he busied himself with tea things. That's what happened to seafaring! If he compared the world when he was a boy to the one he had, at sixty-five, retired from, time had gone quietly tame on him. This was his complaint. Did I, as a woman, understand this?

Unfairly (you'll say) I thought of my years with Kier and asked him, 'Is it also a meaner place?'

Meaner maybe, he agreed, though he tried to occupy his days sufficiently to ignore the world's meanness. He liked this patch under the willow fronds, with the quiet green water gliding just outside his screen door, and yet the GPO within acceptable walking distance. What apartment offered that? The other long-term residents in the caravan park allowed him his peace.

As I looked about the interior, I reflected that the caravan was not such an unlikely home for a man who had spent his life in the confines of one ship or another. The small windows, the close-fitting metal door with its snap lock, the economies of space in cupboard and bench, the constraints, all this had a certain nautical feel to it, and I remarked on the similarity to Albert.

'I see more daylight now than when I worked the stokehold and the cabins,' was his rejoinder, and I watched him rummage here and there for tea and sugar.

The next thing that drew my attention were two small framed photographs propped above the bedhead. The first was a colour snap showing a familiar 1960s' starlet whose name, Jenn, I ought to remember. Starlet's bare arm rested on the white tunic of Ornery Gent, then a considerably younger gent. In the background were the balloons and partying of some cruise ship's lobby, and both Albert and Starlet were smiling flirtatiously for the camera, which, oddly, I thought, did his dignity more harm than hers.

Of course, rather mean-spiritedly, I made my inferences, that the photo of the cabin steward arm in arm with screen celebrity stood there in its gilt frame as a reminder of what may have been a rare highlight in Albert's otherwise under-stimulating career of bringing morning tea, making beds, pushing a trolley of laundry up and down the narrow corridors of an ocean liner. For there were other bits and pieces around the ex-steward's caravan, all rather tawdry, mementos picked up from the ports of the world: Panama, Aden, Colombo, Singapore. But then Albert disconcerted me by, as it were, reading my thoughts.

'You're thinking that there's not much here to show for a life.' Naturally I was quick to retort with my assurances, but the ex-steward was forthright. 'Well, you're right, there's not.'

I asked him if he had ever married, and he dismissed the option with the routinely courteous observation, 'That kind of life, you know, long periods away, not fair on any woman.' I suggested to him that his circumstances were more settled now, and his very prompt response to this was, 'Are you saying I should make you an offer, Miss Fawne?'

I took the question to be a frivolous long shot. Far from it. He scrutinised me for an answer. Had I said yes, I'm sure he would have made his proposal out of that same spirit of casual optimism which, during the fifties, I gather, used to bring farmworkers from the country down to the dockside to call out marriage proposals to any eligible girls lining the rails of the migrant steamships. But I screwed my face into an apologetic expression, and asked him about the second of the two photographs. Thus by a hairsbreadth did I remain single!

The second photo, also in a gilt frame, depicted a sailing ship with its quadrangular and triangular sails nicely rounded in a breeze. In a flash I guessed its name, and had this confirmed by Albert, who seemed able to drop the idea of marriage as casually as he had raised it.

'You're spot on. *SV Bicheno*, skipper Charlie Tilber.'

He took the picture from its shelf and placed it on the table between us, then proceeded to name sails, gaffs, windlasses and so on, 'showing the lady round ship' as he put it. He had found the photo among others in a junk shop upon his retirement to Adelaide in 1978. He deduced it had been taken some years before he, himself, had served on her.

'That blurry hump you can see near the helm might well be your relative.' I looked at it carefully, but it might as well have been anyone, or even a piece of deck cargo.

Then Albert asked me, did I have any theories as to why some images stay in mind all one's life, while others vanish?

'Do memories choose us, or do we choose them?' was the question I supplied in response.

And his reaction, Jenn, was so vehement it took me aback.

'My word!' he exclaimed. 'They choose us. Or we walk smack into them! And get as a result a heartache for the rest of our lives.'

Heartache? I asked him what he meant. What followed during the next hour or so was, in outline at least, the story of Albert's acquaintance with my great-uncle. We got through several pots of tea.

It *is* a story, and you *will* be told it all. Albert has confirmed that we should meet and put the thing down on tape. Forgive me if I withhold what I have learned until then. Once on tape it will become more cogent because I will be able to plan my line of interrogation. I will, dear Dependable, prepare you a complete transcript. Promise.

Until then, yours, Sarah.

PS: Of *course* you can ask me about the business with Kier, though I warn you, he really is at the periphery of my interest just now. So also, I repeat, are the various moveables in that ex-marital home which we will need to divide between us. The thought of driving back across the infinite Hay Plains just in order to reclaim some cutlery, books and bed linen fills me with a sense of the futile and the petty. Kier will stand by the door of the living room and say, 'You must take whatever you want'. But what do I want? Certainly not that progress the two of us will make from room to room, saying to each other, 'No, you must have that,' in an atmosphere of withheld reproach! Not that! There's too much else to be getting on with.

PPS: And also, you ask, do I, post-Kieran, miss the intimacy? Ha! A newspaper survey once asked, *Do women prefer orgasms, hugs or chocolates?* Most, it seems, prefer hugs. Being fully rounded, I'll take the chocs!

But seriously, no, I miss neither sex, nor, to the degree it is distinct, intimacy. Has that energy been redirected into my fascination with finding my way into Hades and back? Once in a while I feel a bit ... I will *not* say incomplete.

But I put the deprivation to use. It lets me imagine the lost attachments of my seafaring forebear. Did he, during all those years on the glassy oceans of the world, miss what you call 'the intimacy of family life'? I puzzle away at that. You see, I suspect that even to *ask* the question is to disarrange the fragile fabric of what a seafaring person actually expected from life back then. The past is so effaceable. Yet, *I've learned myself to be on the other side of the world to the thing I love.*

How has he 'learned' himself, do you think? Incessant physical work, I'd answer, hauling, belaying, reeving, climbing, furling, loosing, holystoning decks, scraping rust from ironwork, painting ironwork, greasing topmasts, casting a log, spells on the helm, spells as lookout, spells on the pumps, sending signal flags aloft, handling the great anchors inboard or outboard with crowbars and catting tackle, pushing a capstan bar, shovelling shingle ballast around a hold, etcetera, with snatched intervals to sleep and feed, and the odd spree ashore in strange places to glimpse how man and woman, mother and son, brother and sister might live in more homely circumstances. That routine, night and day, year in year out, 'learned' my fifteen-year-old great-uncle not to miss the intimacy of the crowded Tilber home he left. *And it needn't be as bad as all that.* What do you make of it? Love, S.

July

The first letter from Sarah this month announced that she was immersing herself 'in the practical, evocative memoirs of seafaring folk'. She provided various titles — *A Gypsy of the Horn, Mother Sea, Fo'c's'le Days* — which, she assured me, 'for all their tatty, brown-paper bindings, Jenn, give me what I want, namely the *geist* of those last decades when the deepwater sailormen vanished from the earth.'

She was, she said, also seeking out the work of marine illustrators, and again provided names: Arthur Briscoe, George Gale, Gordon Grant. For her expedition to the ketch ports of the South Australian gulfs she had a cassette of shanties for the long straight roads, and in this letter she scribbled a verse from one song onto a photocopied illustration.

> *Now we are ready to head for the Horn,*
> *Weigh-hey, roll and go.*
> *Our boots and our clothes, boys, are all in the pawn,*
> *With a rollickin' randy-dandy-o.*

'Catch [she wrote] the melancholy good morale of this. The shantyman wails and the fo'c's'le crowd answer, slow-plodding around their capstan as they warp their towering ship through the harbour lock. You *need* to visualise this, which is why I enclose Gordon Grant's drypoint illustration. Look at his fellows bawling out their song from black, shapeless mouths, barefooted and with capstan bars pressed against their midriffs. Look at the woollen-hatted gent, how his face is starey, adrift, graven with his debaucheries ashore. Look at Baldie with his neckerchief and wisp of beard, and then assess the boy pressed to the next capstan bar with his small piggy eyes and his uncertainty among these veterans. Charlie Tilber's people. Now you can see how I attune myself.'

I could indeed. Like an athlete, like a nun, Sarah was gearing up mentally for the task of giving 'her shrewdest sympathies' to the recovery of her forebear.

She also included in this package several photos of herself at Ardrossan, Edithburgh and Port Victoria. 'I have never seen you looking so pared down and coppery, Sal,' I wrote back. 'You're like one of those solitary adventurer women who lead their donkeys across the Australian desert', and added that by contrast she would find I had become rather a sponge cake.

❧

Next there arrived a short letter written on the twelfth of July. She had recorded Albert's story and was clearly under the spell of his voice.

'Now I believe,' she wrote, 'the voices of old men have a distinctive music. It is a harmony of their frailty and veteran resilience. It's as if the fatefulness in a person's life transfers itself into something we *hear*. This is rather moving, I think. Albert is quite untroubled by the egotism of talking at length about himself to "a young lady", as he calls me (at forty-two!).

'He may disclose his emotions more carefully to me than to a male interviewer, but don't take this to mean we have a natural rapport. The obstacles to that are his prickliness, his self-regard, his bouts of rather ponderous gallantry. This, in turn, makes me gauche. But Albert's mind is clear, Jenn, and he has a veteran's self-possession. When he came here the other day, he sat so uprightly, delineated against the window, his posture suggesting a senior and trusted serving man who has been allowed to sit down for a moment in order to receive directions. At our first meeting I had been allowed to know how, as a matter of service pride, cabin stewards were kept "on the go" in those sleek, creamy passenger ships of the post-war.

'And he haunts me. He possesses the past to the exclusion of the present. You know how I could never credit those self-deluding historical regressions-under-hypnosis that became popular in the seventies. Yet Albert's story does seem to make a claim on me, and it's a claim that startles me a bit. I must get to work transcribing the tape, so you can hear it together with my reaction. To do so, I'll rise before dawn, like a holy person, and fill these pages. It makes such a difference, Jenn, writing *for* someone. The secret of why you and I get on so amicably is that we excite the best language out of each other. Don't you agree? Until my next, then. Love, S.'

Semaphore, July 16th

Dear J,

So, Albert was in my flat for two hours, arriving by a taxi which he allowed me to pay for. I settled him into my one cane easy chair, while I took the wooden kitchen chair, the cassette player and its microphone being set up on my table. The time we began, I noted, was when the afternoon wind shift occurs on the gulf waters. All those ketch and schoonermen of yore would have watched for it, as I do too, when my gauze curtain lifts and fills.

Before commencing, I went over with him what I intended. I apologised for not being able to offer him money for his time. Money, he let me know, was not the thing he wanted. He had his pension. 'I want the business to be at peace.'

I did say to him that, as our project was oral history, we might end up in an archive together, and I noted he perked up at the prospect of being in some library. As I fiddled with wires and plugs I encouraged him to speak freely.

'I was always a talker,' he replied. 'Your average passenger likes the cabin steward to manage a bit of intelligent patter.'

'Do you miss that sociable life?' I asked.

It had fretted him, he admitted. How can you take an interest in people who pop in and out of your life for a few weeks at sea? 'You can send yourself broke on pretended interests,' he ended.

As I switched the machine on I could hear below us

the veritable *sea noise* of cars surging away from the roundabout on Military Road.

'My name is Albert Prideauz. I was born in Adelaide in 1913. My mother died when I was eight years old and I was brought up by my father and my uncle who had a photography studio. I went to sea for all my working life, until I retired here again in 1978 when I was sixty-five years of age.' Thus he identifies himself for my tape. 'And all that time seems to have gone pretty quick.' His head remained quite immobile and the whitish light from the window caught the edge of his profile, the lips moving slightly, so that there was a way his very stillness compelled my attention. Periodically he would glance at his pile of papers as though to take his cue.

'I joined *Bicheno* in September 1927 when I was fourteen ...'

'In the register you're listed as being sixteen years of age.'

'Lots of the fellows used to fake their ages. I was fourteen on *Bicheno* and was paid as a cook/deckhand.'

'For the tape, tell me about SV *Bicheno*.'

She was a two-masted schooner, he said, built on the Derwent from huon pine in the 1880s. He rather thought Mister Tilber had bought his share in the vessel before the Great War. Being in the Hobart trade, she had kept her two topsail yards crossed in order to give her some edge in Bass Strait and down the west coast of Tasmania. Her hull was green, her mouldings, housings and spars varnished, and all the brightwork and paint was kept up. 'Which cost your ancestor a pile, and left him poor at the end.'

I asked about Mister Tilber's other partners — Routledge & Selth who had an office in Santo Street.

'Long gone.' Albert pinched off that topic. Next I asked about the crew.

'Depended on the trip,' he expounded. 'Two or three of us boys, and always Minkus. Minkus was a fixture. I did maybe a dozen trips.' This apparently included one lively passage from Port Adelaide round South West Cape to Hobart.

My next question took him to what I knew he regarded as the heart of the matter.

'The March 1928 trip to Port Lincoln. *Bicheno* has arrived beside Kirton Point Wharf and unloaded. You are going ashore for a spree. Will you tell me the thing you saw that evening regarding your skipper?'

On the tape there is a clearing of the throat. 'I have the kind of mind that re-lives things,' he began. 'It churns them over, like.'

'Yes.'

'The skipper had given us four fellows our liberty for the evening. Minkus had put on the white collar and waistcoat he kept in his dunnage. Jim, Otto and I put on clean shirts with short-sleeved jerseys over the top. We shined our shoes as best we could, plastered our hair down with water. A schooner's fo'c's'le didn't allow much room for four fellows to shuffle into their shoregoing clobber...' Albert paused, then made the judgement, 'But you took trouble in those days when you went to a dance. It's all singlets and spike haircuts nowadays.'

'I teach myself not to think about it.'

He appraised me for a moment, then went on. 'We tumbled out in our spruced-up condition, climbed into the mainmast shrouds and so leapt across to terra firma.'

'Climbed? Leapt?'

'Your small fry vessels like schooners, ketches, will ride well below the height of the wharf.'

'Thank you. That pictures it.'

'Picturing it, if you'll pardon me, is what you'll need to do, because it's sometimes downright impossible to say how common things were different back then.' Albert paused in order that I might take to heart this reminder.

'I also have the kind of mind that likes to re-live things,' I countered. As I say, Jenn, we did not particularly warm to each other, but I think I was convincing him that I was prepared to give my allegiance to those who put on a collar and waistcoat for a dance rather than the spike-haircut tribe. Again he seemed to assess me for a moment, then resumed.

'I listened to our four pairs of boots clicking along that jetty and I felt grand. After what we had accomplished throughout that Saturday —'

'Describe for me what you *had* accomplished exactly.'

'Exactly?' He picked on my word, then gathered himself. 'In four days,' he held his fingers up, 'we had loaded *Bicheno* with a cargo of bagged superphosphate, made a run from Port Adelaide in thirty-six hours with the help of a couple of sou'westerly gales, hefted this cargo out and stowed another of bagged wheat. What common folk had to do for a crust in those days gets forgotten . . .'

'Men *and* women,' I thought to insist.

'And boys down to twelve years old,' I might say he blazed back. I was sensible of his resentment, and it was not just directed at the fact that my knowledge came from books rather than experience. Albert was, I detected, proud of what 'common folk' had done for a crust, and sensitive when he thought I might muddy the fragile ethos which had surrounded those labours.

'Do you feel you missed a real childhood?'

'I never gave it a thought,' he replied promptly.

'Describe the procedure of stowing a cargo for me.'

My request calmed him, allowed him to express what was dear to his heart, an old nous for waterfront doings.

'You take the wheat. When you stow that, you wait in the hold for the bags to come down the chute from above. Clumsy bloody things, three bushels per bag, a hundred and eighty pounds each. You juggle them with your bag hook so as to sit them on a hood of calico which you wear across shoulder and neck, like that, see.' He patted his shoulder. 'You then lug each bag to the far corners of the vessel, layer on layer, working up and back towards the coamings until the last bags are jammed in. These you might bleed of some of their contents so as to get a tight stow. No allowance for being young or lightly made, that's for sure.'

'A test of your mettle.'

'You could say that.' He paused for a moment or two, then resumed. 'By the end of that stint on the Saturday, holy mac, we ached, and Minkus said how you could fire pottery in the heat of that hold. I remember the smell rather than the heat, hessian bags mixed with that sickly river mud all the old ships used to give off. But we were used to that, sweated away until we could knock home the battens and wedges around *Bicheno*'s holds, took a bucket and washed off the grime from each other, then —'

'Then listened to your four pairs of boots on the wooden jetty,' I finished for him.

'Minkus, Jim and Otto in front. I was a step or so behind. It was not yet quite dark. Behind the roofs of the town you could see there was still an apricot flush in the sky. Eastward, towards Cape Donington, night was coming on, with the sea under Boston Island a yellow-silver like that old cutlery before the stainless steel. We passed where a pair of hurricane lamps had been set for some of the fellows to work by who were still loading one of the ketches. A wagon which stood on the little railway had a sad sort of a nag hitched to it, and there was one bloke sending bags down a chute. 'Chop chop, you blokes,' Jim called out. There were moths flitting about around the lamp flames.

'Beer, Jim had promised me, as we had got into our clobber. Fancy food, music, young ladies. It was the thought of the fancy food I relished most.

'We were well out of earshot of *Bicheno* by this. So I said, "Mister Tilber must be the most dinkum schoonermaster on the seaboard I reckon." That was it, verbatim. Maybe I was trying to sound grown-up and in the swim among these three elder blokes.'

'What was their response?'

'My opinion of our skipper wasn't controversial.' Albert paused to sip from a glass of water. 'A niggardly skipper might have gone straight out on the evening tide and saved twelve hours. Mister Tilber gave us our liberty and some pence in our pockets.' Another pause, then, 'It was more how Minkus reacted that affected me in the long run. "Charlie Tilber can be a melancholy kind of a cove," he said.'

'Melancholy kind of a cove?'

'Exactly that, and then he said I would pick it if I stayed with *Bicheno* for long enough. As we walked up through the town, I wondered. I had done nearly six months with the skipper by then. But as I said to you, I didn't have to wait long at all.'

'Yes.'

'Oddest thing! It was...' Albert looked down at his knees, then straight at me, 'profound!' I waited. 'It has stuck with me all my life.'

This time his scrutiny of me was more intent and, finding his gaze a little too fierce, I decided to relieve the tension.

'That was quite an endorsement you gave your skipper.'

Albert took another interval to arrange his thoughts. Then he began. 'A fellow could be unlucky in his choice of ship. Skippers who stinted on the rations, sweet-talked you into extra days not covered by wages. After *Bicheno* I was on *Klara*, a shell-grit ketch. Her skipper was a penny-pinching sod, but I'll come to him, and one or two others. Your Mister Tilber was my first skipper. He's got the front-row seat in my memory. But to get a picture of Mister Tilber you've got to be able to see the life as it was...' At this point Albert looked up at me.

'As I say, I've read this and that. Quite a lot, in fact.'

He shook his head as if to say that mere reading could not come at the essence of it.

'Look! Of course there were the wages. But all that loading and unloading, keeping the schooner shining. That bloke got goodwill out of us. We'd give him his quick turnarounds if he wanted them.'

'Why?'

'Authority.' Albert allowed the word to stand for a few moments. 'Scarcely six trips on *Bicheno* but I had already picked up one lesson about the skipper's authority. It was this, that he could get us to give him a quick turnaround simply by leaning on a pin rail and filling his pipe. No growling. No threats of pay being docked. No trickery, no standover stuff. "You boys wouldn't be so good as to..." he used to say when he wanted that bit extra out of us. It was in his expression. His two eyes were set there, like some gnome's amidst all that facial fuzz of his, and they registered such a — you'd say — complicit kind of hopefulness. "You boys wouldn't be so good as to ..." *Polite,* that was him. It was like he wouldn't have known how to be otherwise. Was your dad a polite man?' Albert fired this question at me suddenly.

'Good-natured, yes,' I told him.

'Family trait, then,' Albert decided. 'But crikey, that was not so *very* common on the waterfront. Funny how, when you think of the goodness in a person you have this vague urge to sob.'

He took a further moment to reflect. 'I remember on that run down the west coast of Tasmania. My second voyage and my first in any kind of weather. It was the middle watch, midnight to 4 a.m., cold, and wet, because both wind and sea were coming at us from the westward. Jim came forward to relieve me on lookout and I went aft to see if the skipper wanted anything else before I turned in. He had taken over the helm on account of the dicey conditions and had both hands on the spokes. The schooner's stern would sideslip down one sea then slowly rise across the face of another. I found those long movements a bit hair-raising to tell the truth, with the white water visible in the darkness along the top of each sea. Phosphorescent is the word. With his head the skipper beckoned me nearer. "Would you be so good as to put your hands in my pocket, son," he said, close to my ear. I did so, and found a pair of socks. They were made from thick wool, and in the binnacle light I saw they were bright red. "Would you be so good as to pull those over my hands," he said next. He presented me one, then the other. "Much obliged," he said, then added, "A ship's always safe in warm hands."

'Do you see what I mean about him?'

'He instilled calm,' I supplied, then thought to prompt, 'I heard from my dad that his Uncle Charles was supposed to have had unusually strong arms. Was that true?'

Albert thought about this proposition for a moment, then said, 'I saw him take in an extra eighteen inches on a headsail sheet after Otto and Jim combined had done their best with it. That was on one of the close-hauled legs of our west coast trip. It's not in the arms so much as in knowing how to use his entire body to get a purchase on the thing.'

'Was he a skilled seaman?'

'A wizard. That's the accepted opinion, a cheerful, untalkative sort of a sea wizard. From one end of a trip to another he uttered scarce a dozen words. The schooner would practically sail itself. He had a repertoire of little signals that you had to learn. A change of course, for instance, was indicated to the helmsman by catching his eye, swivelling his own eyeballs to port or starboard, then pinching his thumb and forefinger to suggest by how much the course needed to be altered. Could have been a chef telling an apprentice how much salt to put into a meat pudding. Another discreet hand signal told you to hold steady when you had brought the ship onto the course he wanted. I think he took a mischievous pride in communicating things without using his voice.'

'Which meant, I suppose, you stayed very alert.'

'Exactly so.'

'Tell me more of this kind of detail.'

'You can see the skipper's trick. *Use your common sense, son. Work things out.* At night, of course, or if a squall came over, he'd stand beside you, hand on the wheel, peering into the binnacle.

'Or he'd materialise beside you in cloth cap, braces over his white shirt, pointing a single finger towards the sky. Which meant that he would like you, if it was not too much trouble, to scramble aloft and hand the foot of the gaff topsail over the peak halyard, or furl it, or unfurl it, or put a reef in the main, or take in a headsail. You always knew what. And if you did it too slow, he was there as you came out of the rigging, moving his hand in rapid circles as though winding a handle, his eye smiling but with just a hint of danger in it. So you did it faster next time, no question. Mister Tilber was the exact opposite to what you heard about those bucko types in deepwater sail. You felt this irresistible urge to behave well to him.'

'You sound protective of him,' I suggested.

'Yes, in a way we were,' Albert agreed. 'He was shorter than each of us four fellows, including me at fourteen, and if you didn't know him you might have thought he was having a joke with you, or doing some kind of humorous dumb show. But it was those gestures, and that hopeful smile on his face. It was charm. I'd say that he liked the company of human beings whatever shape they came in. *That's* what it was made me blurt out my opinion about how dinkum he was. Already my ambition was to be a fellow like Charlie Tilber one day.'

'So you could dispense authority with charm?'

'Arh! Not *just* charm. That little man had such presence. When you joined *Bicheno* somehow you got to know how Charlie Tilber had served during the 1890s on the big nitrate barques that took the coal across the Pacific from Newcastle, then picked up their nitrate from Peru or Chile for a European port. God knows what those hardy deepwater seamen would have made of Mister Tilber's style of issuing orders.'

'As you say, he was a deepwater man himself.'

'My word. Now we've got the TV, Miss Fawne. How do I tell you the spell which the names of those harbours had on fellows like me at fourteen years of age? Pimentel, Iquique, Antofagasta, Coquimbo. Names like that mixed up in his personal details had made our short skipper — what would the word be — venerable? And someone, probably Minkus, had mentioned how Charlie Tilber had served as a boy on one of the crack China tea clippers — *Thyatira*, maybe, or even *Thermopylae* —'

'*Theseus*,' I slipped in.

'Whatever. But in the mind of a fourteen year old with a hankering for the life of a seafarer, service with the old tea fleet made Mister Tilber more than venerable. It made him a bit of a legend. You ever heard of *Thermopylae*?'

'Of course!' I hurried him on. 'We were heading for a dance.'

'No trouble to discover where the dance was being held. The wheat cockies with their wives and daughters had come in from the Gulf country all around, one or two in their Fords, a good many with a horse and sulky. For it was show time, and there were tents on some vacant land with bunting and all. The four of us just followed the drift of people to the warehouse, paid a penny or two for admission, and joined the crowd who were already there.'

'Describe it.'

'You could see hurricane lamps and pressure lanterns hanging from wire around the walls. You could see, way back in the shadows, there were wheat bags stacked up into the roof. Tables selling bottled beer and glasses of cordial had been set up, and other tables with sandwiches, cakes and jellies in grease-paper cups that the ladies in the town had made for the occasion. You can imagine this appeared fairly grand to us after the rudimentary meals of hash or mutton chops I cooked for all of us in the schooner's little galley. On account of my age, Minkus was going to get the odd bottle of beer for me, so I loaded a plate with food and found myself a place near the band from which to observe what went on.'

'And this band?'

I saw Albert narrow his eyes a little as he summoned the band in his memory. 'There was a stout fellow with a concertina, a beanpole with a fiddle, a gent at the piano who wore a bowler, and another in spectacles who played his harmonica like someone warming his hands by blowing into them. All of them quite elderly gentlemen.

Does that picture it? They played old-time stuff, waltzes, twosome and foursome reels, schottisches. Pleasant. I liked the sway of it.

'Jim and Minkus danced. I was too tongue-tied to raise my eyes from the floor. So I stood with Otto, whose English wasn't too hot. We drank steadily from the bottles of beer that Minkus or Jim brought us, and I listened, a bit self-conscious but happy enough. Minkus did his best to urge us both onto the dance floor. Otto got teamed up with one solid matron, but I wouldn't come at the granny Minkus offered me. "Don't let the side down, Albicorus," he yelled in my ear. But I waved him away. That's your loner for you, turning shyness into an agreeable, secretive self-regard . . .'

I eyed Albert steadily for a few moments, Jenn, and then commented, 'You watch yourself very minutely, I think.'

'Maybe,' he said. I waited for him to resume. The dancers had given the impression of kelp swaying in a swell. 'Dizzying, a bit, though that could have been the beer and my age. The band took their breaks. We had been there maybe three hours. Then I saw Mister Tilber had turned up.'

'Was that such a surprise?'

'As a matter of fact, yes,' Albert stated. 'There were a couple of those Erikson four-masted barques in port; they used to sail out of Mariehamn, and one of their masters was known to be a hospitable fellow. We'd heard talk that the skippers from the various small fry were going to scull across and take advantage of this.'

'Was it so strange he should change his plans?'

'It is the effect on *me* I'm trying to get at. He had materialised. Slap out of the blue. That was the force of it. Took me aback a bit, you see. Me, fourteen years old. Too much beer inside me. Mister Tilber, my skipper, probably having a responsibility. *In loco parentis* or whatever. Materialised. I had a blur of dancers before me, shirtsleeves and waistcoats, pleated frocks, trailing ribbons. Then this gets drawn aside like a curtain at a show and there, in his own space on that warehouse floor, was our Mister Tilber. You could have believed it was an act. And your relative was dancing.'

'But not in time with the rest?'

'Not in any time, you might have said.'

'Dancing how?'

'It was an odd shuffle, like a hornpipe. He was quite on his own. Quite.'

'Why had he not taken a partner?' I asked.

'Oh, he had one. That's the point.'

'I don't understand.'

'You're coming in too early. I want to say what I saw.'

'Of course.' I was at pains not to ruffle him.

'The lean fiddle-player,' Albert continued, 'had stepped away from his fellow musicians. As he played, he had his eyes fixed on Mister Tilber, sidelong down the length of his instrument. It was as though he were taking a lead from our skipper. And the tune had changed, not waltz stuff, but something more, well, more fluid, hollow, more ancient altogether. *Melancholy.*'

'That word again.'

'Out of Orkney, Ireland, or some tent in the Sahara. It coiled, coiled as it uncoiled, like a person doing a trick with a length of cloth, making one end chase another. And what I saw was his big nose, his rather kindly eyes, and the splash of forehead in their frame of whiskers. That was the effect of it. He had his arms folded formally in front of him, like so, and, for his part, he kept his eyes fixed on the fiddle-player as though he were taking his lead from *him*. That's how it was, *as if their eyes were locked together*, and, as the dance went on, it was as if the music would stop only when the dance stopped, and equally, that the dance would stop only when the music stopped. Profound! I can see I'm not getting across to you how extraordinary the image of this was —'

'You are.'

My assurance was too pat for Albert. He retorted, 'I'm *not*,' and gave me what I had come to recognise as his hard look. He continued. 'Without paying them special mind, I knew the other dancers were looking on. I stared, fascinated by Mister Tilber's hornpipe. So slight, such a minimum of shuffle, so correct in its steps and its sway from side to side, so deliberate, so gentle, so *comical* in its flaunt. His cloth cap pulled down as though to guard his inmost thoughts. I could see the gold chain of his fob watch bouncing slightly on the front of his waistcoat. And his face! What a smile, what a blissful, angelic smile it was that came from within his facial fuzz ...

'And yet ... I could see tears, coursing down his cheeks. Unstoppable. Tears. They glistened among his whiskers. Oddest thing, a blissful little smile together with tears. You might have expected a rainbow! He looked so ... so humble, so elsewhere. So complete. Does that give you any light on your relative?'

I could see Albert was affected by the force of his recollection. And this tail-ender of a question, like the others, was not so innocent. It irritated me. He had moved my emotions, and he wanted me to admit as much, to prove I was not unfeeling. Why did he need me to affirm as much?

'Yes. Of course it does,' I answered, but I was bound to qualify. 'Though I'm not sure I understand —'

He was quick to enlighten me. 'A *melancholy cove*, Minkus had said. And I had thought how grand it might be to become a character like Mister Tilber. Except that "melancholy" doesn't account for the smile.'

'No.'

'I couldn't take my eyes away as the beanpole fiddler played and played his antique tune. Don't tell me he wasn't as deep in some ... well, you'd call it, *intuitive* arrangement with the dancing man as it was possible for two humans to be.

'And what should I have made of our skipper? The man was known in every one-jetty town from Esperance to Hobart, wherever there was enough water to bring a schooner alongside. He had position. He had his authority to keep up. How could a fellow with such standing be so unguarded about himself?'

'Detached?'

Albert ignored this. 'He looked as casual as a bottle afloat between one wave and another. And, at the time, I didn't know what on earth to make of it.'

'And you know now?' On the tape, Jenn, I find my voice is quite hushed as I make this enquiry.

'It is my opinion he was haunted,' Albert declared to me.

'Whatever that might mean.' It was my turn to challenge, for I feared the word threatened to take our oral history into the realm of the improbable.

He was ready with his rejoinder. 'I wouldn't use the word if I hadn't come to a view on that,' he defended. 'It is when the proper soul of a person gets snagged by a moment in time while the rest of him continues through time.'

'However that might work.'

'I've seen it work.'

I could have pressed Albert on his phrase 'proper soul'. Instead, I asked him to continue his account of the evening. 'Presumably you all got back to the ship.'

'One way or another,' he allowed. 'A couple of brazen fellows on the dance floor started doing their own imitation hornpipe. Impudent tomfoolery, and the indignity of it upset me...' Albert paused for a moment, then resumed. 'But it broke the spell. The fiddle-player retreated back among his fellow band members. I saw Minkus take our skipper by the elbow and lead him away, lending him a handkerchief with which to wipe his eyes. Folk started dancing again and people whirled past my line of sight. I was feeling fairly giddy by this, so I crawled under one of the tables where I was hidden by the white tablecloth, and went to sleep among the empty bottles. All that physical hard work earlier in the day, together with the beer, meant that I slept like a top.

'When I awoke that vast warehouse was deserted and I was cold. The tablecloths had been removed from the tables and the hurricane lamps doused to leave the place in darkness. It seems no-one had minded my curling up among the empties. Outside there was that brightening blue of the pre-dawn. I got a lift down to the Kirton Point Wharf with a fellow on a milk wagon, and as I jumped into the main shrouds and swung down, I heard Minkus say, "Cutting it a bit fine Albicore."'

'You haven't really given me much of a picture of Minkus as yet.'

'You're keen on your pictures.' Albert's condescension was not lost on me. 'Minkus,' he explained, 'was one of those fellows you meet who takes responsibility for things. I worked out later from the press clipping he was over forty, but he could pass for twenty-five. When I saw him there he was astride the main gaff, attaching the throat and peak halyards, mousing the hooks with twine. His short legs dangled down either side and his knife hung by a cord from his belt. Minkus had the best balance of any person I've ever met, an even temper to match. His head was like something you put through a wool press. As was the rest of his body. Not flattened so much as made more compact, more densely muscled. Years later I met him in a bank in Melbourne, and his face reminded me of the way sandstone weathers. His eyes seemed more scooped-out, his forehead blotchier, his eyebrows more tufted and overhanging. But back in 1928 Minkus was the colour of sandstone too, with his blond hair and a yellowiness in his tan.

'I asked if Jim and Otto were back from the dance, and he pointed for'ard where I saw them busy with the headsails. Mister Tilber had been on deck earlier, but had gone below after leaving his instructions, Minkus said.'

'Did you ask Minkus about your skipper's behaviour at the dance?'

'I began to. But Minkus told me to get the stove lit and the pot on, and then to come back out and help when we warped out into the bay. Mister Tilber wanted to catch the ebb. So I went for'ard. Jim and Otto had got the fore staysail up and it just swung there slackly on its boom because there was no appreciable wind at all. Then I saw that the sun had just begun to appear from behind Boston Island. Sudden as it sometimes is. And the sea. Well, it was turning from its night-time no-colour into a silky kind of flat. Blue shot with fiery gold. Like something expensive you might see unrolled on a draper's table. Then a sun ray, like the beam from a projector, caught the raised headsail and turned it to the intense ruddiness of a smoked herring.'

'Very vivid.'

'It was bloody vivid!' He actually rounded on me. I was not prepared for the fierceness. Then he seemed to relent. 'This...' he said, and Jenn, his voice, his posture, it was so *very* intent at this juncture, 'this is the thing I want to pin down. They say it's a kind of brain chemistry ...'

'What is?'

'What I'm trying to tell you. The onset. How I had stopped casually on the main hold. How the eastern sky was immense, cracked with the orange-gold sunrise. How I still had on my shoregoing clothes. How the profile of Boston Island was black as our cooking pots, but behind me a galvo roof was taking fire. How the grassed coastline south was so ... unearthly! How casually I had found myself in the midst of this, a world coming alive, like something out of a great shell. How, oh crikey, I felt such a queer sensation come over me, like I could centre my life on that moment.'

Albert eyed me like one assessing whether I had, not so much the intelligence, as a sufficient fineness of feeling to give him my full sympathy. He went on. 'It was as though there were immense space in my head. My dead mother was in there, but small, having her place. My whole future was in there, unknown, but also having its place. How could I put words to it then? I was fourteen. You charge about in a harum-scarum, then, one day, you look around yourself and think: "Why! The redness of that headsail, the brightness of those paddocks, the silkiness of that sea! How extraordinary that I am alive here." Do you reckon that's true?'

I told him I did, Jenn, and was moved that he should recall his youthful awakening to the world's loveliness with such immediacy. But this was presumptuous of me, for Albert had a more complex, a more *psychological* point to make.

'You see, I wanted to smile and blubber in the same breath. I could not free the joy from an attendant heartache. You'll think me soft for saying that, won't you?' He looked at me steadily.

'Not at all,' I said.

'I can tell you,' he continued, 'I've had my share of knocks from knuckle-boys on ketches or vicious third officers on freighters. During the war there was at least twice when I stood on a deck beside the corpses of fellows I held to be the best mates you could ever wish for. In all the palaver of feelings that come from seeing a person dead who you were having a joke with the minute before, it has never occurred to me to come over emotional for myself or for anyone. But as I stood on the hold looking out towards that grandeur over Boston Island, well, I could have made a right spectacle of myself.'

'What do you mean?'

He answered me with his own question, saying that, well, why should his feelings have taken this particular turn after the performance he had seen the previous evening?

'You make that connection?' I had done so too, uncharitably.

Yes, he did, he declared. 'And have been under its thumb all my life. This was its onset.'

'In what way?'

One moment comes along, he explained, richer, finer, more delicate than the rest, and he comes over all private and downcast. 'I suppose Minkus might have called me a melancholy cove as well. Maybe I was wanting to be exactly that. Melancholy.'

'Was it that?'

He shrugged. Albert had lost the condescension in his manner. Nor was it sympathy exactly that he sought from me. Rather, some hint from my own experience which might shed light on this perplexity in his life. Could I not, as a woman, be expected to have a more refined emotional wisdom than a single man, was the enquiry his gaze appeared to direct at me. For in a flash I comprehended how his entire life had lacked a person with whom to exchange confidences. Oh Jenn, *nothing* in my years with Kier had quite prepared me for the peculiar necessity with which Albert presented his experience to me. It gave me a sense of elation, almost, yet my immediate response to him now was inept.

'You make your skipper's sorrows like something ... well ... one might catch.'

'Not sorrow,' he contradicted. 'Joy,' he held one hand up, 'and sorrow,' he held up the other, and brought them together into a knot of fingers. 'The one tangle.'

I told him I had never experienced that, and across the cassette machine saw him scrutinising me again. So I asked him, 'You told me you never married, Albert. Did you never team up with anyone, I mean, even for a short time?'

'As it happens, no.' Then he thought to elaborate. 'There were knocking-shops here and there. They used to make me feel clumsy and sad, those ladies, and I'd come away not liking the human race any the more.'

'And Mister Tilber?'

'When I knew him, Mister Tilber was a bachelor. I wouldn't know about the other.'

'You use the word *innocent* for your skipper. Was he simply so unworldly as not to be bothered with "the other" as you put it?'

'I wouldn't know. Innocent was the impression of him.'

I brought Albert back to the event of the dance itself. 'Tell me more exactly what it was you think ...' I hesitated to use the word, '... *haunted* your skipper on that evening.'

He deflected my question. 'I think maybe we could take a break now.'

'Was it something you *can* be more exact about?' I persisted.

On the cassette there follows an interval of perhaps half a minute where nothing more than the airy shuffle of a body on its chair and the single punctuation of a distant car's horn is audible. Then at last Albert says, 'Yes, I can be exact,' and his tone is just a little defiant. 'I think that evening the skipper was in the company of Miss Maie Alice Yuell.' He spelt out the surname for me.

'Who was she?'

'She was a little girl, the daughter of a Captain Yuell who was the master of a full-rigged ship called *Kilbride*. She drowned at Valparaíso in the June of 1900. That's what Minkus's press cutting says.' He allowed this information to have its effect on me.

'Yes, you mentioned some press cutting.'

I was told that Minkus gave a document to him on the morning after they picked up their wages. It was a piece about a shipwreck. My relative was one of the personages who featured in it. Albert still had the paper in his possession.

'I would very much like to see it,' I requested.

Yes, I would be able to inspect it, if I wanted, he told me, then repeated his intention that we should take a rest from talking.

At which point, Jenn, I'll give my fingers and my typewriter a rest too.

❦

Continued July 18th

Yesterday I was entirely slack. Now I'll go straight on.

By the time of our break, it had become late afternoon. I had earlier bought a bottle of Irish whiskey — a rather expensive purchase for me. Now I took it down from its shelf and suggested I should pour us a glass each.

'To both reward and oil memory,' I announced. Rather gruffly, Albert declined my offer of liquor.

'Had to claw myself off that stuff once.' He had taken one glance at the bottle on the table and then kept his eyes averted from it, as if surprised that I, a woman, could keep such a ruinous thing in the house. I replaced it in my cupboard.

'You started early, by your own account,' I said, referring to the bottled beer of that long-ago evening.

'My word!' he affirmed, adding vehemently, 'And the sides of *that* hole are as slippery as all hell when you're at the bottom of it.' He would have some tea, black, if I would be so kind. I saw he had risen to his feet and was pulling out titles from my one bookshelf, examining them briefly and replacing them.

'Library books,' I explained. 'I borrow a dozen at a time.' I caught myself in a silly smile. 'My own books got left behind when I took flight from marriage.'

Keeping his attention on the books, his response to this was to say that his views on marriage were probably old-fashioned. 'When there's an obvious thing in your life you don't have, you expect all those who do have it to live up to it.' His moralising was done with his eyes averted from me.

'What was it you didn't have?' I asked.

He considered for a moment. 'Someone at home.'

'That was equally true of our Mister Tilber.'

'He was way beyond home, that man.'

I watched Albert inspecting my books. 'You're a bit severe on me,' I decided to inform him, and then deflected us from the subject of matrimony by asking him if he was a reader himself.

He had borrowing rights at several libraries, he informed. He tramped from one to the other. When an author or subject interested him he churned his way along a shelf, sitting in a chair near the library radiators until closing time. 'Nowadays my second home.'

'And when you were on the ships?'

Paperbacks. When he had finished a title he was as likely as not to toss it into the sea.

'Or pass it on to someone else?'

This, it appeared from Albert's shrug, was not convenient.

'You don't have the wish to own a few favourite titles?' I asked.

He didn't have the wish to own anything very significant, he said, and when I likened my new, austere existence down here to Albert's indifference to possessions, I wondered whether it would have been so very peculiar of me to have accepted his earlier offer of marriage.

I busied myself with kettle and teapot, reflecting, as I watched his restless shuffling of my books, that I would not have picked Albert as an ex-wino. If he was ever on skid row, he has done the repairs to his morale with great intelligence and that seems to show in his well-kept appearance. He is a slender man and, for all his age, his face is still lean, the flesh still taut, tanned almost to a ruddiness that matches the brown on the backs of his hands. His hair is white, thin, and combed back from a tall forehead on which there are furrow-lines. There is a comb in his breast pocket and evidently he takes some care to keep himself as presentable as he used to be, no doubt, when, with white tunic and bow tie, he knocked on the doors of first-class cabins with morning tea.

Now, having glimpsed the flicker of distrust which passed through his eyes when I suggested our quick snort of whiskey, I decided to probe him a little.

'So, were you an alcoholic once?'

I watched him replace the book in his hand and sit down again in his chair. He shrugged. 'Every boozer thinks the world has a right to only one interest. Him.' He would not meet my eye.

'And was that you, craving attention?'

'Listening to me I'd say you can answer that for yourself.'

'But you are off it now.'

'The craving for booze I could beat, not the other.' I thought this might be the extent of his admission, but then he added, 'On a binge I would always be watching myself. Couldn't help it, you see. Even when I knew I could pass myself off as beyond responsibility there was this eye in the mind, watching my antics, like a detective.'

I wish I had got that comment down on the tape, Jenn, because for the second time I felt an impulse of ... I suppose I *should* call it affection for Mister Albert Prideauz. There was this fineness in his introspection. Should I have probed him further on this subject of his drinking past? I suspect I would not have got very far. For had he not been a seafaring man in the rigorous days of sail, shouldered wheat bags three bushels per bag? How could his dignity have permitted me to make of him a victim? Anyway, after the tea we returned to our recording.

I asked him to tell me about Maie Alice Yuell and her sea-captain father. No, Albert had his own ideas about our schedule. He would continue to say what happened on that trip back to Port Adelaide with Mister Tilber. Things would be brought in where they belonged.

'Fine,' I agreed.

So, with his hands spread on each arm of the chair, Albert resumed his narration. Again, Jenn, I transcribe it exactly.

'I was saying before how the skipper wanted to catch the ebb that morning. We took our breakfasts. While I washed up, Otto and Jim took the starboard anchor in the dinghy and sculled out into the fairway a little, laying the cable as they went, then they heaved it over, sculled back, and we got the dinghy on board. Minkus let go the stern line and jumped back into the shrouds quick so he could get the fenders inboard and take the helm. Otto and I worked the rocker gear, Jim feeding the cable down the spurling pipe into the chain locker near the after hatch as it came clank-clank off the windlass.'

'You still have the rigmarole off pat!' I could not help admiring.

My word, he said, he had loved it, the knowing what to do, the greased cogs, the water dripping from the chain as the vessel was warped out. The skipper had made his appearance by this, in white shirt and braces. 'There was a kind of casual thoroughness with which he checked that all the routines were being performed.'

'Did his spirits seem recovered?'

'If I noticed anything odd in Mister Tilber's behaviour as we got under weigh, it was the fact that he had a notion to join in all the heave-and-grunt work, not so much because he fussed, as that he seemed to want (for reasons which I came to deduce after) his share of the sailorising. So, a little stiffly, he climbed up on the rail and led the work of hauling on the halyards of the fore and main sails. You mentioned the strength in his arms. It was there in the torso too, for all his short stature. Strength and nous. I went to coil down the slack on the pins, but he shooed me away on this particular morning and did the job himself.'

'Was this so unusual?'

'Well, I can tell you my impression. It was that Mister Tilber had a thing on his mind.'

'What kind of a thing?'

'You couldn't see the shape of it but you could see him handing the slack as though the weight of a coil of rope had suddenly become of precious importance to him. I reckon that says it.'

'It was a presentiment?'

'I couldn't say at the time. It was an impression. Anyway, he then went aft and indicated to Minkus that he wanted to take the ship out into open water himself, so Minkus handed the helm over to him for a spell. Same thing. It was as if he was greedy for the feel of the vessel. Not that we went far in that morning calm. The bit of bunting we used as a telltale on the backstay would lift promisingly, then drop. The blocks would clunk as the booms shifted across, the sails refusing to set.

'It was not until around eight o'clock that a small nor-nor-easter picked up. This allowed us to beat past Cape Donington and lay a course that would take us to the north of Dangerous Reef and Wedge Island, before bearing south east towards Althorpe Island. It was a slow, lazy sort of a trip, sixty hours or more, big blue sky with the occasional mare's tail floating over, the winds light. I had the notion we were all a bit reflective too on that Sunday, feeling the long fetch of those Southern Ocean rollers lifting us and letting us down slowly. At about midday it fell calm until the sea breeze came from the south west. We could see the bevelled profile of Wedge Island a few miles to starboard. The breeze held until around midnight. As I say, no-one seemed to do much talking that trip. I was too perplexed by that shuffling dancer I had seen the night before, sorrow-and-joy, and the peculiar sensations I had discovered in myself that morning. So I tried no conversation. If I look at the facts of our routine, I can say we each took our spells at the helm, but whenever I chanced to look aft it seemed to be Mister Tilber standing there on the grating, white shirt and braces, that floppy cap of his sitting atop all that vigorous growth of facial hair, one hand grasping a spoke on the wheel. He looked so casual, yet so in charge, as if the blessed schooner was an extension of his own body. On the first afternoon Otto and I were occupied giving the dinghy a lick of paint. As the wind or our course changed, we trimmed sail. I cooked the midday dinners and the evening meals — for pudding we filled up on bread and melon jam from a tin. We lit our navigation lights when it got dark, which it was by the time we picked up the Althorpe beacon. Jim and Otto went below. Sometimes I saw the mast light of a ketch, so still it was hardly distinguishable from a star low on the horizon. I was told to watch for the beacon that indicated the Troubridge Shoal, but with the slack conditions around midnight it was broad morning before we were abreast of that. Then Jim and Otto were called while Minkus and I went below for a spell. In turn we were called. That second day conditions were very light and we went nowhere. A steamer thudded past, so badly ballasted that you could see the top of its screw thrashing the water. Here and there were ketches with their quadrangles of grey or rusty sails as bereft of wind as we were. You'd think the wind had slackened off in order to let time stand still awhile. It was the third afternoon before we were off the beach here at Semaphore, and early evening before we picked up the Wonga Shoal beacon at the entrance of the Port Adelaide River. As I say, sixty hours in total. The slowness of the trip affected our mood, you see.

'The skipper had taken the helm again off Semaphore, while we prepared the tow rope. There was just enough of an evening southerly to get us into the mouth of the river where we took our tow from a small tugboat for the run down Hindmarsh Reach. By the time we came to tie up alongside McLaren Wharf we had the canvas all furled and everything on board stowed away properly.'

Albert stopped, and I couldn't resist saying, 'I'm not the only one under the spell of memory, I think.'

Cont'd in the evening of the 18th

Let me tell you, Jenn, why I made that last remark. As I listened to the minutiae of wind changes, beacons, landfalls, the ship's routine of those several days in March 1928, how could I not be struck by the perception of something radically out of scale in Albert's memory?

I could not help but sense that behind all the detail there was an unusual power of feeling and that it was bound up with something perhaps not disclosed to me during our original conversation in his caravan. So I drew my conclusions about what it might be and decided to forestall him.

'Let me guess,' I put to him. 'This was your skipper's last trip, and he knew it. You're going to tell me that something happened?'

'I'm going to tell things in their order,' he reminded me gruffly.

We regarded each other for a few moments before he continued.

'The skipper had gone ashore and used the telephone. I made the evening meal and we ate it sitting on the forehatch. Then we sat about awaiting the skipper's return to see if we were still needed. It was dark by the time he got back. I looked up to see his silhouette cross from the wharfside into the main shrouds then clamber down. It was a warm, still evening and he hadn't bothered with his jacket, so that as he leaned there between the wharfside and the shrouds, for a moment he reminded me of a spider.

'He came up to where we were and said, "Now we'll maybe unbend all this canvas, you fellows."

'The directive to stow away our sails in the locker surprised us, since it indicated the ship was to be out of commission for a period. Was she to be overhauled? She appeared in reasonable trim.

'We set to, unshackling sheets and halyards. Jim was for'ard, cutting the twine lashings that fastened the hanks to the headsails. Otto and Minkus went aloft and loosed the topsails from the jackstays, while I found myself working with the skipper, unlacing the mainsail from its gaff and boom. There was some light from the wharfside, but Mister Tilber had his back to it so I could not see his face. The two of us worked in silence, our fingers pulling at the lashings from alternate sides. After a time it was like a trance. Above my head I could hear Otto and Minkus talking quietly to each other. And then I found I had addressed Mister Tilber.

"'I was there at the dance, skipper, and I didn't understand what I saw."

'I could not prevent myself from saying this. If it was impertinence, I felt somehow remote from its consequences, and nor did I really expect an answer. But I knew I was the subject of that attentive gaze from across the spar, and that the eyes had their strange, detached, humorous light.

"'Was I there at all?" was what I said to him next.

'Our fingers moved the whole time, drawing the lashings through the cringles, and I was being watched. What could he have told me? What did I have any right to know? He should have said, sharply, "Mind your own business, son." But he did not. Instead I saw the black profile of his head look back at me steadily, like a well-disposed schoolmaster, as though the answer to my question was, well, here was a poser, and if he could have helped me round it he would have done so. We worked on, freeing the luff of the mainsail from the mast rings, folding it, exchanging no words. By midnight we had finished and stowed the sails in their locker aft.

'Mister Tilber went into his cuddy, then came again to where we stood, up near the forehatch. He had put his jacket on now. There was a little illumination from the mast light which no-one had yet doused. For some moments he just stood there with his hands in his pockets, that odd characteristic expression in his eyes that was a mix of the hopeful and the playful. You could never read it exactly. Then he spoke to us quietly. He gave us to understand that we would not be required to help unload on this occasion. Arrangements had been made to load the grain into a German steamer that was due in port tomorrow. The stevedores would look after that.

'I saw him take the wallet out from his inside pocket. Then he said — and these were his exact words — "Thank you, boys. That's the sum of it. You can sleep on board tonight. But tomorrow I am going ashore. I will dissolve my partnership in the vessel. It is my intention to leave the sea." And having said that, he paid to each the banknotes and silver that were due, shook us each by the hand, then turned his back on us, walked to the stern of the ship and disappeared down the companion to his cabin.

'And I remember thinking, his jacket had been in his cabin with the wages in his wallet all the time. He *knew* this was his last trip.'

'Why should that have made a difference?' I asked Albert.

'We might have made some kind of bloody occasion of it.' He regarded me for a moment, then apologised for the language.

Momentarily Albert seemed disinclined to go on, so I took the opportunity to change the tape. When it was ready, I held down the pause button, awaiting his signal that we might continue. It was clear that after sixty-odd years he was still moved by this moment in his experience. At length he gave me a nod.

'At fourteen I was a stringy, tallish chap,' he began. 'I reckon your relative reached about the level of my nose. As I shook his hand I found myself looking down into those hopeful, uplifted eyes. That was a cruel feeling.'

'I don't understand.'

'That hand — it was a biggish hand — had set stunsails on the runs back from Canton and Foochow in the seventies of the last century. Charlie Tilber had been a boy on the celebrated *Thermopylae*, or one of those other thoroughbred tea ships, it doesn't matter which. Where, in the course of more than fifty years on the globe, had he not been? And this was the finish, the cap on a lifetime's experience, an occasion consisting of no more than four fellows able to say, "Thanks, skipper" and "Good luck, skipper" on the deck of a schooner before he turned his back on us. You think of the ballyhoo when some toff retires. And I was looking *down* at him.'

'I still don't understand. What effect on you did that have?'

It was a while before Albert spoke again. Then he stated simply, 'I felt unfairly treated.'

'Why was that?'

He took his time to answer, for he was very little bothered by how much of my tape should be taken up by his silences.

'What right did he have to turn his back on us like that? None that I could see. It was the effect of Mister Tilber's phrase, "That's the sum of it". You don't simply write off a whole working life with a phrase, *the sum of it*. Our skipper was venerable, we could boast to the fellows in the other ketches and schooners when we met them.

Our skipper went back to the days of those beautiful tea ships...' Albert paused, before adding, 'You know what was at the bottom of it?' He paused again. 'I felt unsafe.'

'How did the other three react?'

'I noted they were fairly subdued. We doused the mast light, and went below and lay on our bunks, all four of us. It was semi-dark because Jim had lit the candle we kept in a margarine tin. You could hear the harbour water lick-licking the hull. Then I said, "But he can't let go of things just like that."

'And Minkus said, "The skipper's an old bloke now, Albicore. He can't be far off seventy."

'And I replied, "That still doesn't give him the right to walk away from old *Bicheno* and just curl up in some Seamen's Home." Despite the sodden time of it I had experienced on our run around South West Cape the previous year, I still had sentimental ideas about a sea calling. But Minkus just told me to get some kip and to ask around the docks for another berth in the morning.

'"You're on your own now, Albicorus," he said.

'"And you," I asked. "Don't you and the skipper go back a bit?"

'"We're all looking out for ourselves now," he replied. And then he snuffed that stub of candle between his fingers and I took what he had just said to be his last word on the subject. But it wasn't.

'By this time it must have been getting on for one in the morning. At first I lay with my eyes open, listening to the creak of the fenders between our bulwark and the dockside. And then I must have been asleep, because suddenly there was Minkus, giving me a shake, saying in a whisper, "I want you to wake up, Albicore. You awake now?" "Yes," I told him. "What time is it?" He had lit that stub of candle again, and he didn't answer. Instead he said, "I've decided to give you some things." I heard the slight snoring of Otto on one of the upper bunks, and the sound of Minkus rummaging in his sea bag. Then he came back and I saw he had a book in his hand. It used to be a joke with Jim and Otto that Minkus only owned the one book and he hadn't ever read it. From between its pages he took a piece of paper that was folded into an envelope. Within it were two further folded pieces of paper. One of them was that press cutting I told you about earlier. The other was a certificate of discharge. Minkus said, "You was asking me about the skipper. There's a bit about him written up in that. You'd better read it, I reckon. In fact you can have the clipping because I don't really mind if I'm not the keeper of that story any more. I've had enough of it."

'He put into my hands the envelope with its two documents. The envelope was a good quality paper, though old and grubby, but the clipping was so frail, like the wing of a moth. By the candle I could see it was brown, with ragged edges where it had been torn out of the original journal. I felt like I was neither awake nor asleep during this, but in some suspended state of mind. "Why don't you want the story?" I asked Minkus. He wouldn't give me an answer to that. He just said, "It's yours now, Albie." "But why me?" I persisted. "Because you're in the way of it," he replied, then blew out the candle for a second time and went back to his cot. I don't know whether Jim was awake during this.'

'What was in the press cutting?'

'You'll want it exact, so I'll show you it maybe next time.'

'I take it that, when the four of you woke up the next morning, you did find employment in other vessels?'

Albert would not be hurried. 'Without the usual routine to wake for, we were left to sleep late. By the time we turned to, the skipper had gone ashore. We folded and packed our blankets and personal things, then went to a dining room close to McLaren Wharf where we ordered a good breakfast. With our pay in our pockets we, at least, were going to make an occasion of it. Bacon, eggs, coffee, toast and jam. And then we were finished and there was nothing more to be said. So we shook hands with each other. Jim and Otto went off first. Minkus, in the corner seat near the window, was lingering over his coffee. He looked at me with his wide face all serious.

'"You got a place to go to?" he asked.

'I told him about my uncle who lived in Commercial Road and had a photographic studio. Then he too shook my hand and told me to look after myself, and hefted his sea bag through the aisle between the tables. I followed him and asked, "What about that piece of paper you gave me last night? Won't there be things I'll want to ask you?"

'But he just waved and said, "From now on, let that story float where it wants", and walked off towards the wharf. I realised I had not asked him whether he, himself, had a place where he could doss down. He looked as though he were going to start searching for another berth immediately. As I watched him go, with the drawstrings of his bag across his shoulder, I could see how bow-legged he was. Then he turned a corner and I didn't see him again until the time twenty-three years later in the bank.

'And that *was* the sum of it, because I have to say that never again did I go in a ship — sail or steam — where I did not have to think whether or not I was happy.'

'So what happened to you after *Bicheno*?'

The next few minutes of our taping session relate the remainder of Albert's seagoing life, Jenn. It was clear he had decided in his own mind that this balance between the minutely told three or four days of his last trip with the schoonermaster, Charles Tilber, in March 1928, and the gloss he gave me on the ensuing fifty years of his working career was an equitable counterweighting of two phases of his existence. This was for the reason he had given: that it divided a life before from a life after. It marked the moment of what he had called his 'onset', when he had become 'a melancholy cove'.

So I heard from the old gent how, after a few days ashore staying with his uncle, Albert found a place on a ketch in what he called the shell-grit trade, shovelling the shell-mash into a couple of big tubs in the intervals of low tide off some beach north of Ardrossan. There had been another lad with him, and, whether through niggardliness or mismanagement, the skipper of *Klara* had kept them both hungry.

'We were never hungry on *Bicheno*'.

At the first opportunity Albert had left this employment to join the crew of a small American barquentine that sailed across the Tasman to Whangarei for a cargo of sawn timber. It was no more happy than the shell-grit ketch, and I'll transcribe another snippet from the tape so you can hear his voice again.

'I was fifteen by then and could eat like a horse. But I

was still the youngest on that ship, so last in line at mealtimes. One Yankee fellow enlightened me as to getting my share. If I wanted a fair helping, particularly of the meat, I had to use my knuckles.'

'And if you didn't?'

'"Do without, buddy," he told me.' Albert allowed himself to remember the Yankee fellow for a few moments. 'What affronted me,' he continued, 'was how blatant a tyranny it was. I can say to you, young lady, I dislike hurting any living thing. But I stuck up for myself out of a kind of panic that I'd otherwise starve, and if I bled someone's nose or knocked a tooth out onto the deck, I did also succeed in getting a little of my share. But I didn't feel good about my victories, I simply felt the world was mean and had succeeded in making me mean too. It was a ferociously mean fo'c's'le on that Yankee, oh golly yes.'

Later, Albert continued, he joined a freighter and worked variously as a trimmer, stoker, greaser for the Alliance Steamship Company. This had taken him through the thirties and forties.

'Did you have a hair-raising war?' I enquired.

In the Mediterranean it had been unnerving at times, he admitted, buried down in the innards of the ship. Malta, Tobruk. 'You heard and felt the action, but saw precious little of it. Yes, unnerving. The crack-crack-crack of the oerlikon cannons and the whine of dive bombers. You sensed the hull lift whenever there was a near miss.'

Albert had been rescued from one burning oil tanker in the middle of the Atlantic in '42. So, at war's end he decided it was time to come up for some daylight. He joined P&O and served as a cabin steward on a couple of the well-known liners throughout the fifties and sixties.

'I've been around the world more times than I care to count.' Gibraltar, Naples, Port Said, Aden, Colombo, Singapore, Suez and Panama — he had his tanned face and forearms to show for all that circumnavigation. Then the creamy, purposeful steamers with their yellow funnels vanished and were replaced by the floating luxury hotels, whereupon it had seemed to the steward like a good idea to retire.

'Feeding the well-heeled, bringing them their newspapers while we all sailed round in a serene circle — this was seafaring!' he expostulated.

'No-one with a pair of red socks in his pocket . . .'

'No destinations,' he corrected me, then allowed himself to reflect. 'And no-one to give me back any of what had gone away so quick. For that *was* the sum of it. A working life.'

He looked at me steadily to gauge whether his tone had allowed me to understand. Did he want from me what he might have called *the compassion of a woman*? I've told you how he affected me, Jenn, and yet there was still something cross-grained or hostile in his nature which inhibited my sympathy for the old fellow.

'You saw the world.'

He reminded me what he thought about that. A bus route. Again he stopped and regarded me. I returned him to what I hoped was still the quick of his interest.

'That trip home in 1928. Mister Tilber was taking the helm, doing all that — you called it sailorising — because he knew, after a lifetime, he was about to let it go?'

'That's the nub of it.'

'You'll tell me Mister Tilber died soon after.' Albert looked up sharply. 'That he had a sense of fate?'

'Fate? Nothing of the kind. Your relative lived another twenty-eight years. He died in an old people's home aged ninety-seven. Those short fellows live a long time.'

I did not, Jenn, immediately calculate the year of my great-uncle's demise. I needed to keep my mind on the questions I was asking. But you can see from what I have told you how Great-Uncle Charles Tilber died in 1956. He was actually *alive* at the time young Sarah and her dad were holding the magnifying glass above his name over that family chart at Hardacre Street. He certainly outlived all his brothers and sisters, and the fact that his time on the earth overlapped with mine excites me with a sense of his proximity. Possessed of a few of the facts I now know, Dad and I could have flown around the world in an aeroplane and actually have seen, heard and touched the man!

Howsoever, my next enquiry to Albert was, 'Did you ever see him again?'

'I told you how I ran into Minkus in a Melbourne bank. That was about 1951. Minkus told me how Mister Tilber was now in the old people's home. It was called the Rostrevor Rest Home and has changed hands now. Back then it was run by one of the churches and they employed a few nurses to look after a dozen or so old people who had no family. I should visit the skipper if I had a bit of time, said Minkus, and he gave me one of those looks which said that he expected it of me.

'Well, I had been stewarding for five years by then. I was on *Carinthia,* and she was in Melbourne for ten days.

The company owed me a bit of leave, so I took the daylight train across to here, stayed with my old photographer uncle and, late one afternoon, turned up at the address Minkus had given me. Rostrevor was a rambling, weatherboard place in Seaton, not so far from where we're sitting, as it happens.

'I had the feeling as soon as I was there that I shouldn't have come, that it was false sentiment on my part. For I was being led through a ward of various old fellows. There were some of them bedridden; one or two old codgers, far gone in dementia, who were wandering the lino corridors in their nightshirts, mildly trying to find a way out. You could smell that there was a good bit of disinfectant being sloshed around.

'False sentiment? Here I was, using up my leave with trains and a visit to an old chap I'd known for only a few months of my youth. I was not far off forty and in that shiny American world we got after the war. I wasn't keen on all the human decrepitude which surrounded me at that moment. It turned me up. But I fortified myself by thinking, well, there's something in the idea of gratitude to those spirits who have touched one's life kindly. And I found I believed myself. Don't you think that's so?'

I was not prepared for the question, Jenn, so Albert repeated, more searchingly, 'Don't you think?'

And what I found I had done was nod and say, 'I suppose that makes me think of my dad.' The answer seemed to please Mister Albert Prideauz. He continued.

'Your relative had been put in a room by himself. It seemed that sometimes "the Captain", as the nurses called him, had a habit of bellowing which disturbed some of the others. I told them how the Mister Tilber I knew, you'd be lucky to get five words together from him.

'And when had I known him, one nurse asked me, so I said, "Far off schooner days". "I think you'll find him changed," she warned. She related how the Captain was believed to have suffered a stroke or two before he came there. The church had found him in a room containing not much more than an old bed and chair. "He's not keen on being bossed by us girls," the nurse finished.

'We all three stopped at the open door of a small room with yellow curtains. And there, framed by the doorway I found myself confronting a terribly ancient person who had been propped in a chair beside his bed. That torso which I had remembered in its white shirt and braces beside the helm was shrunken and collapsed. It looked as if it were made of rags. And the head was slumped on the chest as if it were too heavy to lift. Oh lor, what a transformation. You're told to expect it and you don't, do you?' Albert waited for my answer.

'No, of course not.'

'Twenty-three years since I had seen the skipper. That was all. I could have been looking at one of those saintly human carcasses preserved by a church since medieval times. And they had put a vase of flowers on the windowsill behind his head.'

'Yes.'

'I don't say I hadn't brought it on myself. Had I not wanted to catch sight of those months in 1928 when I had been happy ... Well, here I was being given this sharp lesson.'

'Yes.'

'I said to one of the nurses, "He used to have such a thick beard and moustache, ma'am."

'True, she replied, but they'd shaved those off because it was easier to clean him up after feeding him. As a cabin steward, I knew about cleaning up. You've got to go with what's convenient, don't you? And yet the effect of taking away his fuzz was to make his face so meagre! They'd left him with an incongruous tuft of black hair on top. Yes, black, even at ninety-odd.

'"Hello skipper," I sang out as I went in. It was the form of address I had decided on, for all the years of experience I had collected since seeing him last. "Remember me? Albicore!" I supplied one or two other clues — *Bicheno*, Minkus, Otto. And I tucked a bar of chocolate between his fingers, because I recalled that he had liked his chocolate. He looked at the small slab in his hands then his head rolled up to regard me for some moments, slowly, like some poor drowned joker you might pull out of the ocean. His eyes were so tired. *No-one* with eyes like that could be a bellower, I thought. Then I found he had said, "I remember," and nodded once or twice. Social skills. They say the very old retain these even when every other faculty has gone. For he didn't have a clue who I was. I could see that. Then his head sagged again.

'But I'll tell you something, I soon learned about the bellowing, and for all the decrepitude of that ancient head, its freckled, flaky surface, its exhausted eyes, there was something energetic going on in the mind that pointed backwards at a life.'

'Like what?'

'You see, the two nurses who had led me to him encouraged me to take the skipper out into the grounds. A spot of sunshine would do him good, they said. They were nice young ladies, patient, pretty, particularly one of them, and they must have put up with a lot from that ward of old people. They made a fuss of the skipper, and evidently regarded him as a bit of a character. One of them had wheeled in a bathchair.

'Now the two of them lifted that poor sack of a man from one chair into the other. As they did so, I saw there was a moment when the skipper's legs were unsupported. Maybe there was some trouble with the small of his back, or his pelvic bone. To be abruptly yanked from one chair to another was probably excruciating for him. But what came out was a bellow. I wasn't prepared for that. "*Get to the fuckery!*" he roared in that instant as those two pretty nurses shifted him across.'

Albert regarded me, and again asked me to pardon his language. Then he continued.

'But crikey! That oath sounded as though he wanted his very own childhood to hear it across the years.

'Next the skipper repeated the oath, but more quietly, as though he had considered it and decided it should stand. "Get to the fuckery," with a kind of snarl on the "get". The first time it had been like an animal. But the second time his eyes seemed to come alive for a moment and look sidelong, and the curse had such . . .' Albert looked to me to supply him with a word.

'Enmity?'

'Enmity's about right. As if something bottled up had been let out.'

'So this was the bellowing. Was it that he didn't like women in general, do you think?'

'He didn't like something.'

'How did the two nurses take it?'

'Oh, they laughed. "Captain!" they exclaimed, and told him off for using such language. They had all the authority now, didn't they, and no doubt had heard these oaths before. But I minded, my word I did, on their behalf perhaps.'

'Were you not over-reacting?'

'The skipper had a grievance. Don't you see?' Again Albert was watching me to see whether I understood. 'And I immediately took it to be a grievance ancient as all hell.'

'It probably was.'

'Well, that grievance was the last detail given to me to add to my picture of Charlie Tilber, who is your relative, my first skipper, and a person I would call the most naturally likable man I've ever come across. I would have told anyone how that man could not know what a grievance was. *Innocent as the angels*, I was prepared to swear. What did I want that opinion of him muddied up for?'

'Did you get nothing from him while you were in the garden?'

'Nothing. He just slumped there in the bathchair. Sometimes his eyes would flicker as I chatted away. But the impression he gave, like a lot of old folks, was that he was absorbed by some inner, remote object of contemplation. He was like a person looking down a tunnel. They say the long-term memory takes over. But I couldn't tell you whether his inward-looking expression was fixed on something in his remote childhood, or in the present aches and pains that had been roused when he was shifted from chair to chair. I took him in for his evening feed and said goodbye.

'Would you believe how he dismissed me? "Come again," he said, rolling that tired head in my direction. This invitation was the nearest we got to his old self. In the garden I had talked to him about old times, about myself, about whatever subject came into my head which might stimulate him to a response. Was there a mind registering any of my patter? I couldn't say for I only ever got those two sparks of attention from him. "I remember." And "Come again". Social skills.

'I gave one of the nurses the address of the company and asked to be posted when the old fellow passed on. I also wrote to Minkus, care of the Melbourne bank, to see if he knew anything of the destitute circumstances in which Mister Tilber had lived before he entered the home. But I never got any reply.

'On the strength of what I saw in that bathchair I would have given the skipper a few months. It was five years before I received a card saying he had passed on. I was on the other side of the world by then. But as I held the card in my hand I had those two oaths of his in my mind still, because they didn't seem to fit along with the polite, eccentric manner of his dealing with us, his crew of lads. Had I misremembered him? When you recall the time you were young, there does seem to be a great deal of light falling on things.'

'Had you?' I enquired.

'No, I hadn't misremembered. I was right to ask where the angelic little man had gone, and why that hint of such …

well ... if you like, woman hatred — for what other explanation is there? — why that had surfaced. It was like something bared and unhealed over a lifetime. Four words, and they seemed to carry such anger, such ... such ... Ahh!'

'Disappointment?' Again you'll say I was prompting my witness, Jenn. On this occasion the word I offered did not satisfy Albert.

'Grievance.' He came back to this. 'That has to be the only word gets round it. There it was, as if it had always been like an ugly patch on his exemplary good nature. And yet I'd never picked it, and I'd swear the other fellows never did either. I have never managed to make it fit with what I knew. And that was that.'

'Did you ever see him in any dealings with women?'

'There was a lady worked in the office of his partnership. I never heard he was rude to her.'

'Nothing else?'

'No. He was offshore most of the time so his company was men and lads.'

'A working life.'

'I suppose you'd call it.'

'Do you think he might have harboured any long resentments against his family, his mother perhaps? Did she pack him off to sea at a tender age, or ...?'

'I can't say what I don't know.' Albert put an end to my speculations.

It was my turn to allow the tape to run for a few moments while I regarded him. Then I asked, 'So, in the end, what are your feelings towards Mister Tilber?'

He took his time to answer. 'I would be happy to find myself in his corner of eternity.' Some moments passed before he added. 'It would be a place out of harm's way. You'd have to say that.'

'Who else would you find there?'

'Unattached fellows of one sort or another.'

Again I was moved by the old gent's sentiments, and, for all his egotism, I took it as a privilege that he should take me so far into his confidence. He had loved my ancestor. That was the nature of his loyalty. Love

I had one more question I wanted to put to Albert that day. 'There is also the subject of Maie Alice.'

'I will show you Minkus's press clipping,' he repeated. Then he announced that he had talked enough and requested that I phone a taxi for him.

Some ten minutes later I escorted him down my concrete stairwell and, with a contribution from me to cover his fare and a handshake through the car window, he took his leave.

Continued July 20th

Tuesday's effort of transcription, dear Jenn, left me bleary-eyed, fatigued and dissatisfied with myself. So yesterday I took another rest from Great-Uncle and went fossicking among the opportunity shops. I have acquired a handsome teapot striped with gold and carmine to add to my collection, price two dollars! And a couple of practical corduroy skirts, price six dollars.

I believe it is the aroma of op shops that draws me in. Those jackets, skirts, trousers, overcoats on their chromium racks do seem to retain the smell of the wardrobes they have hung in and the bodies they have covered. It is *not* a very agreeable smell but it is inescapably our common leftover presence, isn't it, somehow both communal and bygone. The idea of this teases me.

In the evening I came home and perused what I have written to you. This is already such a bulky package and will poach rudely on the time you should be giving to the boarders at your school. So I had better conclude it soon. But first let me encapsulate for you what it is I appear to have accomplished so far. And also what it is I have let myself in for.

(1) Those two question marks on Dad's family tree have now been dealt with. Date and place of death for Charles Harling Tilber have been established as: Seaton, Adelaide, 1956. My elder brother, Brian, has all Dad's genealogies, and I shall write to him with these details.

(2) Dad's question marks have been replaced by question marks of my own. CHT has a life story which, in part at least, seems more riddling, more intriguing, than anything I know of the dyke reeves, thatchers, launderwomen and ordering clerks who appear in Dad's charts and pamphlets.

(3) Albert's picture of CHT as a benign, charismatic, private person, an immensely confident and experienced mariner, is moving and intense. So what of his bellowing? Howl of pain or deep-seated grievance? (I do feel intrigued by how well he might have got on with his mother, but *must* not impose on the story as it might be.)

(4) And Maie Alice Yuell? Sorrow-in-joy? How seriously do I take Albert's word 'haunted'? Why is Albert himself just a little haunted by my forebear?

I have to say I am moved by this notion of a man locked into some particularly intense emotion who in turn affects another. What is this strange, binding claim one man can have on another that clamps them into some unresolved, comradely melancholy down the years? It is the psychological pulse behind ancient heroic poetry, war memoirs, etcetera, isn't it, and also somehow male-ish, don't you think?

You, with your common sense, will say, 'But Sal, your Mister Prideauz would inevitably have found *something* in his life to be "haunted" by.' 'Maybe,' is my answer to you, 'but it was *this* something, and it did involve *my* ancestor.' So I want to know more and have high hopes of this press clipping.

In the meantime, dear Jenn, I am well and truly embarked on my journey down into the past's murk, and so offer you here all these ill-typed pages for you to be patient with and please, please, to favour me with your reactions. Yours, Sarah.

August

This package of July, the 'big one' as I recall Sarah's various parcels of the ensuing ten months, consisted of nearly forty closely typed pages. It arrived towards the end of our summer term in a padded envelope covered with colourful stamps. As she expected of me, I found her transcription of Albert's story poignant, and wrote back to her as encouragingly as I could.

I was troubled. You have seen how in our friendship I have known myself to be the passive one. In part this has meant I am the more adept at disguising my feelings. Sarah is forthright. Now I was twelve thousand miles away from the two intent voices around her recorder. The English school year was coming to a close with drama productions and inter-house athletics competitions. Did I enter the spirit of Sarah's long remittance with quite the sympathy she wanted? As I sat at my kitchen table composing my replies to her, I tried, and you have seen one instance of her quite effusive gratitude for my efforts.

But did she occasionally see through me? In my response to 'the big one' I had suggested, lightheartedly, she was in danger of immersing herself too meticulously in the past for those of us who still inhabited a present where speech day, school reports, and clothing lists for the new intake of September had to be juggled with. I was startled when a postcard bounced back from Australia, taking me up on my chance word 'meticulously'.

Semaphore, August 11th
    Dear Jenn,
    One part of your response to my package I don't understand. *Why* do you advise caution when it comes to bringing the dead to life so (your word) *meticulously*? Do you think I'm haunted too? I'm restoring the right of my great-uncle to be remembered and, by extension, all our unnotable forebears. Is that so dangerous? It's democratic! Biographers do it for notables every day! Yours, S.

❧

When I received this — how shall I say — *hair-trigger* reaction to my casual remonstrance, I felt nettled. I contemplated bouncing a card back to Australia saying no more than, 'Sal!'. But what was it that had nettled me exactly? I felt infringed, I realised. My own existence was being crowded out somehow. Yet had I not, through friendship, volunteered to be her 'sounding board'? In an instant I saw that it might be possible I could become indifferent to her interests. This recognition frightened and disturbed me.
    So I sent no postcard. Besides, the holiday came and our family went to France. On our return, three further

letters from Sarah were waiting for me. The first contained a copy of the press clipping mentioned by Albert.

Semaphore, August 13th

Now Jenn,

I have seen Albert again. The *unfailing* Mister Prideauz! Last Thursday he walked from his caravan to the University building where I was about to give my class. His express purpose was to present to me, in person, the envelope of documents he had been given by Minkus in the dark of that schooner's fo'c's'le sixty-one years ago.

I found him in the Arts Building foyer when I arrived. He was reading a notice board in the quizzical manner of a foreigner trying to make sense of a bus timetable. On seeing me he removed a book from a plastic bag.

'*Your* relative,' he said. 'These bits of paper are more yours than mine.' His book was a compendium of TV personalities, and he took from between its pages the envelope of fragile documents and gave it to me.

I protested that I should merely borrow and perhaps copy them.

'*Your* relative,' he repeated as he put his TV personalities back in the plastic bag.

'But they're your memories.'

'People think they want to hang onto things. But memories shrivel up like anything else.'

'That's bleak,' I said.

Albert shrugged. The envelope was blank but for various random striations where, anciently I suppose, the light had faded different parts of it to different degrees. I unfolded it and saw the pages of the press clipping which, as Albert had described, were ragged on one edge where they had been ripped from the original journal.

Not quite knowing how to thank him properly, I asked, 'Will you not reconsider joining us for our class?'

He would not. He had given me his reasons already. Yet he hesitated, and I wondered if the fellowship of my elderly folk tempted him at all. It would not have done to ask him. We stood watching each other in the airy foyer, hearing the klung-klung of rubber shoes coming down the iron stairwells, and the hubbub from a nearby canteen. I looked at the papers in my hand and said, 'You didn't say what became of Minkus after he left *Bicheno*.'

'He never found another vessel to suit him,' said Albert. 'He wouldn't look for a berth in any ship that wasn't sail. In the bank that time he told me he worked on the docks, Port Adelaide for some years, then in Geelong and Melbourne. He got involved in the Union. When he told me that, I said it didn't surprise me.'

'Why did you tell him that?' I asked.

Albert paused before he answered. 'I said on your tape how Minkus watched over our welfare. Some people have an instinct for it. They visit folk who are crook, get money for families going through a bad patch. You find fellows in the unions who do all that. Natural charity, I suppose, and Minkus had it.'

'The politics?'

'Ignored them, my guess. And the graft. Minkus would have made a good husband and father, but he left his run for that too late. Like your relative.'

'When did he pass on?' I asked.

Albert didn't know that. 'People come into your life and go out of it. You can't take a hold of them all, can you?'

I was suddenly moved to ask him this question. 'Is that what you would like to do? Take hold of them all?'

He regarded me and shrugged. 'I'm past caring, I reckon.'

'But would you once have liked to do that, as though they were some . . . some Splendid Company?'

I could see he did not trust this direction in my questions and would not volunteer an answer, so I prompted him. 'I would like that.'

'I told you how I would spend eternity. It would be the same as what you're asking,' he confided eventually, and I tried to indicate that I was grateful for the confidence.

'You would all do the hornpipe,' I suggested. He appraised me, but would not reply. 'It is the thing in which everything gets reconciled. That dance of your skipper's, I mean. Isn't it? Not just joy and sorrow, but the whole compass of what a person can feel in this life.'

'It was a dance. If the skipper could have said those things he wouldn't have danced, would he?'

'No. Of course.' I had seen my class file into the seminar room. 'I have to go, I'm afraid,' I said. 'I'll come and see you at the caravan if I may.'

Again, I had this impulse to regard Albert as a dear, but he shrugged once more, as if to say that he didn't care one way or the other whether I called on him or not. And with that I watched him make off down the corridor, presumably to walk all the way back to his camp site. His knees, I noted, have that slight crookedness of the old, though he manages without a stick.

I slipped the big envelope into my folder, gave my two-hour class, then came home. I was, naturally, excited, but disciplined myself (as you'll recall from college) by disposing of several humdrum chores and then taking a long walk on the Semaphore sands. 'Sarah going into focus mode', as you used to call it. Only then, quite late last night, did I carefully unfold the envelope on my table, place the pages under my lamp and read them through.

They seem to be from a North American shipping monthly. The article concerns various dangers of the Chilean coast and is dated April 1909. In a long section subtitled 'Il Norte', the sudden winter storms of this region are described, and the tempest of June 1900 at Valparaíso in particular. I have photocopied for you only the parts that are relevant, and I'll paste them in at this point for you to read.

> But by far the most tragical drama of those few hours concerned the loss of the English full-rigged ship, *Kilbride*, 1637 tons, under the command of Captain Yuell, which had anchored in the bay late in the afternoon of May 31st, laden with Vancouver Island timber.
>
> By sunset of May 31st, the wind was blowing fiercely from the north, and the harbour master signalled that the loading barges should return to dock. By midnight, it was gusting to hurricane strength. With two anchors ahead and two astern, seventy-five fathom of cable on each, *Kilbride* held on well at her moorings until shortly after 3 a.m. when the starboard cable gave way at the clench

on the keelson. After the most strenuous effort, the crew, led by the first mate, William Fordyce, managed to get a spring onto the cable and make it fast around the foremast. But no sooner had they done this, than the ship began to drag her anchors, and it was then Captain Yuell realised that nothing more could be done to save his command. Fearing the worst, he went below and directed his wife and child to prepare themselves in case they might need to leave the ship.

In a very short time, the vessel was driven broadside against the town's waterfront, where she continued to be battered by the mountainous seas and the powerful backwash produced by the steep shelving of the beach. That part of the timber cargo which had been carried on the deck now worked itself loose, and the battering of the logs against the foremast and mainmast soon took these spars and all their hamper over the side. The lifeboats and their skids had also been swept away, as had the charthouse. The ship lay with a slant towards the land, being rolled nearly upright with each surge of the backwash, then falling back again. In addition, she was bumping on the rocks, with the result that the members of the crew, who had by now taken refuge in the mizzen rigging, were strained to their utmost simply to hang on against the ship's jarring efforts to dislodge them from their precarious hold.

The Captain had assisted his wife into the mizzen shrouds and entrusted his small child to the second mate, a Charles Tilber. Neither Captain Yuell nor Tilber were able to ascend far into the rigging on account of the men already seeking shelter on the ratlines above them. Captain Yuell used his body to shield his wife from the force of the breaking seas, and survivors of the disaster record how Mrs Yuell continued to call out encouragements to the sailors through the dark hours before dawn, until she was obliged to desist through sheer exhaustion.

As they waited for daylight, the plight of the *Kilbride*'s crew was desperate indeed. Their cries for help were answered by cries from the shore, but seventy yards of murderous white water divided them from their would-be rescuers. At the high tide, the savagery of the seas had already carried boulders, heavy iron pipes and timber across the railway lines to batter the warehouses and habitations on the Avenida Errazuriz. Several great hydraulic cranes had been torn from their mountings, while the Calle Blanco and the Bellavista Plaza had been blocked by the debris of smashed boats and floating tins of paraffin.

Believing that the mizzen mast would soon follow main and foremast over the side, the first mate, Fordyce, made a decision to seek shelter in the wheelhouse. This was a fatal error, since, no sooner had he reached the deck, than a sea came up over the counter and took him off, never to be seen again. An apprentice, the sailmaker, and two seamen perished in a similar manner.

So, throughout the dark hours, the survivors clung to the mizzen shrouds. At the first signs of daybreak, it was noticed that the lumber cargo had been forced from the holds by the sea and, for a short interval at least, was forming a precarious raft between the stricken ship and the shore. Two apprentices, seizing their opportunity, managed to scramble by this means across the confusion and onto the embankment. They were followed by the second mate, who had tied the little girl to his back. Tilber was observed to lose his footing, slip from a plank into the smother and vanish from sight for a period. The watchers presumed him lost, but then, bleeding profusely, he was seen to have gained the shore, where he was immediately assisted by several onlookers who plunged into the surf. The little girl, still secured to his back, unfortunately had been struck by a rock or baulk of timber, and was no more. Both were taken to the stationmaster's house, where the child was laid down and the second mate's injuries were attended to. Tilber refused to leave the child's side until later in the morning, when the father was brought by stretcher into the presence of his daughter.

Meanwhile, several attempts had been made to get a line to the vessel using the rocket apparatus. The third attempt was successful, though it was after 7 a.m. before the tackle had been secured to the mast and the volunteers ashore had been organised to hold the guiding lines. These needed to be manipulated with great attention as the ship was still rolling violently when each sea struck her broadside. An Australian apprentice, George Milliken, who was later interviewed, gave the following version of the morning's events.

'That there rocket got the line laid across the mizzen top at last and we was able to make it fast. But them instructions that were sent across for rigging the actual cradle were useless on account of them being in Spanish. No fellows there could make head or tail of it, but with a bit of know-how we got the thing rigged anyway. The first man we sent over was our negro cook, Joshua. You could see how he took a fearful ducking and a bashing as the ship rolled shoreward and the line went slack too sudden for the blokes on the lines ashore to take up. Then he was almost flung out of the cradle, like as if from a catapult, when the ship jerked upright in the backwash. But the line held, and we saw how he was got ashore with no more (as we later learned) than some bruises. Then it was decided we should risk the Captain's wife, Mrs Yuell, on the second run. She had been a real pillar of good cheer through the dark hours with all her calling out and hymn-singing, but she was now done in. Myself and another seaman were able to secure her in the cradle, and the shore people commenced to haul away.

'But Mrs Yuell was unlucky, because over the ship at that moment broke such a tremendous sea you had to have been there to have believed it. You'd swear it was high as the mizzen top. As a consequence of this wave, and the backwash, the roll of the ship got so violent that them shore people on the guy ropes again were not quick enough to give it some slack. This time the rope parted near the tackle on the mast, so that Mrs Yuell went down into that frightful mix of timber and white water. We could hear the groan of the crowd when this happened, and we saw a man with a line round his middle plunge into the surf in the effort to save her. But it was a while before we saw them dragging out the cradle from the white water, with Mrs Yuell still secured in it, and we feared the worst, which proved to be true. They took her to the place where her little daughter was. How much of this the Captain would have seen was hard to say. He looked done in himself, his head hanging back limp. Being higher up in the shrouds, I could see a bit more in the intervals between each sea breaking.

'There was quite a long time before a further rocket was fired. With this first shot, the line fell across the mast, and we were able to get into the top and get the hawser across and secure it. For a time, the people on shore couldn't produce the cradle which had gone across with Mrs Yuell, so two of the fellows made the journey to safety hand over hand. The first was plucked from the sea just as his strength gave out. The second got his share of dunking and bashing, but we saw that he succeeded in getting ashore also. Then the cradle was sent across, and we got everyone, barring the

Captain and myself, ashore. Captain Yuell had his limbs twisted through the ratlines, but, as I say, his head lolled, and I wasn't sure whether he was dead. I was fairly done in myself, and could not get the skipper into the cradle. It was then that two Chilean fellows from the shore came across, and we three managed to get a bowline under the Captain's armpits and fetched him onto the land like that. I was next, and got some knocks on the way, then, one after one, them two Chileans. When they took Captain Yuell to the stationmaster's house, where they had put his daughter and Mrs Yuell, I went there too so that the cuts on my hands could be treated. Mister Tilber, the second mate, was there in a room near the dead girl, but I could not get him to speak to me. They had put a picture of the Saviour on one wall, and had covered the two bodies with a couple of oilskin coats. I did not like to look at them. I was told it took several hours before Captain Yuell came to, but I had gone with the consul by then. I was glad I did not have to witness Captain Yuell's sorrow when he came round in that room. I know that Mister Tilber stayed there the whole time. I think he took the little girl's death very hard, and I felt sorry for him because they had been good mates, him and her.'

This is all I have copied for you, Jenn. The journalist goes on to quote the views of other crew members who came off the wreck: that my great-uncle 'was a quiet man, and had been well-liked'. There follows some account of the loss of two other ships during the same storms, an American steamship and a Chilean barque. The article ends by recording that 'the wife and daughter of the English captain were buried in the Protestant part of Valparaíso's cemetery. Captain Yuell and the surviving members of the crew spent some time in the care of the English consul, before taking a passage home on the steamship *Valdivia,* bound for Dieppe.'

Eighty-odd years have foxed and stained these pages. Nonetheless, they describe (as though exclusively for my benefit) the event that haunted my lovable, melancholy forebear. Well, the survival of these pages has not been wasted. They have reached a forceful imagination! Clear in my mind's eye my Great-Uncle Charles sits in this railway house. He is small under the high ceilings of the room and his face is turned away from me because, even with Albert's description of it, I cannot delineate his features exactly. His injuries (I presume to the head, given all that blood) have been bandaged. Someone will have lit a fire in the grate, but his clothes are still sodden. Is he shivering from the cold, or from a delayed reaction to his ordeal in that tumult of sea and loose timber? Mrs Yuell and her child, we're told, have been laid side by side. Are they on the floor, or have that unknown Chilean stationmaster and his wife, awed by the tragedy, directed that the two *Inglesas* should have been placed on their own large bed? I favour the second image. We know there are oilskin coats spread over them both, and that a picture of Christ looks down upon them. No doubt the wind still howls outside, and, though probably not as strong as it had been, it is even now blowing odd pieces of the lighter wreckage across the railway lines and into the streets of Valparaíso.

And my great-uncle? If I can judge from the character Albert paints of him, he has placed himself at a respectful distance from the bodies of the woman and child, but his vigil is evidently profound. For he does not respond when the apprentice, Milliken, speaks to him. Something dogged, sorrowful, no doubt sentimental, is keeping him there beside the little girl who had been entrusted to his care. He will wait until the father is brought in, whether that man be alive or dead, and he will answer to his skipper for the failure of that trust. He is a Tilber.

Yet what, Jenn, do I really know about his feelings? Dogged, sorrowful, sentimental, these emotions are going to be durable enough to prompt him, some twenty-eight years on from this moment, to shuffle about on a dance floor in an odd expression of sorrow-in-joy, played to by a beanpole fiddler who, probably without understanding why, colludes in this ritual. It is his *separateness* that baffles and intrigues me.

And the pair will be watched by a fourteen-year-old boy who, like a relay runner, will carry the image of the dancing mariner for more than sixty years until he is able to drop it into my imagination. I find the fortuity of this so moving, I don't know whether to laugh or cry.

Well! You can see what it is I need to divine now in order to make sense of things. I need to reconstruct whatever friendship it was that grew up between the second mate and Maie Alice Yuell on that voyage which ended in Valparaíso Bay on June 1st, 1900.

But there is one more item which these brown-stained pages disclose, and which I have been saving for you until last. In the margin of the last page is a pencilled message. It is a little faded but not difficult to decipher, and it reads as follows:

> You see, Albicore, I know more about this than I let on this morning, because this here George Milliken is me, Minkus. What this reporter bloke writes I saw [underlined] and I was the age then that you are now. Twenty-eight years I've knocked about with Mister Tilber and now all those years are shot. You think you've a right to feel a bit sore. M.

I imagine the message was scribbled by Minkus onto the page on that last night aboard *Bicheno* in 1928. This led me to have a closer look at the second of the two documents Albert had given me. Before reading the article I had glanced at it cursorily. I noted the word 'Valparaíso' in the box marked Place of Discharge, but had neglected to pay attention to the name of the seaman being discharged because, in my eagerness to acquaint myself with the contents of the journalist's narrative, I had assumed the certificate was the discharge paper of my great-uncle. Why else would Albert give it to me? However, it was not that of second mate Tilber, but the apprentice, George Milliken.

Albert was inviting me to make the same inference as, no doubt, he had been compelled to make himself after Minkus gave him the documents in the small hours of that Wednesday morning in 1928: namely, that they went together. The association between Minkus and Mister Tilber had endured for a quarter of a century. They had, after the wreck, become inseparable sailors-of-fortune and ended up on a schooner that traded around the South Australian gulfs, the one as its skipper, the other as his steadfast deckhand on a few pounds per month.

Or should I say 'follower', because that is the word that suggests itself. I checked this by going back to our Mortlock Library records and confirming that the name Milliken, G, Deckhand is linked with the name Tilber, CH, Schoonermaster from at least 1910. Do you see? That discharge certificate is a testimony of rather extraordinary human loyalty. It is the point in the life of one Milliken G, Apprentice, where he made a decision to follow — how should I say? — his sympathies rather than his best interests. Clearly Albert understood this.

Now, Jenn! Can you see the power of feeling being restrained in that cramped fo'c's'le after they had got in from Port Lincoln? Minkus goes and burrows in his sea bag, then gives away these two documents to a fourteen-year-old boy. 'You can keep this story,' says the voice in the dark. 'I've had enough of it.' For one assumes it was the end of an association. My great-uncle had reached the age where he could retire. The seaman Minkus still had a crust to earn.

And what, you ask, is the effect of all this on me?

Possession of a story might be like the knowledge of a crime: there is a 'time before' when you can recall being free. You will know the way this story of Charles Tilber, Minkus, Albert, moves me because you can see how imaginable I find it. As I say, I cannot think of that friendship between the first two named without my eyes prickling. What a queer sensation! Why should the discovery of a straightforward loyalty of one human being for another cause this emotion? Remember, George Milliken was an apprentice in June 1900. His future could have been to rise in his profession until, perhaps in his late twenties, he might have gone for his Master's examination at the Board of Trade and skippered his own ship. This prospect, I assume, he decided to give up. Why? His was a generous temperament, and something had touched him in the sight of a short whiskery fellow keeping watch beside the corpse of a little girl to whom he was quite unrelated.

I should consider, I suppose, whether it might have been a homosexual attraction. It is the interests of my own time that apply that pressure on the matter. My instinct is to believe that it was not sexual at all, but sentimental in a way that epoch allowed and ours doesn't. I think an impressionable George Milliken had bumped into the peculiar charisma and purity of my great-uncle, Charlie Tilber. Of course I'm guessing, but I have Albert's own testimony that roughly the same thing happened to him. With Minkus it must have been kindled while the *Kilbride*'s survivors stayed in the home of the British consul in Valparaíso, or on the steamship that took them to Dieppe.

So, where have I reached in my ambition to live on the inside of another person's time? Four months ago I had a relative who was little more than a name on my dad's genealogical chart. There is also his 1875 letter from China, but now I can almost sense his presence in this small flat of mine. A photograph of Great-Uncle Tilber would be useful, but might be too much to hope for. Besides, I do know a good deal about his character, occupation, and even some details of his appearance. I have, so to speak, seen him at a dance. And yet, sometimes I lie awake before the dawn comes over this city's eastern hills, forgetful of my hours in the library or my sitting opposite Albert with the microphone, and I can believe I have simply conjured this intimacy out of nothing.

But there are great gaps in his story and I want to fill them. That means more archives, maybe more from Albert. Ideally I would like more money so that I could go to the places of my story — Whampoa Reach, Seattle, Valparaíso — to walk along wharves and streets where my great-uncle might have walked, Jenn, and track down in the written record each of those tall sailing ships he served on, read whatever might be known about them and study the pictorial evidence that depicts them.

Bother the money. I will! I will! Wherever I can, in museums and the like, I will handle the machinery and the materials with which he might have been familiar — pumps and their handles, belaying pins, capstan bars, rope, heavyweather and lightweather canvas, tea chests and wheat bags. With the attentive eye of a portrait artist I shall renew my studies of old photos for the characterising physiologies of his century, for the former landscapes of that time now hidden behind our own skylines. For is it not possible to concentrate all of history within the story of a single person? And you are not to tell me I am either monomaniacal or haunted, dearest Jenn.

I'll write when I have decided upon how to proceed. I feel so free. If I won ten thousand dollars in a raffle I would feel freer still. I could claim from Kier half the value of our weatherboard home — and would get it undoubtedly — but will not, because I am quite undeserving of it.

This screed has been all Sarah and no Jennifer. How *do* you manage with your busy family round, the duties that accompany being wife of a headmaster, mother of four, to say nothing of your patience with the immoderate enthusiasms of your grateful, oldest friend? S.

Her next letter was jubilant.

Semaphore, August 23rd

Oh Jenn,

I have a face! I have a physique! I have a human presence, for I have tracked down in the museum's collection here a photograph of Charles Tilber! Hurrah for all collectors, official and otherwise! Particularly those with sharp noses and lank hair! And hurrah for Sarah Tilber's luck! If only Dad could have lived to see the face of his uncle. To think that I know more than my father about his own father's brother.

Here's what happened. I paid another visit to the maritime museum in Port Adelaide. From my flat it is a short walk down Semaphore Road and across a bridge in the blast of heavy traffic. Once at the museum, I asked to see the photographs in their collection. Was I looking for any ship in particular, asked the slender, pale curator, he of lank hair, sharp nose, and a whimsical tilt to his eyes and mouth. 'Ah! *Bicheno*.' He recognised it immediately. 'One of the schooners. Captain Tilbrough —'

'Charles Harling Tilber,' I corrected. 'Born 1859.'

We busied ourselves and quite quickly we found the photo of SV *Bicheno* that I saw in Albert's caravan. But Lank-hair, who, like me, cannot resist a research project, was not satisfied, so we continued thumbing through the folders of photographic material. As we did so, he chatted about the personalities of the different moustachioed and bowler-hatted gentlemen who looked out from the pictures.

'They look so indispensable, don't they?' At length Lank-hair put his hands on the picture he recalled. 'I was sure it was Tilbrough.' He pointed to where the photographer had scribbled some names across the bottom of the picture: 'C Tilbrough, Master, *Bicheno*.' Indisputable!

For a small fee, Lank-hair made two reproductions of the photo for me, one of which, Jenn, I enclose for you. Captain C Tilbrough/Tilber, schoonermaster, is the fellow standing middle row, second from the left, with the jacket buttoned to the throat and the squashed bowler on his head. The others are various ketchmen, schoonermen, shipping clerks and lady visitors. The pic is taken on an August Sunday in 1911 at the McLaren Wharf, Port Adelaide. You'll see how C Tilber conforms with Albert's picture of my great-uncle: shortness of stature, thickset torso, thick beard and moustache obscuring so large a part of his face, yet somehow the air of one who gives directions.

Lank-hair handed me the two copies, then contemplated the picture for some moments. I had told him that Captain Tilber was my great-uncle.

'Will you now correct the name?' I asked.

Instead of saying yes, he would, he looked at Great-Uncle standing there amid that group of people, and said something I thought was rather perceptive.

'Why does this picture tell us this man was unassuming and perhaps rather solitary?' I watched his eyes, which were crinkled up in scrutiny of the small figure in the picture.

'Well...' He straightened, and took another photo from a folder. 'Here's a studio portrait of one Captain Rory Miller, who owned the ketch, *Erith*. We know a good deal about Captain Miller, but then the way he appears to outstare the camera's eye doesn't put in doubt that we would, does it? Your relative, on the other hand. Look at the way his details have already started to wander off. A careless photographer adds a "rough" to his surname and immediately he's drifting off towards an identity not his at all. Does he look concerned by that? I think not.'

'I agree,' I said.

'Now, Captain Rory is being photographed because he wants to be remembered. Your ancestor looks as if he has wandered into this group portrait by mistake and is keeping still for the moment of the picture in order to be obliging, nothing more.'

'Perhaps he never saw the picture.'

'Or if he did see it, with the "Tilbrough" appended underneath, perhaps he was amused by just how precarious his identity was.'

There was a phone ringing and my helpful friend had to go and answer it. 'Your mind works in the same way mine does,' I managed to slip in, and thanked him for his trouble.

I have had the picture magnified because I wanted to scrutinise the eyes. The resulting focal quality is bad, but good enough to show the eyes' expression of hopeful goodwill, of *expectancy*. 'So this is the world!' they seem to say with such an untroubled composure.

The original group photo I prop on my desk; the enlargement I hang on my wall so that I may get used to Charlie Tilber's visual presence. Does he resemble Dad at all? It would be wishful of me to think so, though Dad in his armchair could look up from a newspaper with that same expression of good-natured expectancy sometimes.

Now that I possess an actual face for my mind's eye, can I coax Great-Uncle Charles into talking to me, into re-establishing contact with his lost family, as it were? I don't mean 'talk' in any silly psychic sense. I mean *communicate* with me at whatever that plausible level is where we recover the fine detail of a past life. Study the enclosed photo and tell me. S.

And a few days later a fourth communication arrived.

Semaphore, 2 a.m. August 27th
    Dear Jenn,
    These past days I seem to have become an insomniac — more than usual, that is. At present there's a high sea wind funnelling through the apartments. I've just come

back from walking out to the end of the jetty where I listened to the shallow sea coursing and shuffling over itself. After some time I found I had been joined by a youngish-seeming fellow out there. He was dressed in nothing but jeans and a white T-shirt which gave him a spectral appearance as he leaned against the rail with the white caps of the small waves behind him. He reminded me of that Barney odd bod who lived in the attic room at my Lincoln digs which he plastered with various New Age posters — you met him once, I think.

To this fellow tonight I wished a good evening, to which he made no reply. Then I offered another remark, perfectly commonplace, and I heard him swear at me. *Really* swear.

'I'm sorry, I didn't catch what you said,' I told him. Again came a string of quite extraordinary curses, after which he turned and walked unsteadily back down the length of the jetty. But in the instant he had spoken his oaths, I saw his face and he wasn't young at all. It was a little wizened face, shrunk around its eyes and nose like a rat's.

Of course I was immediately put in mind of the curses of CHT that Albert heard at the nursing home. Perhaps this fellow on the jetty was drunk. Nonetheless, I wish he had stayed since I would have quite liked to strike up a conversation with a total stranger at that point. His rudeness disappointed me and I searched my mind to think what I could have done to have provoked it. Why does enmity come out of the blue like that?

Thus, instead of making me sleepy with sea air, my walk made me preoccupied and dismal. If I sit up in bed and unburden myself in a letter to you, will I succeed in tiring myself out a little?

I'm looking at the enlarged photo on my table. I ask, 'Why will you not disclose yourself to me, Mister Tilber? Or should I call you Mister Tilbrough? After all, that lady beside you in the picture can feel the worsted texture of your coat as it brushes her wrist, can smell the tobacco impregnating your clothes. Does it smell the same as the aroma that escapes from the pages of some of the secondhand books I buy, fragile vestige of the breath of some reader back in the fifties or twenties?

'And the cravatted man behind you in the photo. Might he be on the point of making a remark to which you, Great-Uncle, will respond in a manner perhaps half anticipated, integral to *just there, just then*? Will the deckhand on your right smirk knowingly? Why must I suffer from this moment an absolute exclusion?'

Oh, this is self-indulgence! I interrogate this face beside me and ask, 'Have I not, Mister Tilber/Tilbrough, concentrated my sympathies sufficiently? Must I believe I cannot come at the quick of your existence because our lives did not conveniently overlap in time and place?' And as I do this I recognise Great-Uncle's interest is so elsewhere. Together with those seamen, shippers and visiting ladies in the picture, he stares past me.

Of course I see the danger of straying into some spiritualistic murk. (Well, maybe I don't entirely appreciate that danger.) But I ask him, not to *be* alive, rather to be *as if* alive. And I thought I had learned from Albert enough detail about CHT to have some kind of a relationship form. Obviously I am expected to know very much more. I feel at an impasse. Do I sound petulant?

There *is* a problem I have to consider and it takes me a little into the spiritualistic murk, I fear. When I confided to Lank-hair that I wished to recover a sense of my forebear's actual presence, he asked, reasonably, 'What age will he be?' It makes me think. What is the age that the 'proper soul' of a person decides for itself? How will CHT appear should I succeed in finding his presence at the end of this odd tunnel I am in?

Practicalities! I know the insomnia is my own fault. I must drink less tea, and take meals at regular intervals instead of grazing on cheese and crackers at all hours. Kieran was good for me when it came to routines, Jenn, as you were at college. Yours, S.

September

On the evening that we returned from our holiday in France, I recall sitting beside Mike in our room. The bedside light was still on, and Sarah's letters lay, open and just read, in my lap.

And then I said to him out of the blue, 'It's the sneakiness of change that I hate. It makes me feel vaguely endangered.' He glanced up from his book and asked me what I meant. I indicated all Sarah's pages. 'I don't quite know how to cope with the ... the pressure in these. What if a day comes when Sal is strange to me? Against the endurance of our friendship I have always measured the way most other things don't endure.'

Mike didn't answer, so I spoke the image that was in my head. 'A person passes a glass each day and casually looks into it. Then one day, unaccountably, there is a fracture right across it. That's how change presents itself.'

'You and Sal are inseparable.' Mike was watching me rather closely.

'I *want* to give these the attention she expects,' I said, picking up the bundle and dropping it again. 'But I begin to fear I will fall into a habit of faking my interest.'

'Sal is your oldest friend.' Mike turned out the lights. For some time I did not sleep.

Some days later, I wrote the following letter to Sarah. All my correspondence with her was returned by Kier to Hazel.

St Walstan's School 19/9/89

My dear Sal,

If I can give you assurance on one thing it is that you *do* make yourself so very present in your letters to us here. Across those twelve thousand terrestrial miles I quite believe I hear the sound of your footsteps on the boards of your long Semaphore jetty with your 'shuffling' sea and those distant gantries as a background.

You sound, not lonesome exactly (you've never been that), but so very *solo*.

This is to tell you that you are present in our thoughts. Last night, after the junior boys' lights out and when the school was at last quiet, I sat for an hour with your three recent letters and the grainy photocopy of Mister Tilber.

The aspect of your great-uncle was quite striking. So tough, so watchful, so benign. Yes, take away some of that facial hair and there *is* a small resemblance to your father. In unguarded moments, Ben Tilber sometimes had that *So this is the world!* expression too. Mike came past and, glancing at it, said, 'Sal is under the spell of a vanished mode of authority.'

This evening I sit with the last of our autumnal daylight outside, trying to decide how best to help you with your 'impasse'. I find two voices in my head, and they do not altogether agree.

'What can Sal possibly hope to achieve?' says Voice One (not unlike Mike's).

'To identify with this man's life,' argues Voice Two (not unlike yours). 'To try the limits of what a historical imagination might encompass in a given case.'

'She'll get nothing but heartache,' pronounces Voice One. (Mike is sometimes overfond of pronouncements.)

'Why should it?' Voice Two objects.

'Because,' Voice One explains, 'to try this is not history. It is hallucination, seance, a kind of ancestor worship. She wants this person as though present in her life . . .'

'As *though*,' Voice Two interjects.

To this, Voice One replies, rather unfairly perhaps, that a psychologist would say your involvement with your great-uncle was a case of transferred grieving for the loss of your father and the estrangement from your husband during the past two years. 'It is her father's shade she is looking for in Hades, not her great-uncle's,' Voice One trumps.

'It is what Sal says it is,' rejoins Voice Two sharply, and reminds Voice One of the resilience and cheerfulness of your temperament, the finesse of your historical imagination. 'You must allow her the thing itself,' insists Voice Two.

In this fashion, Sal, I wrangle on this page as the blue of the twilight grows more inky in the rectangle of the study window. I should turn on the standard lamp, except that the crepuscular light suits my present mood.

There! You see how you divide me? It is because I have known you so long that I am confident I have apprehended the nature of the thing which animates you, even if I cannot fully understand it and explain it to myself or Mike, who will sometimes behave like an Archbishop (whether he be outside or inside my head!). I know my rational dismissals of your Retrieval Project are not *entirely* fair, though I cannot refuse them entirely either. You must bear with me, for as I try to think myself into your project, I am still hearing those curt (Mike-inspired) cautions from quite close at hand.

Firstly, of course I remember from our days in college what a night owl you were, but *do* stop prowling the night and do start eating real meals. It is not like you to behave as an anxious person.

Secondly, you require me to 'enter the plot' as it were, by asking if I think Charles Tilber will 'talk' to you now that you can look into his face.

My instinct tells me this. Charles Tilber appears to have been a reticent man. It was your good self who, in talking about your dad, put into mind the notion that people who are of the good-natured, ordinary type leave curiously little imprint on the memory of those who survive them. So I believe that Charlie Tilber will not 'talk' to you, or otherwise make his presence more suggestible, by any long-staring at his picture or 'direct' addresses of this kind.

He will be prompted to 'talk' when, in your imagination, you place him, as it were, in the presence of someone from his life who was more egotistical than he was himself.

Indeed, you have already mapped out the path of research you must follow. I think it is the mysterious Maie Alice Yuell who will allow you to know at least something of the quick of second mate Charles Tilber's spirit, is it not? How you will investigate her short life … Well, if it is possible, I am sure your resourcefulness will be equal to it.

There! I have allowed myself to offer advice in what Mike would call the manner of the seance rather than the discipline of history. I do worry about the degree to which you seem engrossed by this. Should we not be just a little wary of the past? The warning I gave on this score in my last letter to you was meant more lightly than your postcard shows you took it, but I do believe there's some truth behind it too.

What Mike and I both agree on is that down there in your new Adelaide home you need companionship, someone to go to a film with, a family that invites you to dinner, or on a picnic. I wish you were here with us and we could offer our friendship to you in the everyday. For lively company, perhaps, we'd give you the Second Formers to look after! A cocky bunch. Seriously though, if you feel the separation from Kieran is permanent, perhaps you should leave Australia altogether and return to old haunts and old friends. Our love to you, Jenny.

When I had finished composing this letter I read it over and observed those parts of it where I had entered her project with my cleverest sympathy. The effect then, and re-reading it after it was eventually returned to me, was to make me feel like a hypocrite. Nonetheless I sent it. Sarah's postcard reply to my letter was telegrammatically swift.

Semaphore 23/9/89

Dear Wise Owl!

About the reticence of Great-Uncle, your instinct is quite right. Voice One is a rational Archbishop. I'll give some thought to that question 'Why?' and tell you the results in my next. In the meantime you must not bisect yourself for my sake.

I write this on the beach with a fierce wind blowing sand grains in my face. There's the inevitable windsurfer getting a fearful bounce-and-bucketing out there in the waves.

No real interest in cultivating new friends. I'm not a cultivator. Love, S.

Then followed her more considered reply.

Semaphore, September 25th
    Dear Jenn,
    Yes! For the concerns you voice in your letter you *do* deserve an ampler response than I was able to squeeze onto last week's postcard.
    So, your voices warn me against what you call the heartache of dwelling on past things and lost attitudes. 'Heartache' was the word Albert used about his life. Well, let me try and give expression to my state of mind at present.
    To do so I must start at a tangent.
    I realised the other day that, for all the things you and I had in common as children and teenagers, our taste in reading matter differed widely. I refer to the time we used to read freely, before school and college pushed us towards 'canonical' books. Oddly, it was you, wasn't it, who used to be the diehard historical romancer? Henry Treece, Rosemary Sutcliff, Roger Lancelyn Green, Alfred Duggan, with all their bearded Norse and Celt heroes, the heroines

with braided hair and (if one trusts the illustrations) such big, believing eyes. And even though you have ended by marrying your Archbishop, who is a bearded Celt, it is you, I think, who have turned out to be the more sure-footed of us when it comes to dealing with the present. Coping with schoolboys must do that, which is why I was not a good classroom teacher.

By contrast with your reading, you'll remember, the authors I devoured were the same as those my dad used to like — John Buchan, Rafael Sabatini, Maurice Walsh — 1930s' adventure stories where the heroine was there for the romance element, but where the *real* friendships, the rich life of experience and fortune, was *for* the men and *between* the men. In that world we girls were not permitted friendships with one another.

Then, in the aftermath of university, I sat down with all those newly discovered women authors from the feminist press who turned the old conventions topsy-turvy and told us about the lives of young, sensitive things growing into their awareness of what it was like to be a sexual being, and having their inevitably grim encounters with unsavoury chaps. Abstractly, I accepted the claim on justice that was being made in such books, but this kind of heroine left me irritated and unhappy. Were my own encounters with chaps so grim?

Well, you'll remember that awful character from the boarding school called Jeremy Smy and *his* plans for both of us. But more often — and I would include Kier in this category — the chaps were simply less than I might have hoped, less disclosing, less consequential. Furthermore, my disconsolate mood left me immensely curious about the way men behaved when they lived in a context that was unaffected by us women. Is it any wonder the genders are more at ease with their own company than with their opposites, given a million or so years of dividing in order to do the hunting and the gathering?

All this theorising makes me feel overcast! But if you re-read my various consignments to you, it will explain why the story Albert had to tell stirred me up so. It is not just that I am retrospectively envious of those five schoonermen on their craft with its tannin-brown sails, and all those tacitly understood things between them to do with work, equipment and conversational exchange. I feel gratitude for its strangeness from my own experience.

Sarah Tomboy, you will remind me.

As far as my being enchanted by 'a vanished mode of authority' and affected by 'transferred grief', the first is true, the second is untrue. With authority, I believe history is at its keenest when we study what people have obeyed, and the manner in which they have obeyed it. *That* is fascinating psychological stuff. Furthermore, I am *intelligently* conscious of my enchantment with the elusive, mutable nature of authority.

As for transferred grief, pooh! I miss Dad and know why. I do not miss Kier, and (heartlessly I regret to say) am only mildly concerned about my detachment in this.

With regard to my Retrieval Project, let your Archbishop smile, but I do feel mutinous about *tempus fugit*. Why should an ordinary person's life not be retrieved from the oblivion history tries to draw over it? 'They all go into the dark.' No! Why should they?

As you now see, I have uncovered something of the mystery of who exactly my Great-Uncle Tilber was, and, as a result, I have come upon a further mystery. Hades is a corridor, and it leads me like a person walking into one of those bewildering fractals that science programmes are fond of showing, where one pattern is forever being unzippered by a further, then a further pattern. Does that explain anything, or allow me an excuse with Voice One? Love, S.

'She really has become very reliant on you,' Mike observed when I showed him this letter. 'You are the witness to her life. Whatever your feelings, you will need to sustain Sal's morale.' He paused, then added, 'That's the charitable response.'

'But that makes her a person on the outside of me,' I replied. 'Being charitable will make me detached.'

October

So I wrote to Sarah something charitable, and friendly and muddled, about how she should not obscure the essence of what she was doing — objective historical research — by imposing too-powerful metaphors upon it like 'Hades' and 'corridors of fractals'. The letter that came back was the one I cited in the opening pages of this story where she told me, 'No! I think in your last to me you are missing my point. It is this...' I allowed that one to remain unanswered. Eight days later, there arrived the following account of two adventures in her life that she required me to witness.

Semaphore, October 12th
> Dear Jenn,
> This will be a long one, for I have much to tell.
> I have two more classes to go for the semester, then I shall give them up. The University offered to employ me again next year, but increasingly I have stood before my very loyal elderly folk mouthing things about their writings I did not warmly believe. The fact is I have lost the impulse to be useful, in a social sense, anyhow. A great

deal of The Present — my present at least — makes me feel like a puppet being put through motions. Am I, as your Voice One (or should I say, Mike) obviously believes, going too deeply into my own interests? Don't answer that.

And, after trying to act on your advice, I'm afraid I have also taken up my night-time meanders once more because the night allows me to feel less puppet-like somehow. No, this is not reckless. I find the dark is *not* crawling with sinister types. Somewhere out there bad things may happen, but mostly we prowling insomniacs are as far apart as the stars.

Here are two indications of how safe my life is.

A week ago I walked out of my flat quite early in the evening, and spent a couple of hours among the amusement booths along the Esplanade at the ocean end of my street. I wandered, or sat, savouring the intermixing aromas of doughnuts and hamburgers that pervaded everywhere, watching all the young fellows and their girlfriends being swept this way and that by the whirligig contraptions of the fairground as the plump ticket sellers (all with bad skin) counted their takings and looked bored.

You see, I really can stay among *some* things of the present if I have a mind.

I was strolling past a shooting gallery where there were three fellows in a group. They were tanned, with short combed hair and cleanish chequered shirts. They looked like soldiers on leave, but weren't. One called out, would I like to try my luck with the air gun. If you like, I said, and ended by having several turns with the so-called firearm as each took great care in showing me how to hold and sight it. This involved their putting their arms around me, and breathing beerily at me rather more closely than I might have liked. 'Phil, Victor and Damian' they allowed me to know at some stage in my shooting lesson. They were crack shots themselves, of course, and won several trophies, glittery plastic things like some of the memorabilia I had seen in Albert's caravan, and which, with laconic gallantry, they presented to me, their 'lady from Pomland'. I learned they were in their early twenties and were on two days' holiday from a wheat farm on the Eyre Peninsula. They had driven the entire distance via Port Augusta that day and were going to find a beach south of Adelaide to sleep on. Their uncouthness would have horrified Kier's mother.

From the shooting gallery we went to the dodgem cars. 'Why don't you drive?' the one who shared my dodgem suggested. He sat down at my side, put his brown arm round my shoulders, and every now and then, with great hilarity, used his other hand to disrupt my driving if he suspected I was not ramming the cars of his two pals often enough. These other two flouted the rules to leap from one swerving car to another, and were shouted at by the proprietor without effect. Indeed, all three behaved with that Australian countryman's indiscipline and assurance that they had the freedom of whatever was to hand. That arm resting across my shoulders gave me a self-consciousness I had not felt since my teens, but I was not especially displeased. There was a brazen courtesy about it for all that the whoops and catcalls at the frequent jolts and jerks were high animal spirits.

They led me then to the House of Mirrors, where they called raucously to each other from the misleading reflective corridors. 'Hey, Damian, stay where y'are.' 'I'm not there, I'm here.' 'Where's here?' 'God knows. Is Sarah with you, Vic?' etc.

From this we went on to some tawdry video-like games into which, on my behalf, they shoved a copious quantity of coins that allowed me to defeat assorted sword- and karate-masters by jerking levers at the right moment. I can say my own animal spirits were also quite raised. After this we sat beneath some pines eating hotdogs, which again they would not allow me to pay for, drinking beer from bottles they had brought with them in the boot of their car.

Taking my opportunities, I told them of Sarah's Great Preoccupation with Schoonermaster Tilber and the difficult, scattered nature of the evidence.

'Jeez, but you'd need to be dedicated, I reckon,' declared Damian.

'*You'd* need to learn to read first, Boof,' rejoined Phil, whereupon further badinage followed.

I quizzed them about the waterfront at Port Lincoln and any of the one-jetty wheat ports along the east coast of the Eyre with which they may have had acquaintance. (My own journeys have so far ventured no further than Yorke Peninsula.) Their answers had more of bravado than knowledge, I suspect. Nonetheless, I found them agreeable, though their laughs had a slightly immoderate excitement, and they did not, like Albert, apologise to me for their language. Should I have felt endangered? I always keep my knife about me, though it never occurred to me I might need it. They showed me their car, but when I declined Phil's offer to ride down the coast with them, they seemed quite unfussed. I had half a mind to accept the adventure of it, for my flat has felt to me like a cell in recent weeks. No doubt I would have been propositioned because Phil had allowed me to know that I was an attractive-kind-of-a-person, to which Vic and Damian had murmured an assent. I suppose I would have smiled back apologetically and told them I wasn't very interested in all that, though thank you anyway, very flattering, etcetera.

Would I have been in real danger? If danger did not admit itself to my imagination, how could I believe it? They did nothing to suggest they could not be trusted to behave decently with a lady from Pomland. And they *did* behave decently to me, so why should I paint them in the worst colours because of things I might have seen or heard on news broadcasts?

Besides, this is all conjecture, for I was not pressured. We stood around their car, looking up at the stars and identifying them, then parted not long after with each of them shaking my hand and saying how it was always a pleasure to meet such a nice person, and 'Good luck, Missus'. What had I done to attract such kind attention, I wonder, from a Phil, a Victor and a Damian, who it is unlikely I shall see again? I thanked them and told them I had enjoyed myself.

Cont'd later

So! What is it about the small hours of the morning? There is no traffic on the Esplanade now. The whirligig contraptions of the fairground are immobile black profiles, the booths are all locked up. Jenn, you could believe the sun was extinct and the earth populated by one or two resilient survivors who, on my walks, I see behind windows, vacuuming office space or throwing floppy mounds of dough for the day's bread. Hades indeed! Yet I love this sensation of both being *in* myself and feeling remote *from* myself. 'Being elsewhere, deeply here.'

Does one adventure trigger others along the same theme? A couple of nights after the above encounter, I had this one.

I left my flat at about 3 a.m. and walked along Semaphore Road, across the bridge to McLaren Wharf. I often do this walk at night because I like to see the lights of the cargo ships that are tied up along Inner Harbour, and the moon on the water of Hindmarsh Reach. I also know that Great-Uncle would have known this dockland intimately during the last forty-odd years of his life.

In Commercial Road there's a café that stays open late, and I bought a sandwich and a takeaway coffee, which I took to a bench at the edge of the quay. Having listened once more to the last part of Albert's tape during the afternoon, I thought I would sit and meditate close to that spot where Schoonermaster Tilber had stood under the mast light in 1928 and said to his three fellows, 'Thank you, boys. That's the sum of it.'

I was not left in peace for long. My thoughts were interrupted by the caterwaul of someone protesting. This protest, though in English, was with a heavy accent. His 'fockinghe this and fockinghe that' appeared to be directed against some Port Adelaide bartender in particular and women in general. Then I saw these two characters emerge from the darkness beneath Birkenhead Bridge and lurch in my direction. I watched their progress. One was in a very bad state and I thought he might topple into the water. I could have walked away, I suppose. As they came near I saw that the drunker of the two was a gangly blond fellow with one of those Scandinavian boyish faces which (do you remember from Ipswich docks?) when drunk seem to fall open in a kind of pleading. His friend, a rather handsome, athletic individual in a sports jacket with flashy buttons, was supporting him. They collapsed together onto the bench next to mine, where Blondie continued to rave.

I went over. 'Would your friend like some coffee? I have this. It is black,' I said to Sportsjacket.

He was a bit surprised by my sudden appearance at his side, but after contemplating me for a moment, he said, 'You are being very kind. Iss very dronk, my friend.' And, taking the styrofoam cup, he proceeded to administer it to Blondie.

'Shall I call you a taxi?'

No, they are not requiring a taxi, thank you.

Perhaps I could get some more black coffee.

Was that possible? 'Very kind. Iss very dronk.'

I returned to the Commercial Road café and bought three styrofoam coffees with lids, and several sandwiches. They were still there when I returned ten minutes later. Blondie had gone to sleep along the length of the bench with his feet sticking over the end, so Sportsjacket had moved to the neighbouring bench. I sat down beside him, gave him a coffee and a sandwich. Very kind, he kept telling me. His name was Emil, he was a radio operator, and he was from Denmark. His friend was Paul, an engineer, and he was a Faeroe Islander by birth. They were on shore-leave from their ship, and had been to a club but had been asked to leave.

'Please do not be thinking bad of my friend.' Emil turned and looked at me seriously.

'Of course not!' There were some moments of silence, then I complimented him on his English.

Thank you. It was one of the requirements of his job on the ship that he is speaking good English. This ship, it seems, was a container vessel and was due to depart from Outer Harbour at 7 a.m. They are requiring to be back on board by then, but there is time still.

Not quite three and a half hours, I was prompted to remind him.

Yes, he agreed, time *will* be eventually running out. And here he is, at the end of his shore-leave in Australia, sharing coffee with the kindest lady he has ever been meeting in his life.

'Hardly!' I laughed.

'Indeed yes!'

There was a suave animation in Emil's manner of talking to me. Either he had not consumed nearly the quantity of liquor his friend had drunk, or he had a remarkably good head.

'For one must not be losing opportunities to say what is true.' Did I not agree with this proposition? Emil liked the sweeping generalisation. But before I could reply he proposed that perhaps I would like to be coming with him.

'Where?'

On ship. I could be his wife. He had a good salary — so many thousands of kroner. His officers were understanding people. There were cabins available for marrieds. There was also the moon on the water — we could drink to it. He had some duty-free schnapps. Rummaging in his jacket pockets, he produced a flat silver flask.

For the second time this year, Jenn, I found myself turning down a marriage proposal, and my declining it was greeted as casually as on the first occasion.

Never mind! I should be sharing his schnapps anyway. For some minutes we sat, passing the little flask to and fro. The gangly Paul murmured in his slumbers and curled his legs up so that the bench might better accommodate his length. Where was Emil's ship bound? Nagoya in Japan. Had he been all over the world? Of course! Well, no. Mostly he is in the one place which is his radio room several metres above the sea. With a view of wavelengths. We both laughed at this.

Then, out of the blue he said, 'You see, here and here I am touching the world, but the world is behaving as if it is not touched by me. I go everywhere and am thinking, "This Emil is the most important guy", and wherever I go the world is thinking, "Emil Who?" And both these thoughts I have in here at once.' He tapped his forehead. 'And you?' He turned his attention to me. I was moved by this sudden avowal of his status in life. We seemed to be establishing confidence in one another. His face was wedge-formed with shapely cheekbones and expressive eyebrows, topped with straight dark hair. Perhaps his eyes were a little too close together for my taste.

Instead of giving my opinion, I asked, 'Does the world behave so indifferently?' and began to explain how I was trying to recover an ancestor who had passed through the world in order that I might restore something of his presence. 'I look for his traces where I might expect to find them. And I *do* find how the world has been touched by him. It is slight, perhaps.'

'Is this your work?'

I said it was and told Emil about Great-Uncle.

'But give this person his new place *where*?'

'In the mind.'

'Your mind? It is generous of you. But one day your mind will be *phut*! I hope not soon because in my opinion ...' He placed his long fingers over mine briefly. 'You deserve to live a long time. But one day it will be so.'

'The common mind, perhaps.'

'I do not know what this thing might be.'

'It is ...' I tried to explain, 'wherever, whenever, anyone brings to mind what has been leftover. This takes place. Now, in the past, in the future. It is where history lives.'

Emil considered this and then said, 'Of course! But look.' He bit his fingernail and spat out the paring. 'There. Emil is leaving his leftover. Now, permit me.' And he took my right hand and, with great gentleness and precision, bit off a piece of my fingernail, then spat it out. 'There! Sarah is leaving her leftover.' He contemplated this for a moment or two before he said, 'Maybe in the future there will come a marvellous machine which will sort through and will be — how do you say — *analyse* ...?'

'Yes, analysing.'

'So, will be analysing all the leftovers in your Port of Adelaide. It will find those fingernails and will be able to say, "Hah! Emil was in this place sometime at the end of the second millennium! How strange, because Sarah was here too!" Do you think so?' Again we laughed, then fell silent for a time, taking the schnapps and coffee in small sips. The moon made dancing scallops on the surface of the harbour water. A motor launch with a red light was proceeding downriver.

'Also you will have left yourself in people's memories,' I said.

'In the memory of one angry bartender, I think.'

'And in mine. And others you have encountered during your stay here.'

'In yours, I am hoping.'

'Thank you.'

'But I am thinking you will forget me.'

'I have a very good memory.'

After some moments he asked me to tell him more about my great-uncle, so I gave him the outline of Albert's account and the bits and pieces I had gleaned from elsewhere.

He appeared to listen, and then interrupted, 'He is puzzling you very much, this uncle, I think.'

'Yes,' I agreed.

Whereupon he revealed what had actually been preoccupying him during my narrative.

'Forgive me,' he said. 'I am coming across a woman who sits by herself on a bench at this strange early hour of the morning. It is usual in such circumstances, I think, to discover either that she is unhappy or that she is hoping for a customer. But neither of these things are true of you.'

'Customer?' I asked, and then it dawned on me what he meant. I laughed, and told him that it would surprise me greatly if anyone took me to be on the lookout for a customer. Furthermore, I meant it. I *was* surprised. Is this so very naive of me? 'As for being unhappy,' I continued, 'it never occurs to me to wonder whether I am or not.'

'Then you must be happy.'

'There are things that make me sad on occasion. *On* occasion.'

'Please, you will perhaps permit me to know what these things are?' He watched me attentively, and his scrutiny was not disagreeable, for all that it was somewhat cinematic. Of course, Jenn, I was being chatted up. But his attention was also sincere, and this fact seemed to have taken him by surprise.

'In the way that is usual, I miss my father who died the year before last,' I confided.

'Ah,' he breathed. We had established some common ground in our experience. For Emil it was a mother who was no longer. 'It is hard that we cannot live forever and take all the other opportunities to make better relationship.'

We compared our deceased parents for some minutes. He was a youngest child. 'When I am a teenager, much trouble. I am causing much disappointment to my ... *Mor*, my mum. She has been a kind woman. Like you.'

'I am not very kind. I have to think before I know when to be kind.'

But I could not escape by this self-deprecation, for this returned him to the subject of how unorthodox I appeared to be when compared with the womenfolk he encountered in his different ports of call. 'You are having the atmosphere of someone who is not minding what people's opinion of you might be.'

I told him that it did not occur to me to consider they might form an opinion of me, and was rather surprised to hear myself saying this, Jenn, since it made me realise that, for the most part, it is true.

Again he was thoughtful, until he said, 'So that you will not forget me so easily, will you permit me to be kissing you? I would very much like that.'

'Oh,' I said, then, being at a loss, I heard myself enquire, rather absurdly, 'Would it help?'

He assured me it would, so I agreed and all at once found the wedge of his face rather too close. At first he brushed his lips once or twice across my own, and I found the hairs of his moustache tickled and irritated me as spider web might. Then he pressed his mouth against my mouth with more pressure than was quite agreeable. It felt toothy and bony, and I must have recoiled for I found that he had said, 'I am trying to kiss you and you are bouncing off me like ping pong.'

I laughed and told him I was not very used to the kissing side of things any more, and when he asked me if I had ever been married I provided a few details about Kier.

'Ha!' He understood, of course. He himself had a wife, he said, and two children. They lived at Ringkøbing in Denmark.

'Ex-wife,' I said, having in mind his recent proposal.

'No. Wife,' he stated, not troubled in the least by that bigamous offer. For a moment later he declared with an impish smile that he could be of assistance to me in getting used to the kissing side of things once more. If I cared to. Our knees were touching and I could feel the warmth of his hand in the small of my back. Did I have my apartment nearby?

What were my feelings? I was not aroused. Kier used to make hurt little jokes as to how slow I was in such things. But I did not much want to be pawed all over by this fellow with eyes slightly too close to each other. One concern, would you believe, was on behalf of the lanky, mumbling form of the Faeroe Islander on our neighbouring bench. How could we leave him there?

Yet I would not have minded going along with ... what? I have to be careful. The drift of things? The haphazard of them? Our talk, the scallops of moonlight on Inner Harbour, the icy lights of the two or three ships that were berthed there? All these things affected me. But mostly it was the sensation of touching The Faraway as though it were a palpable thing. So what if it had ended with my body being penetrated by something attached to his, and all the sordid stickiness? I think I would not have liked that very much. But I weighed it against the fact that I might have enjoyed the corners into which our conversation, our proximity, our remoteness from each other, led us on the way to that conclusion of matters. It was the circumstances I found lovable.

So I heard myself saying that yes, I did not live far off and I could probably find some coffee in one of my cupboards, though was it right to leave his friend asleep on the bench?

Perhaps Emil considered his friend; perhaps he detected the nervousness in my answer. His hand touched my cheek once, and he said, 'You are not wanting this, I think,' and again I heard myself saying that perhaps I did not, but thank you, thank you. Whereupon he told me I said my thank yous like a person who has received directions from a policeman, and it was very charming.

Our conversation lapsed for five minutes or so, and we sat, side by side, taking in the sights and sounds of the harbour at four in the morning. During this time he had put his hand over mine, and leaned slightly against me. At length, he said, 'This is enough. I am touching the world. You will be remembering me or not. Perhaps now we are looking for taxi.' There was a lift to my flat if I wanted it, but I said I preferred to walk. He stood up and went over to his sleeping shipmate.

'Now Pauli,' he called, lifting the big boyish head in both hands. It was a tender motion. 'Pauli! Now we are looking for taxi.' There followed something in Danish, or perhaps Faeroese, and Paul stirred, and was helped to his feet. 'You are taking the other side. Please!' Emil called to me. So I supported the poor fellow on his left, while Emil took most of the weight on his right, and we crossed the open space towards Commercial Road, where we found a taxi.

When Paul was arranged on the back seat, Emil turned to me. 'Next time in Port Adelaide we will be meeting and maybe buying an apartment together.'

'I'm rather a private person, perhaps.'

'Of course. I will be respecting that. I will be watching over you. You will be watching over me so I do not end up like poor Pauli, eh.'

I said that I already have my ancestor to be watching for, and Emil considered this for a moment before saying, 'I think not quite.'

'What do you mean?' I asked.

The look he gave me, partly amused, partly knowing,

caused me another tickle of irritation. He said, 'I think you are watching also what is happening to you in this,' paused, then added, 'and in everything.'

Had he been quite the cinema hero, I suppose he might have tried to kiss me again at this juncture. Instead, the last thing he said to me was, 'Is better we shake hands, I think.' We did so, and the taxi drove away.

So there, Jenn, are my two adventures over the past fortnight. If I look at my life as though from a distance, I can say that this kind of contact with others is characteristic of me. Except where you are concerned, I should say. But I know I have come such a distance since our days of bicycling down the lanes and sitting on the Cathouse Hard. I am freest in these letters to you. But that is at least something continuing. Love, S.

November

One after another these extended missives arrived and the distrust I felt in myself increased.

'What is the point of my being the witness to Sarah's life?' I asked, and when Mike didn't answer, I repeated, 'What is the good of it?'

'She is adrift with regard to her place in the world.'

'I can see that!'

'Your friendship is her fixed point.' Mike fiddled with a fountain pen and would not quite look me in the eye.

'Yes,' I answered, but would not say to him how the word 'friendship' was beginning to feel strange in my head. I wrote back to Sarah, of course, but how could she expect my replies to be as disclosing, as headlong, as venturesome as her own? She placed more value on experience than I did. Did I not have the present moment to deal with, forever cresting with its pressing matters?

The October mists came, whiting out the playing fields and classroom blocks. As I went about my duties as teacher and headmaster's wife, I meditated on our differences, and how I might frame my correspondence to Sarah wisely and with tact, 'see her through', as I put it to myself. In the corridors and dormitories I was able to watch the spontaneity with which the boys formed their alliances and, equally casually, broke them.

Surely, I thought, were I able to be in Sarah's company I could, with care and discretion, recover the trust I had in our longstanding friendship, win her back towards a point of view that opened, not onto the past, but towards the future. She knew herself that this distinction in our viewpoints was the main difference between us. Could I but take her into my charge, I would have had her do as I did each morning at school assembly — gaze upon the boys' faces where they sat below the school stage singing the hymns. She would attend as Mike read them the sporting results or day's announcements, and she would see for herself how automatically their features expressed a forward-looking cast of mind.

Then, one wet morning in early November, this postcard arrived from Sarah, and the very opportunity I had imagined appeared to present itself.

2/11/89

Dear J, I fly to London next week. How very expensive of me! But the cost must be accepted if I'm to see for myself whatever documentary treasures Greenwich, Kew, Cardiff, and maybe Lowestoft, might possess. Odd how the town of your formidable blind granny draws me back. More outlandish, how a journey into Hades requires a round-the-world air ticket, bought through the paper at two-thirds of the price from a retired linguistics prof who must miss his conferences because of a fractured hip! I'll ring you. Love, S.

∝

She didn't ring. Instead she turned up on a Thursday morning halfway through third period. From the window of the English classroom I saw her pay the taxi, then stand at the edge of the rugby fields with her luggage. There was a light drizzle and she seemed dressed for Australia, not autumnal England. I sent a boy to direct her to the headmaster's house, and, at the end of the lesson, greeted her in my kitchen.

'You're not a sponge cake,' she said immediately, and we laughed.

'I thought you would have gone straight to your mother's.'

She said that, as a matter of fact, she was rather hoping I would go over with her. She had not seen her mother since her dad's funeral. 'It will be a jollier homecoming for her if you're there too.'

'Of course.'

She borrowed a cardigan from me and, after a school lunch, I drove her to Felstone.

Sarah was to visit me on one further occasion during her month-long stay in Britain. I was to find the force of her interests as troubling as they had been in her letters, but I had forgotten the effect on me of her vital presence. It took us time to find our naturalness with each other, and on this Thursday, face to face as we were for the first time in twelve years, Sarah having come more or less straight from the plane, our conversation was clumsy, a succession of false starts, hanging sentences, self-consciousness, and, at some level, anti-climax.

Acute as ever, she touched on this awkwardness as we drove from Haverhill to Felstone. 'I'm feeling momentarily shy,' she commented, and then, sensing the two things were connected, added, 'You *will* tell me if my deluge of letters to you is making too free with your interest in my affairs?'

'I will and it doesn't,' I assured her glibly, and stated that she had made me as keen as she was herself to learn what the various British archives might yield about her interesting forebear. I was aware I must have sounded like a camp leader out to instil good morale.

We drove in silence for a mile or so, and then she said, 'Shyness, you know, may be the key to it.'

'Key to what?'

'Well, Charles Tilber — all seafarers. Think. They go away from their place. For long intervals they live *cocooned* in the great solitudes of ocean. Meanwhile the incessant waves of fashion change, modify and preoccupy the communities they've left. Then they arrive back at their place, take one look at the disarrangement of what they thought they knew. Everything has moved on from what they remembered. So, suddenly they feel simple and overwhelmed by it. That's the psychology of it.'

'For some, perhaps.'

'You know,' she ignored my qualification, 'I have read that it was not uncommon for seamen in port after a few days to stop a stranger in the street and give away a fiver. "I don't need it," they'd say, "I'm going away in the morning." Can you imagine how hard-earned that fiver had been, grappling frozen canvas, shovelling a cargo of coal that had shifted, or —'

208

'I can, Sal. I can.'

'Or you hear how they used to get paid off then go back to the same prostitute, hand over their entire earnings and be told something like, "Eight quid, Jack? I'll keep you for a fortnight." "All right," Jack would reply equably. And apparently the girls played fair, at least the ones in Liverpool that I have read about.' Sarah was quiet for some moments, and then, 'I bet Great-Uncle had something of that temperament.'

'You must be careful how closely you identify with him,' I chose to say.

'Why?' she rejoined, and I had no ready answer, so we drove for some miles in silence.

To end this silence I complained politely that we had her with us for only a month. Could she not manage Christmas at Felstone? I remonstrated. It seemed not.

I suspect that Sarah's reunion with her mother *was* the jollier for my being present. We were given tea and cakes served from a trolley. Hazel and I did more of the talking, and some of the talk, I was aware, served as a cover for what might have been embarrassed silences had mother and daughter been on their own. In the early evening I left the two of them together, with the arrangement that Sarah would contact me after she had been to the Public Records Office at Kew and the Maritime Museum at Greenwich.

Some days later I received a letter with a Lowestoft postmark. She had borrowed her mother's car to make this excursion and, in two days' sifting through harbour archives, she had managed to probe Charles Tilber's origins a little.

November 12th

Dear J,

Not sixty miles from your home, and yet I still write to you! Forgive the cowardice. Somehow it seems easier to order my thoughts on sheets of paper.

Thank you for coming with me to my mother's. It was a silly, *confused* request for me to make, but you are so much more generous in your interests than I am. I wish I could be *offhand* in my expression of kindness to people, as you are.

Here's what I now know.

Charles Harling Tilber began his seafaring from this town in February 1870 when he was signed on as a 'rope boy' on the herring lugger, *Lillian Crane*. His age is given as thirteen, though he can hardly have been eleven, and the document is signed by the ship's owner and Maud (Lackford) Tilber (1826–1917), CHT's mother and my own great-grandmother.

With photocopies of this 'agreement', and one or two items that mention the career of the *Lillian Crane* and other vessels, I sat on the bed at my B&B and pondered the signatures. The shipowner's is confident and flourished; my great-grandmother's is laborious and crude. I tried to visualise the story leading to these two squiggles. We know it was the winter of the year. Was there snow on the ground between the Tilber home at Lakenheath and Lowestoft? I can check that. Did the mother and this, her third child, travel all the way on foot, or perhaps pay a third class railway fare as far as Norwich or Great Yarmouth? Whichever, it would have been a slow, gruelling journey all for the sake of making a signature, and Maud

Tilber already expecting her next child (Jesse, 1870–1941). But then she must have been a resilient lady, for as you can see, like her son, Charlie, she lived into her nineties.

Now, like a television presenter, let me try to address questions to the boy, CHT, such as:

'Did you have a vocation for the sea, Great-Uncle?'

No response.

'Did you pester your father and mother for that signature? (All I know of you does not suggest a pesterer.)'

No response.

'Was it the harsh necessity of an overcrowded rural artisan's cottage that required you be sent out into the world sooner rather than later? Did that make all those snowbound miles worthwhile for the hard-pressed mother?'

No response.

'Did you, during your life, ever learn how many children survived to Maud and John Tilber?' And for this question I can at least deduce his answer, that he probably never got to know the final tally, *having got used to being on the other side of the world . . . etc.*

Yet I persist. 'What were they like, Great-Uncle, those three years on the *Lillian Crane*, the *Bridget* and the *Delft*, sailing out of Lowestoft, Aldeburgh, Great Yarmouth, Woodbridge?' And again, Jenn, I must provide the likeliest words for his experiences. Cold, sodden, dunked, hungry, cuffed, verbally abused, tumbled, bruised by every protruding cleat, chesstree, ringbolt, boom-block, what-have-you. Ropes dripping from the net as you coiled them down. Sleep, if any, on a coil of ropes. Deck, rail, coaming, scuppers, all slippery with herring. Into port, unload the creels and straight out to sea again if there was what used to be called a 'shimmer' of herring running. Arms aching from work at the pumps or halyards. Night-time, daytime, the sea lifting, falling, combing around you, breaking in such a white glitter, harsh, pure, smothering you until its crescendo and battering underlie every motion your mind is able to make.

'And how *did* you like this, Great-Uncle?' I finish by asking. Again the eleven-year-old boy has no answer because I cannot see him. It is the bearded face of the man on my desk at Semaphore which answers me with his patient, hopeful, enigmatic smile, and an inner life in him that can cause him on occasion to dance for sorrow and joy.

So why did his family shed *him,* and not one of his two older siblings? Do I presume too much if I see him as a less-favoured child? Biographies reveal instances of this — General Montgomery, George Bernard Shaw. I cannot, I simply cannot, penetrate the interior of that Tilber cottage at Lakenheath. I see the smile of the veteran seafarer on my desk. Innocent, hopeful. Is it also fatalistic? Or is that smile a genetic fixture, an expression which, at the rudimentary supper table in that Lakenheath cottage, might have had an uncomfortable suggestion of idiocy? 'Get to the fuckery!' roars the poor old fellow from his bathchair in 1951. *As though he wanted his very own childhood to hear the curse...* This, you will remember, was how Albert felt moved to describe the outburst.

By 1870 had not laws been passed by the House of Commons to protect eleven-year-old children against being shoved off to sea in this manner? Charles Harling

Tilber seems to have been able to slip through the mesh of that epoch's social reforms easily enough.

Stop it, Sarah! It is futile to be angry on behalf of a bygone thing.

I can hear you telling me that, dear Jenn. To do so (you continue for me), is to disarrange the fine determinations and customs of Charlie Tilber's era. His fortune presented itself *naturally* to him, and I must learn to live within his attitudes as I search for him. That is the essence of going back among the shades, isn't it, leaving the fragile, severe circumstances of their lives undisturbed by our prejudice.

I go back to my mother's tomorrow, then to London, and then, if you're willing, to you at St Wal's at the end of next week. You mentioned that you had weekends free. Let's take a long country walk. Love, S.

And on the following Friday evening, before, so to speak, I had time to take breath, she was there at the railway station with her, 'What an *intent* time I've had of it, Jenn!'

Unlike her first arrival, she was now jubilant, having made due observance at her mother's and the family of her elder brother, Brian. Having also, I detected, recovered her focus. For had she not spent days among the archives at Greenwich and Kew, finding the voices of those who were really her 'people'? She had also taken a train out to Shoeburyness on the Thames estuary to see where her Yuells had lived. Thus it was that as we drove along the lanes to the school I heard about 'Little Miss', about 'dearest, overstrained John', and Mister Fordyce.

'It is so moving, you know, seeing their *necessity*.'

This made things easy for me. I let her talk. I relaxed back into my listening role, and was amused when, as we got out of the car, Sarah remembered to ask, 'But what about *you?*'

For a time, Mike's presence and that of our children at our evening meal constrained her. Sarah's manner with Mike was convivial enough, but I could pick the effort in it and the fact that, as with her mother, her interest simply did not attach to any of the topics of conversation Mike proposed. Both being strong personalities, they were shy of each other, and he excused himself, saying he had his rounds of the boarding houses to make. The children went to their homework or the television. We were left to ourselves.

'Was I rude?' Sarah glanced at me quickly.

'Uneasy.' I opened another bottle of wine and refilled our glasses.

'I can't pretend interest, you know. I *ought* to hate myself for it, but don't.'

'You need passive listeners, like me.'

She pounced on this. 'I don't take you for granted, Jenn.'

'You should. You're allowed to,' I heard myself saying.

'Well, yes, I know I do,' she rejoined. 'But where else in the world is passivity so alert, so generous, so intelligent? That's you.' She looked at me and then at the carpet, more embarrassed about her effusiveness than I was. 'You keep me up to the mark.'

'Cheers.' I raised my glass. I told her how good it was

to see her looking so well. 'Now tell me about Mister Tilber.' I settled into my chair. I believe I smiled, felt almost motherly towards her for a moment.

She rummaged in her bag and produced a notepad and a sheaf of photocopied material.

'Just think how dark the afterworld would be without the plain paper photocopier,' I commented, looking at this material. It was her turn to smile.

In the hours that followed we drank more wine than was the custom of either of us, and I was given the full benefit of her researches. I heard how Seaman Tilber, obviously having deserted the East Anglian fishing ports for London sometime before 1874, first turns up in the records of deepwater sail on the crew list for the tea clipper, *Theseus*, bound for Melbourne, Newcastle, Whampoa, then returning, tea-laden, to New York in the November of that year. This is the voyage from which comes CHT's only extant letter. Other sources kept at Greenwich included the abstract log from the *Theseus*, and the captain's more descriptive log of the voyage, which last, it seems, is a leatherbound notebook with marbled endpapers whose pages lend Charles Tilber his first glimmers of existence beyond a name on official documents. In the Maritime Museum's reading room Sarah had been allowed to handle the volume with white gloves, but had to handwrite into her notepad any material she wished to copy from it.

'I'll give you the entry for Christmas Day, 1874. The ship is near the equator, twenty-eight days out from having dropped her pilot.' She put her finger on the page and read.

'Fair conditions notwithstanding, I shortened to
upper and lower topsails in order to observe the
Season by serving all hands with an issue of spirits
at the end of the forenoon watch. Cook provided
proper fare at midday, dandyfunk &c. Some jollity
in afternoon watch, hornpipes &c. Boy Tilber had
crew amused with hornpipe antics. Many of the
people sleeping off effect of spirits.'

Sarah looked up at me for my reaction. 'I note he begins
life by dancing a hornpipe,' was what I thought to say.

'But the character? He cannot help but express joy!'

'Yes, there's a glimpse of something.'

'A glimpse? It's palpable!'

'You are more attuned, Sal.'

'Look, there's more.' As she turned over the pages of
her notepad she filled in the progress of the *Theseus* on
that voyage, how the vessel had discharged her general
cargo at Melbourne, proceeded in ballast to Newcastle
where she loaded coal for China. From the Pearl River we
had Charlie Tilber's letter to his sister, Mary. Then there
was the homeward voyage, the vessel laden with its
'ground-chop' of middling teas and its 'top-chop' of
Flowery Pekoe, etcetera.

All this was gone through so that I might be, as she put
it, well-briefed.

'Now. It is June 21st, 1875. We're told the ship is in the
vicinity of the Paracel Islands in the South China Sea.
There are squalls from the south east, it's the morning
watch — which is to say between 4 and 8 a.m. — and
Mister Elhinney's starboard watch is engaged in taking off

216

this or that sail one moment, clapping it back on the next. Then the captain writes:

> 'Ship's boy, Tilber, broke his leg in fall from the fore upper t'gallant yard. Fortunate to fall into topmast shrouds. Laid up. I set the bones and splinted the leg myself, the boy uncomplaining. Mister Elhinney, the mate, very solicitous for the lad. And I had thought Elhinney a brute of a man.

'And for the 24th (weather the same):

> 'The mate's toing and froing with beef tea to our injured party will make the former a little soft in the head, I fear. Carpenter has fashioned a crutch, so I gave Tilber light duties in the galley. Boy has the most trustful expression of any I have yet met in the human countenance.'

Sarah looked up from the page. 'Now tell me, what was it that motivated the shipmaster to make that last comment?' she demanded.

I was at a loss. 'People find him likable, don't they. He seems to inspire affection. He seems to have had some...' I hesitated. 'Well, special qualities, even as a ... What is he?'

'Sixteen year old.'

'What do *you* make of it, Sal?'

She sat, upright in the easy chair, her knees together and the documents gathered on her lap. She was forty-two, yet had the tensile posture of someone twenty years younger. There was a gingery grey tinge in parts of her otherwise dark, bobbed hair. She drained her wine glass and pushed it forward for more.

'I'm not allowed to be . . .' For a moment she was lost for the right word. 'Poetical,' she said at last. 'I'm a historian.'

'Tell me anyway.' I poured her more wine.

'Since you ask. All that I learn suggests he is a child of fortune. As if, after that early casting out from the Tilber cottage, he were being watched over by . . . by whatever.'

'Whatever?'

'I can't say what. Powers. It is like a fairy tale.'

'I think you *are* allowed to say that.'

'No I'm not! Fairy tales! There *is* a determining set of reasons for things. The psychological is the historical. It is the geist of *that* I want to grow close to, not some murky meta-historical force.'

'What else did you discover in the records?'

Much, she affirmed, a lot of it inferential. She shuffled the papers. She had pursued her great-uncle's career in a series of ships from the mid-1870s to 1898. I heard their names: *Lalla Rookh, Thermopylae* (Albert's memory had indeed served him accurately for Charlie Tilber was an able seaman on the celebrated tea clipper's 1879 voyage to Sydney), *Glengarry, Falls of Ettrick, Avonlea, Lady Armitage, Glen Morie, Mooltan*. In 1882 some benevolent shipmaster called Lyell had paid money for Charles Harling Tilber's indentures. Thus, at the late age of twenty-three he had become an apprentice and so commenced his training as a ship's officer. The progress appears to have been up and down. He is a second mate by 1887 on the *Lady Armitage* and first mate by 1891 on the barquentine, *Aliwal*. But then comes an episode with a Norwegian barquentine and an American six-masted schooner, and both in the mid-1890s.

'He must have taken a berth as an ordinary seaman on these.'

'Why?'

It seems CH Tilber and another 'Britisher' had deserted the American schooner in 1896. 'It was the time of the Klondike River gold rush,' Sarah reminded me. 'But look. He next appears on a crew list in 1899, when he has the berth of second mate on the *Kilbride* for her voyage to Seattle and Valparaíso. I suspect he might have felt himself lucky to get that after the Klondike business, and rather beholden to Captain Yuell. *That* is his frame of mind on this voyage.'

'You don't know he went to the Klondike.'

'I'll confirm my instinct on that one day,' was her unsatisfactory response to my objection. She proceeded to outline more of the career of Charles Tilber, rattling off a great deal of incidental nautical history and terminology as she did so.

'I go to Cardiff on Monday.' Sarah apprised me of her schedule. The Registrar of Shipping and Seamen would have material on the *Kilbride* since Captain Yuell's ship had begun its last voyage from that port. She would stay with her younger brother, Derek, who lived nearby at Briton Ferry.

A little before ten, with the school now quiet, we went for a stroll around the grounds together. The night was damp but not cold. There had been some rain earlier and the bitumen of the school driveway gleamed before us.

'Show me your school library,' Sarah requested. We entered the main building and our shoes clicked across the wooden floors of foyers and down linoleum corridors. I turned on the lights and watched her orientate herself among the shelves.

'I always go straight to the atlases,' she remarked, making for the stand-up desks where these were housed. 'Ah!' She had seen a particular atlas of which she approved, and began flicking over its pages. 'Now...' Her eyes were those of the expert wanting to make something plain to an enquirer. I stood by her side, attentively. 'Here's what I mean by the exhilaration of being able to "lift" a moment from the past. Look how I can go to this book, open it, put my finger on an exact set of coordinates in the middle of the ocean and say, my great-uncle, aged fifteen years, was here at noon on the 19th December, 1874, when the wind was light from the north west and the starboard watch, of which he was a member, was engaged in getting the fairweather sails bent to the yards under the supervision of the first mate, a certain Mister Elhinney. Isn't that marvellous? A dreary old abstract log with nothing more than the mundane routine jottings of the officer of the watch allows me to lift from oblivion this human, this unobtrusive but real Tilber family circumstance. The exactitude of it.'

'Not such a rare thing, Sal,' I suggested.

'No animal can do it,' she responded immediately. 'Not one. Besides, however mundane it might be, it is still so exhilarating, so tantalising.'

'Why tantalising?'

'Because it offers us the idea that nothing that has ever been in existence need be lost to the mind.'

'If Mike were here, he would say you are looking for a faith.'

'He's not. And I'm not.'

Yet, as though to confound her, in that moment Mike appeared at the library door. For some moments he stood regarding the two of us with the expression of one excluded from a secret. 'You'll turn the lights out when you leave, won't you,' he said.

We walked some more in the grounds, and by the time we returned to the house Mike and the children were asleep. I showed her the guest room, but it seemed Sarah still had a great deal of talk left in her. We had moved away from Charles Tilber to other topics. I opened another bottle of wine, laid one of the boarding school mattresses on the floor and made up a bed for myself beside hers. We passed the bottle to and fro, feeling for where the other held it in the dark, taking short swigs.

'You're a headmaster's wife,' she said. I could not see her smile but knew there was one.

'Not tonight, perhaps.'

After a time the conversation went back to her great-uncle.

'Ask me questions, Jenn.' I heard her voice from the dark. It crossed my mind to say, 'No Sal, I want to broach the subject of how the force of your personality makes me feel somehow infringed upon.' But I was moved by a contradictory feeling, a desire not to hurt her. I had heard that evening about the boy Tilber being brought beef tea, and watched over by the 'Powers'. Was I under the spell of that story's obscure benevolence?

'What kind of questions?' I responded at length.

'About my life. I am Charles Harling Tilber.'

In what follows, the wine, the dark of the room, our two voices as though disembodied, all contributed to give our exchanges a trance-like sensation. I can only say that, after a false start or two, my own imagination seemed to move willingly with hers, and I accepted this, my actual collaboration in her journey among the shades, as though my own part in it had always been determined.

'Tell me how many years you have spent at sea.'

'Fifty-eight years.'

'And where have you been in the course of those fifty-eight years?'

'I have set my foot on every continent on earth, and sailed on all its oceans.' Sarah made her forebear's claim quietly, not as a boast, but matter-of-factly.

'Every continent? Including Antarctica?'

'I have sighted Antarctica.'

'When was that?' As I waited for her answer, I abandoned my own made-up bed and lay down beside her. I had decided that I wanted her answers to come as though from inside my own head. She accepted my presence.

'It is in the January of 1893,' I heard her state, and noted how she had shifted to the present tense. 'I am third mate on the four-masted barque, *Glen Morie* (Captain Parvis), homeward bound from Sydney with wool. Our ship falls in with great ice masses ... So vast, like a country has come unstuck from its continent.'

'I wish you would describe them for me,' I ask her.

'There are some bergs here fifty miles long or more,

and fifteen hundred feet high. Their edges are so sheer you'd think they'd been taken off with an axe. We stand by the rail and can make out the ocean breaking over the southern end of them in great clouds of spray. And some among these bergs — look, you can see — they are jet black where they have turned over and show the growth on their undersides. And that one there, right there on the port quarter, it is maybe one hundred yards long, and is strewn with what looks like pumice stone. Do you think it is pumice stone?'

'I can't say from this distance. You must tell me with precision where this meeting with the ice masses is occurring.'

'I can do that. These sights are seen in latitude 51 degrees south and longitude 46 degrees west. They are verifiable because later we will learn how the *Loch Torridon* has encountered similar ice masses in this month, and *Turakina* the same in March of this year ...'

'But such things are rare in your seafaring life, surely? The sea is mostly a mundane occupation, is it not? You live in discomfort?' She didn't answer, so I supplied for her, 'Sodden clothing, sodden bedding, a sameness in the food each meal, a sameness in the sea's horizon from one day to the next, the atrocious strain on the arms, the intractableness of ropes, canvas, the unremitting slow, giddy movement of the vessel above the waters ...'

'Never mundane,' she replied. We lay together as we had not done since the unselfconscious days of our early teens, two women in their forties. It was chaste and I could feel her heat. 'I do wonder though, about what my Danish radio operator said ...'

'Leftovers? Fingernails and such?'

'Yes, or a dark hair or two, perhaps undisturbed since 1875 between the floorboards of some old building that had once been a barber's shop on the waterfront of the Pearl River at Canton ...'

'We would both need to be extraordinary super-sleuths.'

'We would be,' she affirmed immediately. 'In Calcutta, for instance, we could enter a junk furniture shop near the river. We could point to the faint discolorations in the board of a century-old table or cabinet and say, confidently, "Look, that was caused by the sweat from the fingers of my great-uncle as he negligently rested his hand there in 1883 when the *Avonlea* was loading jute in the Hooghly."'

So we murmured these fantasies to each other. I remember we had plans to reconstitute the very particles of breath the man might have breathed out in Sydney, Cape Town, Lyttelton, when he was at these places in the 1880s, and reconfigure exactly the weathers he might have experienced on his visits to Antofagasta in 1895, to Pensacola in 1906, Valparaíso in 1900. Fantasies they were, but there was no doubt Sarah had absorbed very thoroughly the material that was to be known about Charles Harling Tilber by the time of this visit to me.

'I don't know what I will come to, Jenn,' she said, after an interval of silence.

'Is that Charles Harling Tilber or Sarah Tilber?' I asked. I raised myself on my elbow and tried to make out her face against the whiteness of the pillow. It was indistinct, a darkness around the eyes, whose expression I could not distinguish.

'Both,' the indistinct patch replied, and we were silent for some minutes.

Again I could have tried to introduce the subject of my own feelings. Instead, I said, 'It *is* about belief though, isn't it? Belief that when you have turned all the data into a retrieved presence, it will matter somehow.'

She wouldn't answer. I wondered if it would be charitable to hug her, stroke her hair or cheek, kiss her maternally on the forehead. The rigidity with which she held her body discouraged all these things. She seemed unreachable. 'All that wine has made me dismal,' she concluded. And with that, she curled up on her side with her head towards the window, and I returned to the mattress on the floor.

On the Saturday morning, a little seedy perhaps from the red wine, we took our country walk and discussed the evanescence of wallahs, skiffle and sculleries.

December

This was the month of postcards. After leaving me, Sarah drove with her mother to the home of her younger brother, and from there I received this.

Briton Ferry 1/12/89

Dear J, It seems I am an aunt, indeed a live Aunt Sally. This is brought home when my two nephews from Derek's second marriage fling things around the family room and I must duck as some Lego masterpiece hits the wall near where I try to read. My mother cajoles me to push swings in playgrounds and help with homework, which pressure only makes me impatient. I would be the happiest being on earth if I were not conscious of the selfishness in me. Love, S.

And three days later, this, in minute handwriting.

4/12/89

Dear J, Oh for Dad to share my retrievals. Derek's interest in CHT is quite token. 'Whatever you say, Bub,' he tells me, if I try and interest him in his forebear. I've done the Registrar of Shipping and Seamen, and have *Kilbride*'s last voyage off pat. She loaded for Seattle here in July 1899. I scrutinise the streets and buildings for what CHT (as he trudges beside me) might recognise around Corporation Road and the Bute Dock.

From 1899 to 1989 is a juggle of two numerals, yet all is changed. Juggernaut lorries roar past me. Cyclone fences guard the windy dockland acres where Martian gantries and monstrous forklift trucks shift orange containers into teetering stacks. Photos of the venerable old docks help. The museum has a photo of *Kilbride* and Captain Yuell who has striking fine features, poor man. Love, S.

❦

Then, back at her mother's.

Hardacre St 6/12/89

Tomorrow, dear J, I fly westward to St Johns, then the long haul home via Newark, Seattle and LA. Before leaving I bought the flingers-of-Lego a present each to prove I was an aunt. It is the remoteness rather than the privacy of Semaphore that I look forward to. The lovable old seafarer is following me back towards the light. He takes form in a solid brick of photocopies and jottings tucked into my luggage. Love, S.

❦

From Seattle airport, three postcards came in the one envelope.

Seattle 11/12/89

Dear J, Here's an odd thing. The loony from my house at Lincoln in 1977 was on the flight from Newark to Seattle. Do you remember the one who called himself Barney and liked showing off his yoga? Since then he has had a haircut and put on a shirt. He recognised me as I boarded the plane at Newark, took a vacant seat beside me, and prattled all the way across North America. Computer software, it seems, sustained him when yoga failed. With his earnings he intends Mexico, then all South America. At one point I had to say, 'If we took a break from talk we could maybe see the Rockies.' He had seen them on his last trip, he assured me. 'Well I haven't,' I said. 'Cool. Feel free,' he licensed me. 'Thank you,' I said. Voluble pest!

I want to tell you more, so I'll buy another card.

(2) We touched down here at Seattle just after dark. Imagine, Jenn, a thief who has made a snatch-and-grab raid in the biggest jewel shop in the world, and dropped his loot in the haste of his getaway. That is the beautiful effect of order-within-chaos of this city at night. Is the world no more than Albert's bus route? No!

Passing the bookings desk, I saw an English family waiting for a flight home. My purse contained some English coins I had neglected to change at Heathrow, so I approached them. 'I don't need these. I'm going away in the morning!' I said. They were puzzled, while Barnaby B, who watched this said, 'The same old Sarah.'

(3) B has hung about suggesting we collaborate to find a cheap hostel together. I suspect that, for all his patter, he's an insecure creature. I'd better be his minder for now, which means a distracted stopover here. I intend to see Skid Row and the waterfront unaccompanied, however. Home by the 15th Oh, and Happy Christmas to you, Mike and the kids. Sarah.

March 1990

These postcards had arrived as the Michaelmas term came to an end. Then, for three further months I heard nothing from her.

After she left the school on that Sunday night in November my mind continued to work on the things I might have communicated to her. Had I not found her actual presence endearing, vulnerable, dissolving my doubts? Could she not regulate her presence so that it was just a little less ... less concentrated?

I rehearsed in my mind how I would write to her about this, and did not. Meanwhile, I expected further letters or postcards assuring me that she had arrived back in Semaphore safely. None came. In February, with the spring term under way, I sent a short note asking after her.

'You need a neighbour or two,' I wrote, 'or better still, a person already pottering in the kitchen when you come down in the morning...' And in a subsequent card in mid-March I asked her, 'Is teaming up with Kier again so very out of the question?'

Finally, near the end of March, a letter came from her.

Semaphore, March 28th 1990

Dearest Jenn,

To answer your last card, no, of course I am not cross with you for wanting me decently partnered. Moreover, you may be surprised to learn that, since you last heard from me, I put to the test your enquiry as to whether Kier is so very out of the question. Here's my report.

I thought that at Semaphore privacy and remoteness would suffice, but in the week before Christmas I became very unsettled, no doubt due to the pace of my gallivanting about the world in the previous month. (Can you imagine CHT 'gallivanting'? That would be a misapplied verb!)

My visit to Canberra was in part prompted by the dismal prospect of Christmas alone in my hot, under-furnished room. In part also, it was the dutiful thought that self-centred Sarah might have it in her power to give a little joy. Anyway, I locked up my flat, garaged my poor Datsun, took a Greyhound bus and, early upon a Sunday morning, turned up on Kier's doorstep. This caused him to be pleased and troubled.

'You have come back.' He held the flyscreen ajar that I might enter the familiar hallway.

'I have come for Christmas,' I said firmly.

But why had I not phoned him first? He followed me down the hall and into the small kitchen. 'Imagine if you had travelled all that way only to find I was away,' he marvelled. I said that I did not imagine it, and in return he told me that I was looking very well.

'Wilder,' he added. We stood on each side of the formica table. Nothing in the house had changed since I had left it ten months previously except that it was a little neater.

Oh why could I not have been moved by generous sentiments? Misgiving was the feeling which rose in me as I sat down and accepted coffee; misgiving, that signal which tells one to break off the parley, restore proper distance, make soothing noises while one withdraws. Misgiving, it is as old as our oldest forebears, I bet, one of those power points in the primitive cerebellum.

What right have I to complain? In the days that followed Kier could not have been more intelligent or perceptive in his dealings with this returned so-called wife and lover. 'Wilder' is how I appeared to him, and there is no telling what this suggested to his imagination as to how I spent my days and nights in Adelaide. Yet, appearing to make no marital assumptions whatever, he gave me my own room, the sunniest at the back of the house. He did not try crassly to revive the past by taking me to favourite pizza haunts or the houses of old National Library acquaintance. Instead we went to new restaurants, and took walks in wooded corners of Canberra I had not known from before. If I ever ventured anything penitent, he shushed me.

It was almost as if, day by day, I could see his intelligence in x-ray. He was tackling the tricky business of bringing vitality to an old intimacy, keeping hidden his own still-gaping injury at my original desertion, hoping that my turning up on his doorstep meant we were going to resume where we had left off, while at the same time not quite daring to have hope at all.

I was there a week. Once or twice, through gratitude, I knocked on his bedroom door and went in. But I found this brought back to me my sense of the old — I hardly dare use the word — oppression. I lay there listening to his breathing near my ear or the odd sucking noises from whatever he might be doing to me. I would grow morbidly self-conscious if my tummy gurgled or my arm got pins and needles from being trapped under his shoulder blades and I had to move it without wanting to make him feel I was retreating from loving kindness. I tried to imagine what he might like me to do for his pleasure, but whatever I tried made me feel clumsy and self-conscious too. Worst of all, I just felt so indifferent to the thing, and could not look in his direction in the morning until I had taken myself for a long walk beside the pretty lake and its dark mountain. I am not bloodless! I am not! Yet, to tell the truth, I was more engaged by those characters I met during my nocturnal prowls: Emil, and the gentlemen-hoons from that Eyre Peninsula wheat farm.

For Christmas Day we went to the Fawne seniors for lunch. Patrick and Tamzen's house (did I ever tell you?) is an extensive redbrick bungalow that backs onto a mountainside where people walk their dogs. (Dogs have a bearing on what follows.) There is a frowning porch, a lounge room that requires at least thirty people standing about on the parquetry with sherry glasses in order to feel it is inhabited, and a smallish garden planted with those dwarf cypresses whose branches look like upended yellow lace tablemats. Kier's sister had returned on leave from her Cairo posting. During the turkey and plum pudding courses the subject of my running out on Kier was carefully ignored, though they were wary of me at first, as though I were just home after a prison sentence. I suppose the meal was not altogether disagreeable. We sat around the table, passed comments on harmless subjects, pulled crackers, wore paper hats, and gradually our cheeriness became a little less forced.

Nonetheless, as we drove home in the evening, Kier said, 'You've had enough of us already, haven't you?'

'No!' I assured him.

But he brooded on the subject all that night, for the next day he proposed, 'We could set up together in your Semaphore flat, or get a bigger one.' I had found him at the formica table with a teapot before him. He had been awake for hours. 'I'll resign from the Library,' he added.

Oh Jenn, this prospect filled me with dread. I was so sorry and looked at him with what I hope was an apologetic expression, for I could not tell him that his proposal aroused in me pure, simple claustrophobia. I *could* not.

'Of course if you don't think it would work . . .'

Kier would never plead. His reflex was to anticipate disappointment, and prepare for it. Presently I will tell you a story that might account for this. Whenever, as now, he was glum, he would glance sidelong at a person, slump in his chair and fiddle with some nearby object.

'I don't want to cause you unhappiness,' I replied, and assured him that he deserved, *and would find,* I insisted, someone far easier to get on with than me. 'We should probably formalise a divorce so you can do that,' I ventured, which was a mistake.

'I don't know why you came.' He looked out of the window.

Rather desperately I answered, 'Because it was Christmas and I wanted to see you again,' realising as I spoke how selfish and stupid I had been to arouse his hopes. 'For all that has passed, we *can* see each other sometimes, can't we?' He would not answer this. 'I don't want to lose you completely,' I blundered. He was turning a pepper grinder around in his hands as though the object puzzled him. Still he would not speak. 'I'll ring up about booking a bus,' I said at last.

'Yes.' Kier looked at me and his hurt little smile suggested he was grateful that our circumstances had at least been given a direction. He went for a long walk, and seemed all right when he returned. But next morning, when he had driven me to the terminal, and we stood at the door of my Greyhound with the fumes and the roar of the several engines of waiting coaches, he started crying. It was that soundless crying, no sobs, no recriminations, just water oozing from the eye-corners and leaving a trail down the cheek. I had to shout above the noise to be heard. 'You'll make me miserable too.' He turned his face away. There were people looking at us from inside the coach. 'I'll phone you when I am home,' I shouted again, and climbed on board. He stood outside my window, not looking up, not going away. I hated being so utterly helpless to cheer him up. I had gone to Canberra wanting to find company and give it, and I knew I had muffed everything.

Cont'd in the evening

I haven't, dear Jenn, finished being dismal yet, for there is all the thinking I did on the long haul back to Adelaide.

Had I just experienced what people call the 'messy' part of marital breakdown? It never occurred to me that my experiences could be like the ones described in the weeklies. I had packed a book I intended to read on the bus, the cover blurb of which had promised me it would explain why Ancient Egyptians took such elaborate trouble when sending the dead on their last journeys. I was going to use it to clear my head of all these claimant personal matters and examine the motives for my own Retrieval Project in the light of what was ascribed to these three-thousand-year-old folk. Instead, as the coach covered the smooth moonish miles of fawn hills and arid pastures, my mind churned away on the subject of Kier, his family, and your friend, this clumsy, unconsidering Sarah Tilber.

Here's the story that I found myself remembering as my bus swallowed the miles. It occurred on the occasion of our first visit to his parents after our arrival back in Australia in 1978 when Sarah was still very much the immigrant bride.

We had pulled up outside the redbrick house. Then Kier decided to warn me, 'These days they are more tranquillised than they used to be.'

'Tranquillised,' I reacted. 'But I know them already. They were at our wedding.'

They were. Kier's father, you will recall, Jenn, is a shortish man with a florid face. He had been a diplomat, a rather high flyer with a reputation for solving problems where the 'clean broom' approach was required. But he had taken an early retirement on medical grounds that Kier had never quite explained to me.

'When I bring people home,' Kier explained, 'I just feel I have to ... well, prepare the ground.' He was nervous about this visit, as he had been when he first took me to meet them in their hotel room before our nuptials.

'Prepare me then,' I concurred, whereupon he volunteered the following.

'My father used to be a workaholic. When he was still with the Department, I used to come home from school sometimes, and Mum would take my sister and me into the lounge room and tell us to sit down. Then she would inform us that our father had ordered the latest dog to be put down.'

'The *latest* dog,' I said. 'You make it sound as though it happened more than once.'

'It did,' Kier went on. 'After one dog had been put down, inevitably our father brought home another pup in a box and we kept that one for a while.' I remember noticing, Jenn, how Kier preferred to avoid using the pet name of 'dad' for his father.

'I don't understand. Why did he not just keep the one dog?'

So Kier explained. 'When our father was working at full pace he was prone to break out with all kinds of different allergies, and while he suffered these he used to get into terrible rages. These outbursts were usually directed at the family pets — notably the dog. This would cause the animal to become a problem: it would bite some passer-by, or behave threateningly towards a child, with the result that it had to be put down. Then our father would miss the creature and get another.'

'Didn't anyone suggest he should do without a dog?' I asked. I was a little anxious that the Fawne seniors might sally out of the house and catch us having this covert briefing session about them.

'Mum did once,' Kier said. He would not look at me while he narrated this. You know his long face and page-boy haircut. I recollect watching it in profile as he spoke, noting its deliberateness and thinking, 'This is the person I have recently married.' I remember the detachment of that thought disconcerted me a little.

'We were all in the lounge room watching television,' Kier was saying. 'Our father announced, suddenly, "Let's get another dog." There was a silence before Mum said that perhaps it might not be a good idea. I remember no-one wanted to take their eyes off the TV because it allowed us to disguise how tense we were. Then I looked sideways at where our father was sitting in his armchair. He had burst into tears. And we all sat there. Our father was blubbering, noisily, and none of us knew what to do except to be embarrassed.'

'How did you and Mel [his sister] feel as each of these pets was put down?'

'We were expected to be very sensible about it, and we were,' he said. 'Besides, our father would go away for weeks at a time and then there was less tension, but also less excitement. For he was always changing cars, or taking Mum to buy new furniture, or bringing home some present after his overseas tours. Maybe we just weren't a pet kind of a family.'

As I leaned my head on the cool of the coach window, I remembered my comment to these disclosures eleven years before. 'I do wish you hadn't prepared me, Kier,' I had told him. 'Now I will feel like a voyeur when we go in.'

I recall he shrugged at this. 'Our schoolfriends used to come around and ask where the dog was. Mel and I had

238

to make up lies — you know what I mean, a watertight case that was untrue. I got to hate that because I could never believe my lies were convincing. Later, at university, I did a history unit one year, together with the philosophy, and I used to go back and back to the sources to check I had the actual facts right. It was suggested I drop history in the end because, while my essays were thoroughgoing, they were said to lack a historical imagination.' He stared at the steering wheel, then turned and, with a smile, added, 'A watertight case that was untrue didn't seem to affect the philosophy.'

The paddocks and fencelines sped by me, Jenn, and I brooded on these things. I can report that nothing untoward in the behaviour of Patrick and Tamzen drew my notice on that visit, or any subsequent occasion. But it was enough to know what I had been told to make me feel uneasy. Besides, the parquetry and crystal did make me, for the only time in my life so far, conscious of my own social origins when I compared the opulence of my in-laws' house to the cramped, homely Tilber dining room at Hardacre Street with its smells of dinners, and Dad in shirtsleeves at his charts.

Indeed, Kier's father, Patrick, far from signing the death warrant on any nearby animal life, was always courteous to me in that way Australian males of the professional class have of tingeing the formal with a hint of the rascally. Not then, or ever, did I see a sign of those allergies and rages, other than in his rather red face and short, pugnacious profile.

By contrast, I found Tamzen to be very proper. You'll remember her as a tall woman, with a long, serene face.

Kier takes after her in looks, doesn't he? Her dark eyes did sometimes suggest to me they had seen a share of trouble, but not in twelve years out here did I ever witness a scene between herself and Patrick or her son and daughter. A gracious woman. Whenever I used to pass those dwarfish manicured yellow cypresses along the front path to that frowning porch, it was Tamzen who I thought was diminished by them rather than Patrick, or Kier, or the sister. Tamzen seemed made for a more generous backdrop. Mind you, she was forever, quietly, trying to push me towards a more stylish taste in dress which, as you will guess, with equal tact I resisted.

The important lesson I learned from that first visit to 'the home ground' was Kier's habit of trying to forestall my reactions to matters pertaining to his upbringing. As you can see, he was not without humour, but the reflex struck me as just a little morbid. In time this habit came to stifle me because it was so killjoy.

'Why must you always frame things for me?' I rounded on him once just before a social occasion where I was to meet friends of his. He was genuinely surprised I should think this, and remained morose all evening.

Of course, I had noted there were stresses in his make-up, but that visit was the first inkling I got that his tensions may have been related to something real. From the days of our first going out together, when he used to pick me up from the Chelmsford College library, I had noted his proneness to the occasional glooms. In Canberra, if we argued about any topic, I found I always won because his reaction to conflict was to become self-absorbed.

'I think I'll go for a walk,' he would say, and wander off for a couple of hours.

'Where have you been?' I used to ask when he returned. We would sit opposite each other in our dining room, not putting the light on. Oh, he would tell me, he had gone down to the lakeside and spent some time staring into its depths. I knew he was directing my attention to his vulnerable sensibility, but I would try to find a flippant defusing response because, to tell the truth, I thought this morbidity was rather comic, poetical, and harmlessly self-indulgent. He *was* seven years younger than me, after all. My flippancy was always enough to cheer him up.

'You should carry an orb and sceptre and wave them about,' he sometimes said, smiling, and a bit shy that I had punctured his romantic glooms so nonchalantly.

And even during this harebrained recent visit, it has not been hard to remind myself of his attractions. Kier is mostly thoughtful, a delightful mimic at times, and he really can talk with such marvellous intentness on those rather bookish subjects close to his heart. So what if he could never *quite* take that close interest in the things which enthused me? That should have left me freer. Did I disappoint him when it came to the bother of sex? Probably. I was tolerant and amused rather than encouraging. He used to tell me my mind was elsewhere. True, it usually was. Did I like him? Yes, and still do in a way. He can be a communicative darling when he is in full flight. Am I happier to have put him behind me? Oh hell . . . Yes, I think so.

And there, Jenn, having thought my way through to that conclusion somewhere near the town of Narrandera,

I was able to switch on the reading light above my head and spend the rest of the bus trip wandering about Egyptian tombs.

I suppose I should have communicated all this tangle to you years ago while it was going on? My reluctance was probably to do with loyalty and the fact I did *choose* to marry him. I will not be burdened with all this. Rather, it is the bit of my life I have put into the left luggage office. I suppose I will have to collect it sometime.

In my next letter I will tell you about Nina Kovacs Musson, a nurse who attended Great-Uncle in his extreme old age, and who I will visit tomorrow. We have spoken on the phone and I learned that she spent some of her hours on night duty sitting by Charlie Tilber, probing him about long ago. Apparently she managed to penetrate his reticence once or twice. There is so much good fortune to be had when you go down among the shades. You'll hear my findings. Yours, S.

April

Semaphore, April 16th 1990

Dear J,

I will continue straight from my last. Of the several ex-nurses of the Rostrevor Rest Home whose memories of Charlie Tilber I tried to jog, Nina's has been the one most useful.

There are two reasons for this, one practical, and the other rather wondrous.

The practical reason is that when Nina Kovacs began work at Rostrevor in 1948 she felt she needed to improve her English expression. So, at the end of each week, she wrote down what she had found notable on the ward by way of idiom, vocabulary, and the manners of these ('so fortunate, my dear') Australians she had come to work amongst. When earlier this month I visited the Musson home at the coastal resort of Victor Harbor, I saw several of these foolscap-sized books. Following the dates in the margins, I was able to scan page after yellowing page where the black lines of Nina's small handwriting recorded, in gradually improving English, the mannerisms and snippets of speech of her fellow nurses and their thirty

243

or so charges who were the ancient bachelors and widowers of Adelaide. They cover the period from 1948 to the time of her marriage in 1956.

And thus, scattered here and there among these observations, bless her, are those she made of the old chap her fellow nurses used to call the Captain, my own dad's lost uncle. The notebooks are a real boon because with their aid she remembers more than she wrote down, the result being that I have now reclaimed telltale details of Charlie Tilber's life that could easily have been irrecoverable. And I tell you, the rescue of these details feels to me so precarious, it is as if I had caught a piece of floating ash from burning papers, cupped it in my hand, and deciphered from it the few ghostly marks of ink that might have survived the fire. You see, my luck holds, except that each new detail creates further, more pressing puzzles — or should I say, fractals?

The wondrous reason I will come to.

Having been, after her period at Rostrevor, the district nurse of a rural area in eastern South Australia, Nina Kovacs Musson is now a fond old lady in her early seventies with a very brown, lined face framed by short straight hair which has the soft colour of a cambric pillowslip. She is slim and sits in a chair with a willed uprightness. Her voice shows evidence of some rigorous elocution lessons early upon her arrival as a refugee in Australia, though I could detect the trace of her mid-European accent behind it. Her husband, a semi-retired sheepfarmer, is equally deep-tanned, white-haired, and, for all that he remained out of our way, he did so with a kind of 'suave tweediness'. He is as patrician as

Australians get, and she has the aspect of a middle-European of 'good family', sharpened by those lessons in the proper speaking of English.

'When you have finished with Nina's memory, you must dine with us and bide the night, for we would very much like to show you the Granite Island fairy penguins,' invited the husband suavely. He seemed to smile with his eyes and one corner of his mouth. 'These penguins, you know, they pop out of the sea like champagne corks.'

Behind the invitation I detected that Stan Musson distrusted the idea of trawling the past too thoroughly, and this was his way of deflecting my interest to a healthier focus. We did go out that evening, along a long wooden causeway, and watched the little creatures come ashore, do their flipper dance, then waddle inland in small gangs to find and feed their young. Very cute. But the valuable part of my visit, Jenn, be in no doubt, was the afternoon. It involved glasses of tea, a cake of wafery chocolate, and two voices talking into a recorder in a front room where there are seashells displayed in glass cabinets and an outlook southward onto the dark blue spread of Encounter Bay.

Sarah: 'Can you tell me the first time you remember seeing Mister Tilber?'

Nina leafed through her exercise books and placed her finger beneath an entry. Well, she explained, he had been admitted to Rostrevor a few weeks after she herself had begun her duties there. I watched her put on some spectacles, poke her head forward scrutinisingly and read the entry, then look up at me and elaborate how, on that Monday in February 1948, a policeman had turned up with the old gentleman.

'My first sight of the Captain was to see him standing in the reception booth beside the constable. Short and tall together, like so.' She held her hands at different heights. 'I remember that the Captain held in his hands a cloth bag with a name stencilled on it. It was drawn together by a rope. I also noted how he had made a rather uneven job of dyeing black his beard and his wisps of hair. His jacket was too big, and suggested his figure had shrunk inside it. The constable indicated the name on the bag and informed us the old man was a Mister Tilber from the docks, and was ... [Nina read from the entry] "a meandering poor beggar ... Couldn't get from the gentleman neither his age, address, nor the date of his last decent feed."'

She looked up from the page at me. 'We nurses also tried to discover these details, but whenever we asked him he would simply look at us beamingly.'

Sarah: 'Beamingly? His face. Can you describe that? I would like to see it.'

But Nina continued her own line of thought. 'It was not as if he was *unwilling* to talk to us. It was as if ... as if ... Hah! You compel me to think.' On the tape she is silent for half a minute or so. 'It was as if he were no longer quite attentive to immediate things, as if his attention needed to ... to *swim* up. To swim up from some deeper distraction. And when it did surface, it left him unsure of where he had arrived. Can you visualise that? He seemed to blink. Many old people have this absence expressed in their features. As a nurse you see it. But your great-uncle, he...' Helplessly she left the sentence unfinished.

Sarah: 'I am struck by how particular was the

impression my great-uncle left on the people I have spoken to.' I mentioned Mister Prideauz to her.

Nina: 'The Captain was — your word is *particular*. Yes, I think so. We wondered if his mind might have been affected by a stroke before he came to us.'

Sarah: 'How else was he particular?'

Nina: 'I think I have never met another person for whom the idea of a home was so unknown. This impression was conveyed in his very being. For many hours on his first day with us, he sat on the edge of the metal bed, quite unmoving, smiling if anyone tried to coax him to have a meal or use the bathroom. Then he lay down, placed his cheek on his hand, curled his legs and went to sleep for an hour. He was like a tramp in a doorway. Another example is that, through all the years he was with us, he kept his belongings in his bag, not in the drawers beside his bed. If we transferred them, he would put them back again.'

Sarah: 'Can you recall what he had in his bag?'

Nina: 'One thing. In the midst of clothing, carefully wrapped in a woollen jersey, there were two or three thick panes of glass. We could not discover from him the use of these, though they were evidently precious for he took them from us and wrapped them again in the jersey and replaced them in the bag.'

Sarah: 'And did you ever discover?'

Nina: 'Oh yes! I can read you that.' She flicked through more pages. 'Here.

'October 14th 1948. We take all the old gentlemen into the garden and we cook for them some sausages. The Captain will not take his sausages. He rolls the bread into balls and puts in his mouth. After a time he has been gone away but comes back later with his piece of glass. I watch him wait patiently until the staff are finished with the fire. He has been sharpening some twigs into sharp points with his clasp knife. Then he goes to the fire, settles on his haunches, and holds his glass over the smoke until it is coated black. Now he takes the glass to a seat by himself, and he begins to draw on it, using his twigs. I am wishing to see what he is drawing so go and stand behind there. I see he is drawing the face of another old gentleman who has fallen asleep on the next bench. The Captain draws him quickly. Maybe he has been doing this all his life. He makes one drawing, then rubs it out with his coatsleeve, goes to the fire and smokes his glass, then tries again. This happens several times. I say, "No! Save that one!" but he takes no notice of me . . .

'There, you see, that is what I wrote. Forty-two years ago!'
Sarah: 'What were the drawings like?'
Nina: 'I think I cannot say to you they were good likenesses because the Captain was an old man. While his eyesight was not much impaired, his hand movements were poor and quavery. But the faces were not unlike in the way cartoons are like their subjects. Perhaps once upon a time he created fine likenesses.'
Sarah: 'What happened to the panes of glass when he died? And his other things?'

Nina shrugged. 'Who should they have been saved for? What was there to save? An old jumper and jacket, a clasp knife and some panes of glass.'

Next, Jenn, I asked her to tell me more about his physical presence, her impression of his face, his stoop, what his hands were like, etcetera. Willingly enough she gave me answers to these things, though I caught her regarding me with a look of slight puzzlement, as though such a nicety in my curiosity was unusual. So I asked about the outbursts of bellowing that Albert had reported.

Sarah: 'What was it that made him angry?'

Nina: 'Once or twice, while he was still on his feet, the Captain used to wander off, and had to be brought back. This made him swear. Then at night the staff used to lock the doors. If I was on night duty, I used to come upon him trying the handles to find his way out. He did this in a mild, methodical way, as though he might learn the trick of it by studying his actions. "Why don't you come back to your comfortable bed?" I used to coax him. And on the first occasion he would oblige me and be led back to it. But then I would find him trying the doors an hour or so later, and this time, if we tried to persuade him and take his arms, he roared at us, and held his hand out for the key as we led him back. You see, I think his logic was that he had obliged us once by returning to his bed, so now we should oblige him by allowing him to go out and roam the streets. And that eye of his could really look quite dangerous on occasion. He did not like to sleep much in the nights, your Captain . . .'

Sarah: 'Those decades of watch-keeping, I think.'

Nina: 'No doubt. In the second year he had his stroke,

or a further one, and was no longer able to move around so easily. That is when he got the bathchair.'

Sarah: 'What do you know of his life before he came to you?'

Nina: 'By enquiry we were able to discover an address somewhere in Port Adelaide. I went there with the matron to see if there were belongings to collect and affairs to settle after his admission to Rostrevor had been formalised. We climbed some iron stairs at the back of a warehouse and there was a small room with a window from which you could just see the funnels of ships across the corrugated roofs. In the room we found nothing but a bed, a straw mattress and a wooden chair. There was also some hair dyeing ointment, black. Otherwise nothing, no pictures, no bits and pieces, no books or magazines. It seems the company that owned the warehouse paid his rent of a few shillings a fortnight. The rent collector knew little of him except that he had been inherited from the previous rent collector and seemed to come and go at all hours. Around the docks, said this man, the old gentleman had been known as an identity, often slipping under a tarpaulin and going to sleep among sacks or curled up in the straw of an open crate. He thought Mister Tilber had been known around the docks during the war, and probably for some years before the war. He knew that some of the nightwatchmen used to turn a blind eye to the old fellow's vagrancy, and sometimes they could coax him into accepting a mug of cocoa.'

Sarah: 'Was he a drinker?'

Nina: 'It is possible, though I never saw evidence of it.'

Sarah: 'And he was called the Captain because you knew he had been at sea?'

Nina: 'Because of those bouts of language! We nurses guessed he might have been a seaman, but began calling him the Captain before it was confirmed for us.'

Sarah: 'The language. Yet he was a quiet, cheerful man, as you, yourself, remember.'

Nina: 'Well, he knew how to treat us to the full colours, my dear.'

Sarah: 'Was it women he disliked?'

At this suggestion the lines on Nina's brown face broke into a helpless smile. 'We nurses would not allow him to think we suspected this to be so. In my opinion he disliked pain, confinement and being bossed about. A doctor in his white coat or a clergyman in his robe could provoke the language. Even so, I was able to talk a little with him when I learnt how.'

Sarah: 'How?'

Nina: 'After he had been with us for a time we thought it wise to give him a room by himself. Because he would not sleep in the nights, sometimes I used to sit there and talk to him of my childhood in Kladno, and the things before the war. For me, at that time, it was a comfort to be speaking of such things even with the likelihood that this very old man may not have been interested in what were, for him, my modern experiences. Yet he lay there with his eyes open in the dark, looking at me. Sometimes I thought there was a curious, rather lovely smile on his face, certainly an expression more pleasant than that when he roared. But when I asked him questions about his own past, he would not answer.

'Then one day I was making up his bed with a new girl on the ward called Mary, and I said to the Captain, "This is Maria", whereupon she corrected me and said, "No, Mary!". And the Captain suddenly said in a husky growl, "Little Mary will be married by now." This caused us both to laugh. But later I thought about this and realised that here had been a glimpse of long ago, a girl he had known, maybe a sister . . .'

Sarah: 'It is a sister'

Nina: 'That also was my guess. Well, that night when I sat with him, I said, "So little Mary will be married by now?" and he responded with an affirmative noise in his throat. "Mother will be pleased," I prompted next, and after a pause he said, "Mother has signed poor Charlie away for the sake of some space." There was a pause before I thought I heard him say, more quietly, "I will not speak to Mother on the train." He was watching me. You can imagine I was intrigued by what I had stumbled on and terribly aware of how tenuous was my hold upon it. "Who will you speak to?" I asked. No response to this. "Will you speak to Father?" After a long time he said, "Father and Matt have gone to Thetford for the work just now." "So who is home?" I tried. He scrutinised me, then waved his arm as though the answer to that question I should very well know. "Did Mother have no choice other than to sign you away?" I ventured. Likewise he would not respond to this. "Is poor Charlie still very young?" I tried, and saw his head nodding in the dark. "Will you never speak to Mother?" was my next question. "Never," he affirmed. "Not on the train nor never." "Will you go home?" "Narrh!" he replied. "I'll make the best of it." I watched his face to see if there was more he might say, and at length he voiced the monosyllable again, more mildly.

"Narrh." Then he turned on his side, and with his head on his hands lay with his eyes open, in the attitude of sleep.'

Sarah: 'Did you speak to him again?'

Nina: 'I tried a few times to learn the thing to which he had been signed away, but without much success. A sailing ship, I surmise . . . '

Sarah: 'It was a fishing smack at Lowestoft in England and he was signed on as a rope boy. He was eleven. His mother's name appears on the articles. I think you have just confirmed for me that he never saw his home again.'

Nina: 'That is very young to be sent away.'

Sarah: 'We cannot judge. It was their time, not ours. Please, can you try and remember anything else he said to you?'

Nina: 'It was difficult, my dear. He got tired and his head would droop. Besides, all the old gentlemen kept us girls on the run.'

Sarah: 'Tell me about any visitors.'

Nina: 'The Captain used to get a visitor sometimes, a Mister Milliken.'

Sarah: 'I was going to ask about him.'

Nina: 'Mister Milliken used to come once or twice a year on the train from Melbourne and stop for a weekend. Milliken it was who told us about your great-uncle's seafaring past, his share in a small sailing vessel and his pride in it.'

Sarah: 'The *Bicheno*.'

Nina: 'Yes, but other ships also. I forget their names. I learned other things, how he had been to the Klondike gold fields and sailed for Norwegian companies and for the Canadians. But when, later, I tried to use what I had learned to prompt the Captain's memory, he looked at me blankly. It was only ever his very long-term memory that I could activate.'

Sarah: 'Tell me about Mister Milliken's visits.'

Nina: 'Mister Milliken knew how to take charge of the Captain, leading him by the arm into our enclosed garden and feeding him slabs of chocolate from a block. He would talk to him quietly all the while under a magnolia tree that was there. Once or twice he took the Captain on a bus to the docks. Mister Milliken was a charitable, lonely man, I think.'

Sarah: 'Do you know what they said to each other?'

Nina: 'Except once, I never heard the Captain reply to anything Mister Milliken said, though he seemed to draw a comfort from his visits. Habitually Mister Milliken sat at his side, looking at his face and keeping up this intent patter. It sounded like nautical talk. Cargoes and so many pounds sterling per ton. Or keeping a good watch for such and such a light to appear on the port or the starboard. Like me, he addressed the Captain always in the present tense or the future, not the past. During this time your Mister Tilber used to stare straight ahead. Maybe in his mind he really was navigating a channel or studying the approach of a gust of wind across water. But if so, these were things in his memory he was unable, or no longer bothered, to find words for. Nor can I say whether he was making much sense of Mister Milliken's patter.

'Then once, as I was laying his lunch tray down beside him, I heard him, without turning to Mister Milliken, say these words in his quiet growl.

'"When I think I might be losing little Maisie, Minks, she turns up again, impudent as you like."

'And then Mister Milliken replied, and his words were, "We all of us know that, skipper, when we see the pair of you promenading on Santo Street." And the Captain said, "There's no sorrow in the thing, is there, Minks, none you can take the smile from?" And Mister Milliken assured him there was not.

'I did not understand this, naturally. But look! It is here.' She showed me a page where she had recorded this exchange. 'Sunday, March 24th 1949.'

I inspected the entry, and was able to give an account of the *Kilbride* disaster. 'The little girl was never on Santo Street,' I felt I needed to explain, and Nina's look was one of collusive sympathy. 'Did you go back later and use any of this to prompt him?'

Nina: 'I did, but he would say nothing. His expression became really quite stony.'

Sarah: 'Do you recall other visitors?'

Nina: 'One man, your Mister Prideauz. You can see here I wrote his forwarding address because he wished to be told when the Captain passed on.'

Sarah: 'So, can you tell me how he passed on?'

Nina: 'In his sleep. We found him curled up on his side one morning. Mister Milliken came for the cremation. I went too, and several of those other nurses towards whom your Captain had been so rude sometimes. We were used to seeing the old boys off; it was part of the job really. I remember Mister Milliken became upset and when we were out on the street again and the traffic swishing past in the wet, I said to him, "He was ninety-seven and could do very little for himself. It was hardly a life these past three years." And Mister Milliken replied . . .

it is here, I will read it to you. June 23rd 1956: "Is it too much to ask that a person might live forever and take up all them roads he never took at the time?'"

Nina looked up at me. 'I did not know how to reply. Then Mister Milliken added, I remember, "And find the place where all them sorrows are made good?"

'He asked us, if we would be so good, to tip the Captain's ashes into the harbour, which we later did. Then he excused himself, shook my hand, and went away down the gleamy street to catch his train. I never saw him again.'

Cont'd in evening

This, Jenn, is the substance of my interview with Nina Kovacs Musson. I succeeded in making her rather downcast, I fear, for it is clear that Charles Harling Tilber affected her as vividly as he did Albert, and has done me.

But the wondrous part of my interview with Nina did not present itself to me for a day or so after I returned to my flat. Do you have one of my letters to you (September-ish), where I mentioned an envelope of folded paper, apparently blank, but unevenly striated by exposure to light? As I explain in that letter, it was given to me by Albert together with those torn pages about the *Kilbride* disaster. I took it for an ordinary piece of folded paper! In the pre-dawn of this morning I woke with a sudden surmise of what it might be. I turned on my desklight, unfolded the envelope completely on my desk, looked at the discolorations and they seemed to be more than random. Then I saw I was right! It was the writing I picked first. It read 'Minksie'. And then I descried the head and shoulders, and they were competent indeed, cartoonish à la *Punch* of circa 1910 maybe, but with the squashy face and eyebrows that Albert had described for me. Here was the likeness of an individual. What a tenuous rescue from oblivion.

I went to the Mortlock Library and had my own guesswork confirmed by a curator there. You see, the yellow parts of the paper conformed to where there might have been lines on a piece of smoked glass. These let light through, whereas the white areas were those where the glass had been smoked and therefore protected from daylight. Do you see what I had discovered? For several weeks in some office, or some boarding room, a piece of glass owned, drawn on and, through a stroke of good fortune, not immediately erased by my great-uncle had lain on top of this piece of paper, masking in some places whatever sunlight might have fallen from a nearby window, allowing it through wherever the drawing implement had marked its surface. This particular pane of glass, no doubt dating to *Bicheno* days or before, was lost along with Charlie Tilber's other meagre possessions. But the paper had been used to wrap one thing or another. Or perhaps, seeing this accidental effect, Charlie Tilber had given it to the faithful subject of the drawing. In any case, it had survived. Minkus had folded his precious press clipping within it, then placed it between the pages of the book in his dunnage which he allegedly had never read. Thus I have the *ghost* of CHT's artwork with me still, preserved by the most fragile of means: the smoke from a fire (the galley stove of a ship most likely).

Oh Jenn, the sheer tenuousness of what I held in my hands to the light! And my realisation that, as I did so, the thing was already in danger of fading from the light it had been exposed to in order to test my supposition.

After I had seen the curator, I went to Albert's caravan with my discovery. Ornery Gent was trying to hunt down a rat that he thought had got among his packets of cornflakes, so all his cupboard doors were open. 'Yes, the paper could well be a likeness of Minkus,' Albert affirmed. 'The skipper did muck about with smoked glass. He come along to the galley and smoked the place out once or twice. We sometimes looked down through the after-cabin skylight to see him busy with his panes of glass.'

'And you had this in your possession all these years without knowing what it was.'

Albert shrugged and went back to rattling a stick through his cupboards. 'I had my view of the skipper, and I suppose I didn't really fit his artistry into that.' I sat with the document spread on his formica table for a few minutes, bringing Albert up to date with my various researches. He rattled away with his stick throughout, half-attentive. So, feeling my visit was anticlimactic, I folded the delicate fabric back into its envelope shape and stood up. 'You really have let go of my great-uncle, haven't you?'

He stopped, but would not quite look at me. 'Not let go,' he said. 'Let rest.' Then he recommenced his rattling.

That was this morning, Jenn. I came home and began to write you this, not knowing quite where I am. I had thought Albert shared my desire to restore the presence of Charlie Tilber to the light of day. And he seems no longer to do so. This makes me all the more grateful to you for your interest in the thing.

I must stop. For the past three months I have been doing a night-cleaning job. I empty bins, clean toilets, and tow a vacuum cleaner behind me, sucking up fluff and crumbs from under computer desks. The idea is that the wage will pay my rent and allow me to keep intact the remains of my capital for another trip I have it in mind to make. Yours, S.

Semaphore, April 22nd

Dear Jenn,

No sooner do I mention money to you than the topic returns to claim my attention. Kier has put our Canberra house on the market, and intends that I should have the *entire* proceeds.

This is what he writes. 'My dear Sarah, I think, when matters are considered, the money from the sale should go to you. Your mounted photos and collectables gave our home such character as it had. And besides, I have a secure income from my work. I will, of course, subtract the costs that arise from ... etcetera etcetera...' He finishes by expressing the hope that the money will give me the kind of freedom I had, so often, told him I wanted.

Jenn, I *never* told him anything of the sort. Never! It is unusual of him to fib. I cannot accept that money, and will not. What will I do if a cheque comes in the mail? I will have to send it back. It is ridiculous. Can you not just imagine Kier chasing me around a bank waving a thick wad of money and calling, 'You *will* take this, you *will*!' And I, while the tellers look on amazed, doing my best to dodge, calling back to him, 'I'd rather not'.

I should be grateful, but instead I feel intruded upon by this. Why is it that, almost involuntarily, my mind takes an uncharitable set against Kier? You see, the worst is that I know him well enough to guess what he is saying by this, and wish I didn't because it makes me feel diminished simply to think it. He *is* being paltry, or childish rather. His letter is saying, 'You are gone. I am hurt. I will not let my life flourish in your absence. By contrast I wish yours to prosper so that you will be ever mindful of how mine doesn't.'

Childish or not, I suppose it is unworldly, for I'm sure he really doesn't care much about the money. I feel nettled by this and guilty. Would it cost me so much to devote part of my life to making him feel happier? In a way it would cost me everything, for Kieran, and his workaholism (he's like his father in that), could easily become my own entire life's work.

I compare Kier's manliness to that of my great-uncle who managed ships, crews and cargoes across the waters of the world without ever raising his voice. *I've learned to be on the other side of the world to the thing I love and it needn't be so bad as all that.* How can I resist the contrast?

This touches the deeper, more delicate reason why I will not take that money. How can I put it? Such a fortune would change the conditions inside my head. I want to work as a night cleaner because by such lonely work I hope I can attune my imagination to living with a lightness in the world, as I believe Great-Uncle lived. I want to find the self-sufficient, perhaps desolating, sensations of that lightness in myself. Having wealth would muddy that. Yours, S.

May and June

Towards the end of May Sarah sent me this from the transit lounge at Sydney International Airport.

May 25th

Dear Sounding Board,

I write this on my knee. In an hour's time I will board an aeroplane that will take me, via Papeete, to Santiago. From there I'll take a train across to Valparaíso. My visa for Chile arrived last minute yesterday. Equally last minute I cajoled a couple of hundred dollars from a wrecking yard for the Datsun, suspended my lease on Semaphore, and stored my few possessions and papers with my agreeable landlady. These arrangements, plus the money from my night cleaning, gets me to Valparaíso, allows me maybe two months' living, then squeaks me penniless back to Australia. I feel a bit heart-in-mouth, like someone who has pledged more than she is able to deliver.

It *is* the money makes me a bit anxious, and I'll need Sarah's luck when I come home. Who knows? At that end of the tunnel I might, like Great-Uncle, welcome the odd tarpaulin or straw-lined crate in a contractor's yard for a bed each night!

Doubts aside, my resolve is to be on a ferry in Valparaíso Bay for the ninetieth anniversary of the *Kilbride* wreck of June 1st, 1900. Call it silly superstition, Jenn, or Sarah's monomania, but that very open bay is the place where my great-uncle's presence expressed itself more intensely than anywhere else in his lifetime. The hornpiping schoonermaster of 1928 attests to that, and I am going there so that my mind might be as concentrated as possible to receive the spirit of him. Spirit? This is not psychic nonsense, it is history. Yet I *am* looking for something that calls itself 'spirit', and must acknowledge as much. How can I not? Furthermore it is a mysterious spirit and I want to bring it back and live with it companionably as a part of my present. Do you remember from sixth form?

> *Though gravediggers' toil is long,*
> *sharp their spades, their muscles strong,*
> *they but thrust their buried men*
> *back in the human mind again.*

Well, Yeats' universal 'human mind' requires *me* to be on the Bahía de Valparaíso. I'm keyed up, and travelling as light as I dare, though my battered cassette recorder is with me in order to use it as an instantaneous notebook when I visit the Museo del Mar in Valparaíso. I hope to see memorabilia from the *Kilbride* drama there. If from this excursion I manage to perform anything conclusive in bringing Charlie Tilber up towards the light from his obscurity, then I'll proceed northwards along the Chilean coastline to some of those nitrate ports that Albert tripped off his tongue so respectfully. Pimentel, Iquique, Antofagasta, Coquimbo. Will their broad bright bays be pricked with the masts of nitrate ships, do you think? Can I *conjure* them to be there?

The loudspeaker wants me to board my aeroplane now, so I'll post this. Wish me luck, S.

When I received this my thought was: now she will bring this thing to a head and be done with it and my responsibility will end and our friendship will be allowed to grow more slight if that is its tendency. This will be more convenient.

I did not like myself for this thought, nor did I harbour generous feelings towards my friend for causing me to think it. Needless to say, I now regret the meanness of these reactions.

While Sarah was in South America she sent me a succession of letters and postcards, the final one posted on the actual day she was last seen. I have arranged this material, not according to the order in which it was written, but according to the sequence I received it here at the school.

The reason I have done this is because I believe my ordering represents the emotional truth of how far my friend was successful in 'inhabiting more than her own time', and the degree to which, alas, she was also deluded into thinking this entirely possible. And it also expresses best my own perplexity at her loss, my unhappiness that

Sarah's life seems to end with her energies, her intelligence, her pursuit of truth, somehow misused.

The first letter to arrive from Chile revealed her morale to have taken a dive.

Hotel Miranza, Plaza Echaurren, Valparaíso. The small hours, May 30th 1990

Dear Jenn,

Since arriving here there have been a succession of annoyances.

Firstly, this hostel may be inexpensive but it is truly bleak. At night things scurry in corners and under the beds. This evening, my second here, I went to the *hotelero* and said, 'I do believe there's something large and alive in the wall cavity behind my bed.'

He sat writing and ignored me, so I tried to find some Spanish for my complaint. Again I waited, and at length, in a rather cultivated English voice, without so much as glancing up from his register, he asked, 'Why does the señora believe that?'

I said it was because I had heard what sounded like the scritching of a reptile's scales against a surface. I suppose I knew how improbable it sounded, but I interrogated him as to whether there were any boa constrictors or giant lizards in Valparaíso.

Had he been *remotely* human, Jenn, he might have smiled and reassured me. However, again without looking up from his writing, he was pleased to relieve the señora's ignorance of Chilean wildlife by reminding her that the *sucuriuba* was a serpent of the tropical forests.

'Sucuriuba?' I asked.

'A big snake.' He took a piece of paper and slowly crushed it in his left hand. 'Not squeeze, like this,' he explained. 'You breathe out, it tightens, you no longer breathe in.' He smiled. There was an English word ... 'succubus', he thought. I was too irritated to compliment him on the extent of his English vocabulary. 'Maybe you will not make tourism over the mountains, but stay here in Chile.' He smiled again, while writing in his register.

I watched his head, intent above the register. Was he put there just to bring out the worst in my character? He owns a simply immense nose and a pair of prominent, lazy eyelids. These, together with the black and yellow shirt he wears, create the impression of a rather sleepy toucan with an ill-natured intelligence. In the office behind him I could see the walls were festooned with magazine pictures of blonde girls with brown cleavages, and motorcycle riders at full tilt. He hadn't bothered to pin several of these back where they were peeling off. Should this seediness have helped me to imagine some of the dens around the world where CHT no doubt found himself? I suppose so.

Toucan finished writing, lit a cigarette and regarded me. Could I be quite sure it was not one of the other women in the dormitory who had been making the scratching sounds? 'Someone shaving the hair from a leg, perhaps.' He had the kind of complicit leer that half-expected I might join him in a snigger. Wretched man! 'In Valparaíso there are rats,' he decided to conclude our conversation. 'Big as cats, and tails like so.' He measured a span with his hands.

Then came the second annoyance. I turned to leave and found myself facing Barney. This was as startling as if

I had turned to be confronted by a leprechaun. He had been watching my altercation, and now he simply bubbled and marvelled at the coincidence of running into, 'would you believe, Old Sarah' at this, the other end of the Americas.

'You get around,' I said.

'*Who's* talking!' he replied.

He had been established in the male dormitory for only a day, would I believe. Since I last saw him in Seattle, he has been to Yucatán, Venezuela and Brazil. He has cut his hair even shorter and looks yellowy. A bout with hepatitis A had put him into a hospital in Venezuela where he could have died, would I believe. Hospitals in these countries, I had to realise ... Well! You were on your own. He had escaped as soon as he could, was still not recovered, would I believe. This chatter followed me down the hostel corridor, ushering me further into the details of his life than I might have wished. Naturally, after my interview with Toucan, the abrupt presence of Barney made me feel peevish and unlucky. Not that my despondency affected his wonder at 'Old Sarah turning up'.

I write this on my upper bunk. The female dormitory is full of Americans and Europeans who wear denim shorts and stout walking boots. Mercifully they're friendly without wanting to team up with me. But Barney, I foresee, will distract me from the solitude I will need in order to stare hard with my inner eye at Charlie Tilber's countenance so that I may catch the exact character of that relationship between the sweet-natured mariner and the precocious little girl.

Why? Why, with two vast continents to lose himself in, does Barnaby B, this quite *incidental* figment from my past, have to turn up here now?

I will have to fit him in.

Cont'd next day

Barney found the café where I was having breakfast. He was disappointed I had not waited for him, for he had places he wished to show me this morning. I was equally determined he should not accompany me around the sacred sites — by which I mean the Protestant part of the cemetery, the waterfront, the Avenida Errazuriz and the railyards of the Estación Baròn, locations you will recall from Minkus's press cutting.

'This morning I'm writing letters,' I told him firmly.

'Oh,' he said, knowingly, 'putting words before experiences, eh?' and he gave me an electrical little laugh. I hate his 'eh's.

'No,' I said, 'just writing letters.'

But then I thought of you, Jenn, your patience. I recognise that Barney's is the presence sent to tempt me. Yes, I will have to fit him in. I have to propitiate. Propitiate what? you ask. The Powers, the Whatever, is the only answer I can give.

'This afternoon we'll take an *ascensor*, find a hill and look at the view,' I promised. How I *do* condescend!

Having shaken him off, I went to the waterfront. There was one building which might have been the stationmaster's house where Mrs Yuell and Maie Alice were taken. When I asked a fellow about it, he nodded his head vigorously, repeated, 'Si, si, jefe de estación,' and assured me it was at least one hundred years old. But he may have been telling me what he thought I wanted to hear. I was allowed inside, and I looked into various rooms, any one of which might have been where CHT kept his vigil beside the two drowned Yuells, watched by a picture of the 'Saviour'.

But I could not be sure. It was the same with other people to whom I put questions about the location of the wreck. 'Yes, for sure. English ship!' I grow impatient with people's eagerness to please. Why can't we just assume everyone will be truthful?

I met Barney for lunch at my café. He is vegetarian and therefore creates trouble for waiters in the kind of cafés I favour. Afterwards we ascended to an eminence behind the town by putting some coins into an *ascensor* and rising to a splendid sea view northward along the coast towards Viña del Mar. The sun was a great puddle of brass on the sea westward.

Ach! As I admired this, Barney, ex-yogi, ex-information-tech, took me through his conspiracy theories: how -isms, -istics and -ologies, how Americans, meat, information, 'the language itself, you realise', all made us so very less pure than we could be. These weary resentments buzzed around me irrelevantly in the Chilean sunshine. Here was the voice of information-tech every bit as instinct with superstition as any ancient shaman.

'Can't we be allowed to follow what intrigues us?' I asked rather half-heartedly at one point.

'And destroy both ourselves and the planet in the process?' expostulated B.

'Why not destroy the planet,' I suggested, 'if that is a consequence of our making the *happiest* use of what has been given us of Time?'

I was asked if I was serious, and answered by giving B an unblinking stare for several moments. I was asked if this was not just a little arrogant of me, and replied with a laugh that I had no idea. 'I hope not,' I added. 'But I do think I am more use if I am content in what I do.'

'Good old Sarah!' was the response to this. 'As out of it as ever you were in Pottergate days.'

'Why don't you tell me about Yucatán?' I urged. 'I like the word.'

Barney is a disconcerting person to listen to. For all his travels, there is nothing in his talk that suggests he has engaged with the particular at any of the places he has visited. It is as though the posters that used to hang in his room in our Lincoln House thirteen years ago still flap about his person. Inevitably I compare him with the man whose spirit I am here to find! *Whampoa Reach, 1875. Dear little sister ... you can choose a serpent from a box of others to have with your dinner ...*

But in truth I am *not* entirely content because I *devise* how I can be good-natured to B, while knowing this is not real kindness. In trying to be charitable I feel fake.

It is now the small hours, dear Jenn, and I write this on my bunk with the aid of a torch. Earlier this evening I gave B the slip and ate alone at a café in the Plaza Sotomayor, then began walking, took an *ascensor,* climbed up steps, down steps, and became lost. How this could have happened in a city which, like Adelaide, has the hills as a landmark on one side and the sea on the other, I am still trying to explain. Evidently I wandered too far, took several wrong turnings, found myself in lightless backstreets and became disoriented. Of course everyone I asked gave me copious directions in a mix of English and Spanish because they were eager to please. This was more confusing, because half the streets here have Spanish names — Calle Blanco, Calle Serrano, Esmeralda, etc — and half have British names — Calle Cochrane, Condell, and Plaza B O'Higgins! Some of my helpers were even careful to see if I had understood, and foolishly I nodded my head, not wishing to offend. There were gangsterish types, and others with that sly hauteur you find in Velásquez's paintings of Spanish nobility. But all were as well-disposed towards me as I could wish.

And yet I became more and more flummoxed, and angry with myself that I should be getting things so wrong. You will say I should have taken a taxi, but at first I would not allow myself to be defeated, and later I found myself on streets where there were no taxis. Finally some fellow from whom I asked the way told me to get into his car. This I did. I suppose he could have robbed me or worse, but he took me straight back to this hostel, chatting all the way. When we arrived the hostel was locked, but he roused the Toucan with boisterous authority, assured himself that I was now safe, and waved his hairy forearm from the window as he drove away.

My uncertainty over, I confess to being in a bit of a state. In fact I cannot recall being so blubbery, not at Dad's funeral, nor at any stage in the break-up with Kieran. Sarah had to hide herself in the ladies for half an hour. When I emerged, there to my alarm, in the dark of the corridor, was the even blacker profile of the Toucan. He could not help hearing that the señora was upset. He sat me down in the little room behind his counter and made me tea. I stared at the tatty cleavages and motorbikes. He didn't ask me what had been wrong. Instead he kept up a conciliatory patter about *pesticida* and maybe building a new wing to his hostel especially for the older women guests.

He was so full of unaccountable goodwill towards me that I've come to bed feeling very confused. In my head I had that image from the *Theseus* log I quoted to you last year, where the young Charlie Tilber with his broken leg is brought beef tea by the solicitous brutish first mate, Elhinney. Tiny acts of kindness in the immensity of time. The Toucan's tea was another case of it. What have I ever done to attract the goodwill of people?

Should I have come to Valparaíso? Is the thing I take to be so important really so? I must not lose sight of what it is I want to bring off. I *must* not.

Cont'd next morning

Last night's scribbling did not exhaust me. Listening to the scritchings in the walls, I lay awake until I saw grey light behind the window, then dozed until I heard the denimed Americans clodhoppering off on their day's jaunts.

I have always thought it vaguely bad-mannered to tell people my dreams, Jenn, but in my doze I had a vile one. I was bicycling in silvery hills (I think in Chile, though it wasn't clear) and was atrociously thirsty. A farmer appeared and I asked if I could fill my water bottle at his tap. He led me up a hill to where a ledge overlooked a tall corrugated iron tank. Then he turned on me and tried to push me in. The result was that I found myself fighting with him. There is such a veracity in the emotions prompted by dream events, isn't there? My entire body seemed possessed by dread. So chemical! We both toppled into the water and neither of us could climb its steep sides to get out again. As we floundered, he said he was sorry and would now help me if he could, but then he sank into the green-grey water of the cylinder until I could not see him. I felt my skirt billowing around me. It was one of those dreams where one doesn't so much die as *pass through* a death. And the time sense was all awry, time that had shed duration, like that hashish experience we once talked about. I woke feeling all trembly. I must drop this morbid mood and focus on why I came.

Cont'd in the evening

In the Museo del Mar, where I went this morning, they have a photograph of the waterfront taken during the 1900 storm. *Kilbride* and a Chilean barque lie aslant against the embankment like the husks of insects. A crowd watches, some with umbrellas. There is much white water in the bay, and a blurry outline of its northern shore. In a cabinet were some items from the *Kilbride*: the ship's bell and steering wheel, some of Mrs Yuell's scent phials, a very water-damaged Dickens. When I finished here, I went to the cemetery, found my two graves and spent an hour there.

Barney claimed the afternoon. He was quieter, and complains of feeling unwell.

Tomorrow might improve my mood when I take a ferry out on the bay for the anniversary. Unlike June 1st 1900, alas, the weather promises to be blue skies and tranquil seas. I'll write again in a few days. Sarah.

Hostel Miranza, June 3rd

Dearest J,

This morning, from the common room, I can hear church bells ringing. On Friday I spent my hours and pesos taking cruises back and forth across Valparaíso Bay. There were several porpoises keeping pace with the vessel at one time, and all day the waters glittered in the sunshine, blue skies no different from Adelaide. How, in such serene conditions, am I to imagine weather so ferocious that it took a sixteen-hundred-ton ship and hurled it against an esplanade with the fury described in Minkus's press cutting? How silly and superstitious of me to have hoped conditions might have put on a repeat performance!

Nonetheless I learned what I could. I saw the view of the town that those on the *Kilbride* would have had ninety years ago: the Muelle Baròn, the industrial strip close to the waterfront, then the hills behind, now settled with many more suburbs than formerly. Upon this scene I superimposed the blurry whites and greys of the photo at the Museo, and saw, I think, a plausible version of Maie Alice's last view of the world.

I arrived back here to find Barney curled up on a sofa in the common room. 'You look rather unwell,' I said. I could smell diarrhoea and he was quite yellow. 'I should get a doctor for you.'

No. Doctors invaded your mind space; he didn't want no doctors. His teeth were bared as he said this, he glowed with fever and his eyes looked terrified.

'I'm getting a doctor,' I advised him, and had the Toucan phone one for me. The doctor arrived, took one look at Barney and directed his immediate removal to hospital. No! Not hospital. He didn't want no hospital mind games.

'Shut up!' I told him, and helped the doctor persuade the sick man into his car.

'Come with me to the hospital,' he pleaded. 'They have to see I belong to someone. *They have to!*' The whites of his eyes were sufficient proof of his fear.

'Of course,' I said, smiling, hating him for this intrusion upon my privacy. We drove. I sat in the back with him, and he was shivery with fever.

'Put your arms around me,' he pleaded.

'No touch, no touch!' said the doctor, looking in his rear-vision mirror. What should I have done? I compromised and clasped his hand and felt awkward. He was got into a hospital bed. Still he did not want me to leave. They gave him something to stabilise him.

He looked at me from his pillow and said, 'I reckon you came to Valparaíso in order to be on hand for this.'

'Well,' I said.

'Old Sarah turning up. Would you believe?' he mumbled, and was asleep.

Cont'd later

I have been back and forth from the hospital. He has told them I am his sister, and I have acquiesced in the lie.

I sit there, while Barney glows, yellow as mustard, on the bed. 'Belonging' to him as it seems I must, I have to do things for him: wheel the drip as he goes down the corridor to the toilet, or hold the flask containing whatever fluid they are trying to make him keep down. Does this make me sound like a ministering angel? I am not. Every kindness I perform I am able to do only because I have seen what someone else in the ward has done — a nurse or relatives of other patients. Barney has a recurrence of the hepatitis A which means I may get it too, having held that hand in the car! He will be here for three weeks! How can I stay?

The ward is lofty, lit with powerful strobes that give to things a pallor which highlights B's complexion. There are grilles on the windows and at least a dozen TV monitors, all of them squawking throughout the day. B dozes and mutters and tosses. When he is awake, already he takes my presence for granted. 'You realise it is fate, your being on hand like this,' he has said a couple of times. And I say, 'I suppose it might appear like that,' and am goaded by the way this mocks the actual reason I have come to Valparaíso. I also think, 'Given it is so hard for me to be charitable, I could at least have gratitude from you, pest!'

Dear, dear Jenn. You are the only person in the world I can talk to in the conviction that I am speaking from the hot centre of my interests. I know you can visualise the intrusion upon my plans and steadiness of purpose that this Barney inflicts with his unmanageable, unappealing life.

And perhaps even with you I am trying to lodge a burden of preoccupations you do not really want. You keep assuring me this is not so, but should I believe you?

And are you right about one thing? Have I done myself harm? I cannot attach to anything in the present because I have thought too precisely, too intently, about a thing that is past. Is this the psychological truth that faced Orpheus as he wandered among the dead people looking for his love? I think so.

So why do Charlie Tilber and Maie Alice Yuell matter to me? Why do Barney and Kier and (how do I dare say it?) my mother, not? Why don't I care what Kier says in his phone calls or what my mother writes in her chatty letters? Yet I fret over the fact that the dancing child and mariner will not so much as look in my direction.

'Drop the business!' your Mike would advise me. 'Find an unruly classroom of Australian children and teach them about something pithy and immediate.' Perhaps he is right and I should get on a plane home.

No! I have come so far I *will* find something. In 1900 a ship went sailing around the world, and a child and a sailor danced a dance and formed an enigmatic friendship. One of them was my dear dad's uncle. So I will contrive to be an invisible third who travels beside them and brings the exact, elusive quality of their friendship to the light again. I have it somewhere in my imagination. And if it is ever done, then maybe I will drop it and be useful to people like Mike again. Love, S.

PS: When I left Australia the newspapers were full of court cases about magnanimous-seeming men who sexually molested children. How easily, how unobtrusively, the mind could entangle the detritus of one's own time around a story like that of CHT and Maie Alice and thus make it impure. This sullying is done by being inattentive *at the instant* of giving oneself to the past moment. Can we remake the past in *complete* good faith? Maybe not. But I can try for as pure a likeness as is imaginable. When I scrutinise what I know about Charles Tilber I still find innocence because his era allowed it. I'm sure of that. Love, S.

∾

The effect on me of Sarah's faith in my loyalty you may imagine. Then, for three weeks I heard nothing. The silence was broken by this short letter in the last week of June.

Hotel Miranza, June 24th

Dear J,

In the mornings I have slept in; in the afternoons I've sat by Barney's hospital bed in order to prove to whatever authority that he belongs to someone. And at night I have prowled beside the fences of the Recintos Portuarios, meditating, then returning here to shut myself in a little boxroom with my recorder. Into its microphone I talk after everyone is asleep.

I have succeeded in putting something on a cassette which, if I can copy it, I will send you. And when you hear it, will you believe I have caught the real light of ninety years ago, or will you see that I have merely trafficked with illusory substance? This, I know, dear friend, is the most trying question I have put to you in all our lives together.

They've stabilised B and have improved his colour. He is leaving hospital tomorrow, so long as I am willing to sign for him. We are going to take a bus north, our destination

Lake Titicaca in the Peruvian Andes. So far I have escaped any infection from him. Hurrah for Sarah's luck.

I like him no better than I did. Indeed, I've noticed most people — waitresses, officials, our fellow hostellers — appear to find him repellent.

Why? I ask.

Because he has no charm, I answer.

But that is not his fault, I point out.

No, it's not. It is his predicament, his character, I agree with myself.

Yes. But why should it concern me?

Because he has put himself in my way.

Can I not ignore that fact, or make excuses? God knows I have sufficient excuse — the money.

No, I cannot ignore it. Barney is there by the wayside, and it's me, Sarah Tilber, who has chanced by. His claim on me is valid. A blessed nuisance, but valid.

Furthermore, it fits the fate I find I have created for myself. It balances the enormity of my self-interest in coming to this town, the impetus which led me here. I must not expect to find selfless acts satisfying or interesting.

That, Jenn, is the quarrel I have with myself. The result is, Barney and I take our holiday. B will convalesce; Sarah will take a break from Sarah, one version of her, at least. After that I will return to Australia and try to make a satisfactory peace with Kier.

This is all cold argument. I cannot, I do not, feel it is near my interest. How can altruism, if that is what it is, be so unfeeling? Love, S.

There followed a postcard and two letters from different harbour towns along the Chilean coast. From Coquimbo:

27/6/90

Dear Wise Owl,

We're on a bus winding northward, the terrain quite eery in its moonishness. I wish B would not photograph *everything*.

I posted the cassette to you, airmail if I made myself understood past the postmaster's frown and the awful acoustics of his glass booth.

Should I have made a will before leaving Australia? Travellers do. Too late now. Kier can have everything, and if these researches come to anything, I'll dedicate the book to him.

I'll stop. B's presence makes me feel dull. S.

෴

From Iquique this letter.

June 29th

Dear J,

A satisfactory peace with Kier? His impersonations *did* make me laugh. Would they do so again? Or, by leaving him as I did, have I made him too mistrustful ever to be unselfconscious in my presence? Would it be the silverfish life again? His, at least, is a useful life.

There! I think of Kier and turn into an unfair person again. I have the power to uncover other people's pasts, but no power to undo my own. Clearly I'm not eligible to be with another person, so I punish myself with Barnaby B who at any moment will come back from the pharmacy where he is having his film developed and brazenly look over my shoulder at what I am writing.

'Good old Sarah, words before experience!'

First I tell you I will go back to Kieran, and then I remember how it was when we used to sit in our small drawing room in Schlich Street after an evening meal. Kier used to stir and stir the teaspoon in his coffee. Once (only once), I cried out in a positive anguish, 'Isn't it stirred enough?'

Or, while reading a book, I would see him surreptitiously scratching his head, then slipping into his mouth the flake of dandruff he had lodged under his fingernail. As though it were a sesame seed! How can I make these instances not sound trivial, or my annoyance sound fair? And why am I writing these things on the waterfront of a foreign shore where sometimes a hundred sailing ships used to anchor, loading nitrate under these outlandish pale hills? There! I describe that for you. But I cannot see it. The sea glitters and is empty. Charlie Tilber came to this port on the *Mooltan* in 1894. In the little boxroom at Hotel Miranza I came very close indeed to his actual presence. Now I feel he is slipping away.

As you have grown older, Jenn, have you ever been troubled by the thought that you have completed all that is within you to do? Of course you haven't. Your work in the school would not give you time to think such a thing. This letter and my mind are becoming bitty. Yours, S.

PS: I enclose some of B's photos of the landscapes we pass through.

And from Arica her last letter.

July 1st

Dear J,

We cross into Peru tomorrow, and I am going to persuade B that we should hire bicycles for a day in order to get our muscles working after these long bus-hauls.

Each day hills and ravines, Jenn, the colour of blotchy human skin. They fold into each other, and not a sprig of vegetation. Meagre concrete houses by the roadside, bunkers more than homes, all defaced by apparently meaningless graffiti. This under a flawless blue sky does nothing to lighten my gloomy mood.

Individuals aren't necessarily lovable. B isn't lovable. At bottom Sarah isn't either. But occasionally, when I look at B's profile, staring dully from the minibus in which we travel, meditating some new complaint about the world's fall from purity, I think, I would not want him dropped from the human race. Is that an expression of love? Do you feel that with your boarders? You must get some odious little creeps (the Jeremy Smys of this world). Yet of course you feel some encompassing attraction towards all manner of folk, and always have done. Why, in all our friendship, has such an obvious thing passed me by? Love, S.

This was the last thing she wrote to me, though not, as I have explained, the last communication I had from her.

Nereid

The final item of communication I had from Sarah was a small parcel, wrapped in brown paper and plastered with several colourful Chilean stamps, which contained the tape of her 'interview' with Maie Alice Yuell. It was posted in mid-June, and did not reach me until November, which was long after the two travellers had been last seen. Whether the item was held up in the mail, or by some bureaucratic procedure of the military regime still governing Chile at the time, I do not know. Suffice it to say, I listened to it when Sarah had already been officially posted as missing and grave fears were held for her safety and that of her companion.

The narration occupies one side of the ninety-minute tape. The recording is unprofessional, of course, and this has the effect of giving to the voice a remote quality both in place and time. In her questions, and the answers she provides for Maie Alice, Sarah speaks in her natural voice, quietly, with some tension, but with no real attempt to enact a distinct role for another person.

A sceptic would say that the subject matter was all illusory: never more, never less than Sarah's imaginings.

Sarah's own claim for the 'interview' would have been that her 'shrewdest sympathies' and her most assiduous researches had placed Maie Alice, Charlie Tilber, the events described in the interview, authentically 'back in the human mind again'; that she had, as it were, led them both out of the realm of oblivion.

My own inclination is to find a truth between these two claims. All too plainly I can hear Sarah's personality talking through that of the drowned girl. Sarah does not escape from Sarah. But she is not limited by herself either. I know my friend's integrity, her self-knowledge, the painstakingness of her research. I am happy to hear in what follows, the nearest approach to the light of day that Maie Alice Yuell and Charlie Tilber can make. I listen to the tape and I believe I hear Sarah's triumph. She went down among the shades and came back with her story, which was as truthful a 'take' from history as intelligence and devotion could contrive. Whatever my impatience with her during the last year of her life had been, I am able to say this. Our friendship was saved from estrangement by the appalling fact of her disappearance.

The questions and responses on the cassette are distinguished by a slight gap between each. The recording begins with some moments of crackly silence, and then the formal, 'Tape identification: interview with Maie Alice Yuell'. She does not provide a date or time for the recording.

A pause ensues before Sarah begins.

'I must know how I should address you. Maie? Maie Alice?'

'When Papa comes home from sea he will sometimes call me Old Granny Porpoise.'

'*Granny* Porpoise? Did he ... Rather I should say, *does* he hold you to be very wise?'

'Of course.'

'Does he have other names for you?'

'Sometimes he presents me to company by saying, "This is my shipping clerk, the Venerable Chilliwack."'

'Yes, I can imagine your papa's affectionate ways for I always rather knew I was my own father's favourite.'

'I cannot tell the future.' (This is spoken sharply.)

'No, of course not. Maie Alice, if I am weightless and attentive, will you then let me enter your lifestream?'

'Shall I?'

'For, you see, I believe I have now followed you as far as it is possible to do so in the public record. I have looked in all the old newspapers and shipping journals and registries. I went to the street where you lived with your mother and to which your papa came home from sea. You cannot know how faint is the trace a child leaves behind! I feel I know hardly anything about you.'

'Recount for me please what you *do* know.'

'You are born Maie Alice Yuell at Shoeburyness on the coast of Essex in June 1890. Your father is John Yuell, a shipmaster. Your mother is Eunice Chandler Yuell and they are married in 1883, seven years before you are born. You have no brothers or sisters that I can find. Should I guess that you received all the affection that comes to a late and only child?'

'Should you?'

'I think I must.' (There are a few moments' pause on the tape here.) 'Now I also know that you drown in Valparaíso Bay, aged nine years, on June 1st of 1900 when your father's vessel, *Kilbride*, becomes a total loss. Your mother also does not survive this occasion. What more can I know about you?'

'I am three days from my tenth birthday.'

'Yes, from the public record I have deduced that too. What more can I know about you?'

'You can try to ask me questions.'

'If I do, will you answer them?'

'I am doing so already and for further back than you think. But if you become impertinent, I intend to be silent, or I may put questions to you in return.'

'Then let me say that I am interested in that one particular voyage you made on the *Kilbride*. It begins in Cardiff, does it not? You sail to Seattle, from there to Esquimault, and from there to Valparaíso. It is during this voyage that you become friends with a member of the crew called Charles Tilber.'

'I call him Mister Tilberry. He is Papa's second mate.'

'He is my great-uncle.'

'I cannot tell the future. Why do you expect it?' (Again the reminder is a sharp one.)

'What does Mister Tilberry call you?'

'Missy.'

'So that I can imagine you, will you tell me what is the first thing in your life that you can remember?'

'If you like, I will tell you that. I can remember when I stand on the seafront near our home. There is a rainy, boisterous wind. (You must learn that I like words! Boisterous! Boisterous!) It flaps my coat and the ribbons of my bonnet.'

'What can you see from the seafront?'

'I can see ships all over the Thames estuary. They are both great and small. Some of the smaller have sails that are the rusty colour of bricks, and they are leaning over. I am in a fright that their booms will touch the water and they will sink. Some ships are steamships with brown smoke pulling sideways and downwards from their black funnels. Some are loaded high with bales of hay for all London's horses. I can smell the rain in the wool of my coat. And sometimes I can smell a snatch of the smoke. It is the coaly smell I know already. Earlier that day, Mama has been given a telegraph by a boy. It says that Papa's ship has signalled its name off the Downs. His ship is called *Kilbride* and Papa is returning after his first voyage in her. We wait until my toes pinch with cold. Mama has perched me on the sea wall so that I may better see. She has told me that the sails on Papa's ship will make it resemble a majestic white bird. "Majestic" is another word in my collection! Then she is pointing into the crowded ships, saying, "There is Father's *Kilbride*! You must wave to him. You must let Papa know you are here!" And at first I am vexed and weep because I cannot tell which, in all that crowd of craft, it might be. Then Mama points to a ship with white masts and so few sails on the yards, and those so ... so ... so *slummocky* (which is my word of words) that I think to myself, why, the wind can blow straight through the rigging and is of no help. Then I see Papa's ship is being towed by a plump, dirty tugboat with a tall smokestack. This tugboat tumbles and dips in the brown water. I can see small figures on Papa's ship, but none of them wave back to me. So I put my hands back inside my muff, for I feel bitter disappointment because the *Kilbride* seems to be the only ship under tow. Why can it not fly beautiful grey or rusty sails like some of the other craft? And that evening, or perhaps the next, we go to the station to meet Papa's train. There is white smoke and many people step from the carriages, but I am able to spy Papa immediately because of the brass buttons on his coat. There is a porter carrying his sea chest and other things on a trolley. Papa gives him some coins as befits a gentleman. Then, when he has kissed me, I reproach Papa for not waving to me from his ship and for using a tugboat on account of his slummocky sails. So he laughs from his fierce face, and there on the smoky platform he throws me into the air and catches me, and we all go home to the tea Mama has prepared. Then, in our parlour, Papa takes from his sea chest a length of cloth for Mama. He has bought it in Hong Kong and it shines like the green in a stained-glass window. For me, from Zebu, he has brought a box of pearl shell and brass in which there is a pair of silver and ivory chopsticks. They are very fine, but I cannot ever learn to use them with accomplishment. And I know in my heart that when Papa comes home from sea we are as complete as we can ever wish. We do not receive company for days and days. And this too is fine. Of course I love Papa, yet there is always something in the back of my mind when he is home. It is a kind of disappointment, as with the tugboat and the chopsticks. And sometimes his ... his ... loftiness from us. There! I have said what I should not have done!'

(Another few moments' pause on the tape.)

'This happens in the year eighteen hundred and ninety-six. It is not the first thing I can remember. But it is the first story I know how to tell whole.'

'When do you and your mother first go with your father in his ship?'

'We only go with him on one voyage.'

'*The* voyage.'

(A gap with no answer here.)

'Are you able to tell me *that* story whole?'

'Perhaps. Relate to me please what you know already.'

'I have seen your postscript to your mother's letter, and I have seen the schoolbook in which you wrote your compositions. This was taken from the wreck and now is in the museum in Valparaíso, very water-damaged, though some pages have not stuck together and can be read. From these things I have learned how to detect your voice. Also, the logbook from the *Kilbride* was salvaged and returned to the company who placed it in the Record Office at Cardiff. I have read those parts of it which are not smudged by water damage. The account they give I have pieced together with an account of the disaster and a picture of the ship that was in the possession of an apprentice called G Milliken —'

'I remember Minkie . . .'

'Together they tell how the *Kilbride* left from Cardiff in August 1899. The vessel is described as carrying a general cargo. The outward passage to Seattle by way of Cape Horn takes you one hundred and thirty days, which is considered a good run. There the *Kilbride* discharges its freight, loads ballast, and is towed across to Esquimault to take on a lumber cargo for Valparaíso. You arrive in Valparaíso Bay after seventy-three days at sea on May 30th 1900, where the ship takes an anchorage near the Baron Station. Two days later it is wrecked against the embankment beside the railway yards as a result of what is called on that coast "a norther". But please, now tell me what *you* remember.'

(There is quite a lengthy pause here, some crackling, the sound of vehicles on Valparaíso's main thoroughfares. At length 'Maie Alice' commences.)

'Mama and I go to Cardiff by the train. We arrive there very late in the night. Papa's ship is in the Bute Dock. If you look where I am looking you can see its white masts rise until they are black. There are men working by lanterns to load the different items in their crates. This is being supervised by Mister Fordyce who is Papa's first mate. The ship is in the dock for two days while we are there, and Mama makes our quarters pleasant with curtains and other knick-knacks. During the day I can watch the seamen hauling one sail and then another to its yard, using the capstan for the big lower sails, then lashing them to the jackstay along the yard. Mister Tilberry supervises this work. The first thing he ever says to me is once when he sees me standing below the lifeboat skids watching their work. "Look Missy," he calls out, "I'm a snake charmer." And then he sings out a tune in words I can't understand. He is like a fakir and the men walk around the capstan, answering his tune. When they do this the big coil of sail rises from its heap on the deck. It *is* like a snake from a snake charmer's basket until other men high on the yard take it, and handle it and lash it, and fasten chains to its corners with shackles. All morning I watch this funny man with his whiskers moaning the sails up. Sometimes the men sing their own song. But there is also much shouting from high and low, and a knocking of hammers around the holds. There are ropes and wires all about parts of the decks where I am not permitted to walk. Papa is usually ashore on business. Then he is with us, and next morning I wake up and the grey sea rolls and curls all around us. It glitters and it is majestic.'

'What do you do to pass the time on the voyage?'

'I have schoolwork. I practise needlework with Mama and am often impatient because the slow up-and-down of the ship makes me dizzy when I stare at the work.'

'Are you seasick?'

'Certainly not! Shall I continue?'

'Yes.'

'After the dinner one afternoon I watch Mister Tilberry cut a length of rope then unravel the three strands. He is so clever. He tucks each strand around its own length in a circle, and in no time at all he has made me three quoits. So, in my free time, and while the weather holds, I am permitted to chalk the squares for a hopscotch game on the main deck. Sometimes, when the sailors are not on watch, they join my game. They are all my friends, but I already think I have known Mister Tilberry from before my life.'

'Why?'

'Because his face has been already in my mind.'

'I don't understand.'

'It's simple.'

'I wish it was.'

(Another pause for several moments before 'Maie Alice' resumes.)

'As we sail, soon I cannot tell one day apart from another, except for Sundays when Papa reads the Bible aloud to us. And when I reflect on how one day is so like another I sometimes feel a little anxious. I write my exercises in arithmetic, geometry and French. On fine days I will do this at a table near the skylight. For my table and chair I employ a biscuit box and a wooden stool which belongs to the sailmaker, who is a Norwegian, and who, at Papa's direction, sets up this open air schoolroom for me each fine morning. Mister Tilberry gives me a shackle to use as a paperweight so the pages in my book will not blow. Days are windy. Days are warm and blue. I watch the sailors climbing the shrouds, one and one and one in line, bareheaded or with their squashy caps and their pipes. And I see them on the yards. They are like sparrows on a clothesline. Then days are still and hot when Papa wears whites, and the sailors have bare brown arms and shoulders. A little later, during the warm days, Mister Tilberry brings me a mat on which I might place my feet when I rise from my cot each morning. This he has also made out of rope. Mister Tilberry never makes me feel disappointed.'

'He has some pieces of glass which he smokes above the stove and on which he then scratches drawings, has he not?'

'Yes, yes, yes. If he has a spare moment, he goes to the galley. He comes back with the glass smoked, then he draws me, or Cookie, or someone, and when he has finished he wipes it off with his squashy cap. His drawings make everyone laugh, and he will never keep one, but he must wipe it off as soon as it is done.'

'You are in the warm days ...'

'Days are cold again and warm again ...'

'Do you remember the period when the ship goes around Cape Horn? Are the storms ... well, quite something?'

'Of course I can remember that! We stay below in our accommodation for more than a week. Papa manages to keep the little stove lit for us despite all. He is away a great deal. He could have been in another country and not on the poop deck just above our heads. Through a porthole I can see the constant white swirl of the sea on our main deck, and watch for the steward to come, battling his way through the white water with food for us. At such times I can taste the salt water in everything and I am scolded by Mama for saying I do not wish to eat it. Sometimes I see Mister Fordyce sleeping on one of the two sofas in his wet oilskins and with his mouth wide open.'

'Mister Tilberry?'

'Mister Tilberry has surrendered his cabin to us at Cardiff so that I might have my own quarters. He sleeps in the after-deckhouse, but joins us regularly at table. And once I wake in my cot and see Papa's shape in the doorway. He is rubbing his fingers trying to get them warm again. Then he has opened the stove door to add coal, and his oilskins gleam in the stove's light.'

'So at last you come to Seattle.'

'We sail on the Strait of Juan de Fuca and on Puget Sound. I see Mount Deception and Mount Anderson in the distance. Papa declares that both are higher than any mountain I might find in my English picture book. They are white with snow. I see the great logs floating in the bays waiting for the ships. It is as if each bay possesses a carpet whose pattern of lines you can't quite follow. And part of me accepts that Papa has taken Mama and me around the big world to see and learn. Yet when I open my atlas on the saloon table and trace where we have come, another part of me, deeper into myself, is appalled and I am unable to puzzle how we will ever return to where we started from.

'Papa takes rooms for us in the town because we are to be there for some weeks. It is a very steep town. I see a street down which the great sawn logs are sent skidding to the water. It is here the poor people live on either side. For a short time I am sent to a school. Then the ship is towed to Esquimault to load lumber and Papa is absent.'

'And Mister Tilberry?'

'At the end of March Papa sends Mister Tilberry to escort Mama and myself on the steam ferry to Esquimault. There is also a new person joining the crew. This is the apprentice called Milliken who I immediately name Minkie.'

'Why?'

'Because it is the right name for a short boy who has bow legs.'

'Tell me more about him.'

'He has been on an English ship, but was left behind in Seattle to recover from wounds made by a knife when he was in a fight onshore. He told Mister Tilberry he had nearly died there. When we sailed again in the warm weather, I saw some of the scars on his arms and hands. But he would not show me the place of the most serious wound in his chest. He is a replacement for an apprentice who has deserted and he is quiet and bashful. I ask him why he was in a fight, but all he can do is fidget in reply as if he were ashamed of his conduct in this matter. That is all I know.'

'And Mister Tilberry. Does he tell you about himself during the voyage?'

'At first Mister Tilberry speaks very little and smiles a great deal. Rather than talk he prefers to act a little charade in order to amuse me. "You are a shy man, Mister Tilberry," I tell him once, which causes him to shrug and move his eyeballs round in all directions. Then, on a hot day when we are near the equator, I ask him, "Shall I teach you about geometry?" He replies, "I think I know about geometry already, Missy." So then I ask him, "Shall I teach you about French?", to which he answers, "I would be obliged, if you're not too busy, Missy." So I tell for him all the French words I have learned and wait while he writes them. His hands are so brown against the white paper! But he will not be serious at his lesson. He *will* suck his pencil, join his hands in a prayer and look at the sky, then pretend to get the answer, and miswrite "père" as "pair". This he will consider, tilting his head to one side, then cross out and write "pear" instead, then cross this out too, and write "pare" and look at me with a twinkle. And it will amuse me to be cross with him.

'I once hear Mister Fordyce pass a remark to Papa about Mister Tilberry. He says he wonders whether the second mate might be a bit simple in the head. I know this is not true and burn to say so, but I hesitate to reproach Mister Fordyce himself, for he is a lofty, stern man. So I later reproach Papa for listening to Mister Fordyce on this matter without rebuking him. Papa frowns and rakes his fingers in his beard, while Mama counsels me not to be so forward. But why should I be quiet when I know something to be untrue?'

'Tell me more of the things that you and Mister Tilberry exchange between yourselves.'

'Mister Tilberry tells me he has been in Seattle once already, when he went to the Klondike River to look for gold.'

'Did he find any?'

'He shows me a tiny nugget he keeps on a string around his neck. He has lost the rest, he says. "How did you lose it?" I ask him. In answer he raises his eyeballs towards the sky and smiles and says nothing. So I give him my opinion. "I think you spent it all buying medicines for your sick friend in Dawson City." "Why's that, Missy?" He gives me a look. "Because I am able to read what I see on your face," is the answer I give him. And this time Mister Tilberry rolls his eyeballs to the right and left and again gives no reply to me. And later, on a day when the sea is like blue silk, I go to the rail on the anchor deck where Mister Tilberry has called me. "Look there, Missy." He points, and shows where there are two dolphins skimming along right under the bows. "That one's my mother," he tells me, pointing to the larger.

'"And the other?" I ask, pointing to the smaller.

'"Can't you tell by her smile?" he says.

'"No, silly!" I reply.

'"Why, that's little Ah Ying."

'"Who's she?"

'"Everyone who knows anything knows that!"

'"I know lots and I don't." We watch the two dolphins weave and skate.

"'She was the prettiest washee washee Chinawoman on the whole of Whampoa Reach," he declares.

"'Is she dead now?'"

"'Dead!' exclaims Mister Tilberry. "Not her! By now she'll be stringy and hard as rope with a voice to wake every blessed creature in China. But you see, she does like to take Sundays off and slip back into the soul she had when she was pretty. So Saturday night, she slips overboard from her washee washee boat and before you know it she has turned up like this, under our bows."

"'No-one but you could have known that!' I protest. And we watch together until I say, "What if our souls go into the bodies of sea creatures?"

"'What if?' he says, and I wait for him to say more, but he does not.

'Then I ask him, "Did you have a real mother?" I have put this question because the thought has crossed my mind that Mister Tilberry's whiskery appearance might mean he didn't have a usual kind of mother. And he says, "Not me." So I pursue this by asking, "Then how were you made?", and after looking at the water for some time he gives me his smile and says, "Like this!" Whereupon he rubs his hands together like the sailors do when they are preparing their tobacco, and opening them he blows on his palms so that whatever it is he has made there floats off into the sea. And I tell him I do not believe him. When I say this, although his smile remains on his face, there is a moment when I see it is no longer for me. So I tell him that, if he prefers it, I will believe it. And he shrugs, and we watch the dolphins until they disappear behind a wave.'

'I know that the two of you invent a dance together.'

'We do not invent it.'

'Are there not occasions when you lead each other in a dance?'

'Yes, but we do not invent it. It comes to us. This is how. The Negro cook has a mouth organ. He has the custom of playing this on some evenings during the second dog watch when the weather is fine and the duties in the galley have all been done. The off-duty watch sit around on the mizzen hatch. One evening I say, "I can teach you how to dance, Mister Tilberry," and offer to take his hands. He takes mine, and I direct Cookie to play a slow tune, whereupon Mister Tilberry and I perform the minuet that Mama has taught me.

'"I can teach you how to dance, Missy," says Mister Tilberry next. So Cookie changes the tune and Mister Tilberry does a hornpipe around the hatch, and I see some of the members of the watch smirking just a little. But they will not dare smirk at me, so I climb up onto the hatch again and the two of us hornpipe, with our arms folded in front and our bodies swaying like a rope trick. And all the members of the watch appear to love our dance, and clap us while Cookie plays on with his big round eye on Mister Tilberry. And I see Papa in his whites watching from the poop. After this, we do our dances often on the warm nights during the dog watches. Sometimes I teach Mister Tilberry to do a mazurka, or a polka. Always we end with his hornpipe. This is at the time of evening when the sea goes through its colours and the stars come out in millions and millions.

'And once Mister Tilberry says to me, "Sometimes, Missy, you make me believe I'm far away from faraway," and I cannot puzzle what he means. The sea is dark and slow, and the sky is pink and lilac and grey. The rail of Papa's ship goes up and down slowly as each sea passes under us. I see the corner of the big foresail dip slowly towards the water as if it will touch, then lift and lift until it hangs a moment on the sky before it sinks again. Next Mister Tilberry says, "Do you think there's a place we can ever go that allows us all to catch up with what might have happened?" and again I am not able to puzzle what he means. Does Mister Tilberry not know there is heaven? So I say, "Of course. Behind there!" and I point towards where the cloud is. For it has become pinker and greyer, like the costume of a rich lady. After a time I ask him how old he was when he first went to sea. And in that moment I look at his face and I see its secret. It never changes from its good-humoured expression, even when he is considering serious things, because it can't. It is to do with the roundness of his eyeballs, and the whiskers that stick straight out like the bristles on a broom. He holds up both his hands with all fingers extended. "Ten?" I exclaim, at which he considers, then holds up one finger. "Eleven!" And he rolls his eyeballs delightedly, as if to say, "I love to amaze you, Missy."

'This prompts me to ask him again to tell me about his own mama. He takes his pipe from his mouth and, with his thumb over the bowl, he shakes the stem and says simply, "We didn't suit each other all that well, Missy." Here is another statement that is more than I am able to understand, and I inform him so. But, after rolling his eyeballs once more, he will not permit me to draw him about this.'

'Is *your* mama happy for you to spend so much time in the company of Mister Tilberry?'

'Mama and Papa have been calling me "Mister Tilber's little companion". They know they cannot stop me roaming about on the ship. So they believe I am safe from being lost overboard if Mister Tilberry has his eye on me.'

'And then you come to Valparaíso.'

'Papa and Mister Fordyce have taken the noon sighting and packed their sextants back into their boxes. I am watching the pilot climb on board from a little boat that has come to meet us. He speaks English. I overhear him use these words to Papa. "You will have seen the glass is falling, Captain." And Papa replies that he has seen it. The afternoon is close and warm, the air like a gauze, even though Mama has told me often it is winter now in this latitude. The pilot has directed Papa's ship past Cape Coronilla to its mooring ground in the Bay of Valparaíso. Through Papa's spyglass I can see buildings and railway yards and trucks loaded with rocks and shingle. It is ballast for the ships, Papa informs me.

'The next morning I see there are several lighters tied up alongside in order to take off the lumber. The work begins but before evening there is a signal from the shore to recall them. It is on account of the rising wind and the seas that are coming into the bay. The seas seem to move very fast and to throw back fine white manes. Papa's crew toil hard, lashing down the deck cargo again and securing the holds. Then quickly it becomes cold. There is rain. And then there are hailstones, for the sky has become the pale grey colour of the sails on Papa's ship.

'At supper Mister Fordyce expresses to Papa his opinion that the anchorage is unsound on account of the steep shelving at this end of the bay producing an evil backwash. "Evil," he repeats. He rises and goes once again to the barometer which hangs in the saloon. I see him tap the glass, give his chin a vigorous rub, then glance at Papa as if he wants to ask a question. Instead Papa says, "If we're in for a blow, Mister, then we will have to make the best of the mooring ground we have been given. We must rely on the anchors." Then Papa requests that Mister Tilberry be relieved in order that he might take his evening meal. So Mister Fordyce dresses himself in his oilskins once more and goes up the companion to attend to matters. Mama asks Papa if there is danger, and Papa's reply is that he has streamed four anchors with seventy-five fathoms on each. He advises us to stay below, then goes up on deck. Shortly afterwards Mister Tilberry comes down and eats hurriedly, then leaves. Mama and I spend a part of the evening playing draughts, which I win. We can sometimes hear the sound of sea boots above our heads.'

'What are you able to hear and see of the storm outside?'

'I hear it, but more, I can *shudder* it. I know this storm will be different on account of Mister Fordyce having said the word "evil". Through a porthole I can spy the long white seas running across the little circle of blackness. I can hear the pelt of hail and rain against the deck and the sides of the charthouse above. It comes in gusts. I can hear the wind because of its long shrieks. But most I can feel these seas that begin to crash under where I lie in my cot. They are so violent, like the heedless half-creatures I have seen sometimes in a dream. It is the way the seas make Papa's ship jerk heavily at its cables. I hear the clunk of a chain going suddenly taut, then slackening, then clunk again. Mama tucks me into my cot and prepares for bed herself. She tells me I should not worry if the fury of the storm prevents me from going to sleep at first. Besides, on the morrow we will go ashore to Valparaíso and take rooms. And there we will purchase a cake for my birthday, she says. When Mama promises this it causes me to feel perplexed, because I cannot see a picture of it anywhere in my mind.

'Do I sleep? I am aware only that somehow I have gone from my cot to Mama's lap, and that I now have my day clothes on. We sit together and Mama reads from Dickens. Then Papa has come down the companion. He stands above where we sit with one hand on the beam overhead. His sou'wester and his face are streaming and his clothes are gleamy. He says to Mama, "My dearest, now you must put on your warmest clothes for we may have to leave the ship." Then he goes up the stairs again. So Mama dresses me and dresses herself in these extra clothes. Then we wait with the one lamp swinging from its brass hook above us. Mama has put aside Dickens and is reading to me from the Book of Psalms. There is water on the floor of the stateroom, not much. It sloshes this way and that about our feet. I don't know where it has come from. Also I can feel now the slow, steep rolling of the ship and the fact that it is no longer moored. I can hear such a shuddering, such a thump and crash along the whole side of Papa's ship. It is near, but if I concentrate my mind I can make it seem to come from far away. In this way, how can I believe any harm can come? For I have gone so deep into my own little sea cave which is my veriest self. But now comes a new noise, a scraping. It is unnatural and dreadful. Mama says it is the keel of the ship and that the anchors must have dragged. Yes, this sound is fearful. It is like someone bumping a cart over stones. Then the cabin begins to lurch over. This makes our chair slide across the floor. Then it comes upright again with a horrible jerk. So Mama and I sing some hymns. Papa comes down the companion again. He says the time has come for us to go onto the deck. And to show I have no fear, I shout, "Hurrah, tomorrow we will be in Valparaíso!" But I hear my shout and do not believe it.

'We climb the companionway into Papa's charthouse. Can I say truthfully I am afraid? I know the ship has moved from where it had been. I know it is somehow broken. Mama holds my head against her shoulder, but I try to look through the door which is slamming like a frenzied thing. And oh, I see! Why can I not find words? Not boisterous, not majestic. Yet dreadful and grand! I see white swirling water. It is like the ocean rising to its feet! Such a boil! Such a slow rage! Then in a moment the charthouse has vanished from around us. It has blown away and left us standing in the blast of rain and sea. For a moment I am able to see down into the well of the ship. There is one white mast and perhaps another beyond it. The lifeboats and their skids have disappeared. But truthfully, what I see and smell most is the wet-wool odour of Mama's coat. She presses my head as strongly as she can. She is panting with the weight of me. She is also calling encouragements to any sailor who appears from the white darkness. I want to see everything and I want to be safe. It is easy to think both these things at the same time.

'And in an instant I know the word I want. Tumult! That is what I see and hear, as though it comes from the inmost thought in a psalm. Tumult, tumult, tumult! Can I really pick nothing above the wind and the sea's crash? Yes, there is Papa's deep voice, shouting. He has taken me from Mama and given me to my friend, Mister Tilberry. "Do your best, Mister," I hear Papa say to him. Now I hear Mister Tilberry bellow in Mama's ear that he will not let go of me as long as life is in him. And it is only now that I feel really afraid and know that I have to behave as if I am not. I glimpse lights on the shore where I had seen them on the previous night. They are much nearer now, and fewer.

'The seas come and suck back, and come. I can feel this. Papa chooses an interval to help Mama to climb into the rigging of the mizzen mast. She cannot climb very high because by now the seamen are all clinging there too. She is encumbered by her coat and skirts. Papa follows her and hooks his arms into the rigging so he is shielding Mama from each time the sea breaks over them. Mama is still calling encouragements to the sailors above her in the shrouds. Now I can feel my wet clothes sticking to my skin. They are cold. Mister Tilberry has followed Papa. He has one hand around me and says in my ear, "Grasp the ratlin', Missy." Of course I know what he means. Like Mama, we cannot ascend the rigging far, so there we wait. I am pressed between the rigging and the body of Mister Tilberry. I can feel his beard against my ear and I can smell tar. Every sea that comes is pluming spray as tall as the mast and Mister Tilberry and I are in its centre when it breaks. Afterwards Mister Tilberry bellows in my ear, "That one is all the way from Japan, Missy." And after the next one, "That one is from Kammy Chatka." I don't know how you tell time when all that you can hear is crash and suck, crash and suck. And all you can see is white darkness . . .'

'You call it *white* darkness?'

'Yes yes. Why *will* you interrupt?! I know we are now waiting for the people on the shore to rescue us. But they do not. I can no longer hear Mama calling out words of good cheer for the sailors. Mister Tilberry has shouted to Papa, "That lumber will break us up, Captain!" And I see Papa nod. His eyes are fixed like a person labouring to uphold immense weight. For the ship will heave upright as each sea wells up around her. It is as if it wants to shake away all of us clinging to the rigging. Then it will fall away on its side again so that we are jolted once more. I can feel the ache in my own arms, even though I am shielded by the body of Mister Tilberry.

'And I can see Mister Tilberry has been gazing over his shoulder towards the lights on the land. He is trying to distinguish something in the mad waters. Then I see him lean again towards Papa and shout, "I believe all that floatin' lumber might be ventured upon, Captain." Papa nods again but I do not believe he has heard. So, with one hand, Mister Tilberry takes his knife. When the seas draw back and the ship lies over on her side once more, he reaches through the ratlines. "We'll have ourselves a length of that buntlin', Missy," he roars in my ear, and draws through then cuts a length of rope that has been hanging slack. This he passes around me and himself so that I am tied to his back. Now he waits his time between the onslaught of each wave. In an interval he climbs quickly down past the steward, who is clinging to the rigging there, and waits his chance. Waters crash around us and I think we will be swept away, but Mister Tilberry has held us to something. I think he wants the ship to roll upright towards the shore again. I can feel it doing so, slowly, slowly. Then I see in an instant what he intends. The white water has become jammed with logs. It is a bridge!

'Mister Tilberry shouts to me, "If we can trust those logs for half a minute, Missy, we'll do the dance of our lives!"

'I see one of the apprentice boys go over the side and I glimpse him leaping from log to log then disappearing in the whiteness. When I sense Mister Tilberry tense himself to jump I shout as loudly as I can into his ear "Tumult! Tumult! Hurrah! Hurrah!" and then we are down and Mister Tilberry is skipping from log to log. He is like a cat. Then he has missed his footing and we are in the middle of the white ocean and I seem to be among huge dark half-creatures. It is, I realise, the lumber from the hold. I am struck by something so that my head feels full of what I cannot understand. I swallow much water. I have no fear and can see light. I go through my life until I pass out of it. And I come to my place in the mind of Mister Tilberry. That is all.'

(The voice on the tape had been gathering momentum as it narrated these events. Then there is a pause before

Sarah continues.) 'Mister Tilberry succeeds in reaching land, and you are taken and laid in a stationmaster's house near the railway.'

'I cannot tell the future.'

'Your mama perishes when the attempt to bring her across in the rescue apparatus fails. Your papa is rescued when daylight comes.'

'I cannot tell the future.'

'Mister Fordyce is lost when he descends the mizzen rigging in order to take shelter in the wheelhouse and is caught in a sea that comes over the stern and carries him away.'

'This I can tell. It happens before Mister Tilberry has cut off the length of rope. I see Mister Fordyce look at me once as he comes down the rigging. Is mine the last face he sees? I think so.'

'Why do you make Mister Tilberry into a sad person?'

(Several moments of silence.)

'Why did you make Mister Tilber into a sad person? . . . Why do you not answer this question?'

'I cannot tell the future. I make Mister Tilberry more complete.'

'I do not understand. You have lost me.'

'You have lost me.'

The voice on the tape ends here. Whatever trance or mood of abstraction Sarah had created in her mind during this narration, it possessed her sufficiently for her to neglect to turn off the recording machine. I continued to hear the blare of car horns, the acceleration of traffic, an ambulance or police siren coming from the night streets of that remote city.

I can say no more about the life of my friend, Sarah Tilber.

∽

The Voyage
Philip Caputo

On a June morning in the twentieth century's infancy, Cyrus Braithwaite—without explanation—orders his three teenage sons to sail from their Maine home and not return until September. The three boys and a friend board the Braithwaites' forty-six-foot schooner and begin a perilous journey down the East Coast, bound for the Florida Keys. A storm abruptly ends their passage, leaving them stranded in Cuba, but when they telegraph their father for help he does not respond. After their ordeal is over, no one in the family ever again mentions the voyage.

Now, almost a century later, Cyrus's great-granddaughter Sybil is determined to know the hidden heart of the story: Why did Cyrus send his sons to sea? Why was their mother in a Boston hospital? What role was played in the drama by Lockwood Braithwaite, the enigmatic child of Cyrus's first marriage? Sybil's discoveries will change the way she thinks about herself, her family, and the America whose ideals the Braithwaites once embodied.

ISBN 0 7322 6842 7